THE NINE DRAGONS SAGA

Morton Raphael

ISBN: 978-1-63490-480-3

Published by BookLocker.com, Inc., Bradenton, Florida, U.S.A.

Printed on acid-free paper.

Booklocker.com, Inc.
2015

Dedication

To my parents and my wife's parents

Table of Contents

Charles Albert Shih Is Born

On a warm day in June, Snow Flake, an attractive sixteen-year-old girl with shoulder length, black hair and large, expressive, dark eyes sat on the side of her grandfather's small outboard motor boat. She wore a rubber suit with flippers and had a snorkel mask perched on her forehead. A seven-foot trident was attached to her right wrist by a long, yellow, nylon rope and a sharp knife was strapped against her left thigh. Satisfied that the ocean was calm enough for a dip, she gently slid into the water.

Her companion was a tall, white-haired man in his seventies with a very lean, wiry build and a face creased by deep wrinkles. His name was Lu Ke Yuan and he was her grandfather. He watched the water around Snow Flake with a critical eye. Wave after wave floated over her body as the girl searched for fish which would be sold to the floating restaurants in Hong Kong harbor. When Snow Flake espied a big fish swimming directly below her, she pulled the diving mask over her head and brought the trident into position. At the right moment, she dove under the water to snare the fish. While she was fighting the hooked fish on the barbed points, Snow Flake used the long shaft to raise the fish's head out of the water. She propelled herself over to the boat where her grandfather was waiting. Using a net, he grabbed the prize and quickly tossed it into a container where fish were held secure by a latched lid.

There were times when Snow Flake missed her mark, but today was a lucky day. She was able to catch more than a dozen large fish. Contented with the day's work, she returned to the boat where she slowly peeled off her rubber suit. She dried her hair with a towel and put on a pair of jeans and a shirt. Lu Ke started the boat's engine and headed for the Hong Kong floating restaurants which might buy their catch. On the way, Lu Ke briefly cast a glance at the girl's adult body. The look of the teenager was already pretty enough to attract many a young male suitor. Her grandparents regretted taking Snow Flake out of school, but without her help they couldn't conceive a way out of hunger. In their hearts, they hoped the girl could have a better life than the one they had endured.

Reading romantic novels was Snow Flake's favorite pastime. She fell into a habit of daydreaming, imagining herself in the place of the heroine of each of the dream stories that she read. This allowed her fancy to interplay within the dramas. Her current book told a story about a poor young woman who left home for a job in a big city department store, where she attracted the wealthy young son of the store owner. They fell in love, married and had children. Later in the novel, she became a famous author.

A calamity had occurred years ago, when Snow Flake was three. Her mother, Little Mai, was the strong one in the family. She would be working on the sea daily while her husband, Big Rock, tethered Snow Flake to a rail on the vessel so she wouldn't fall overboard. He tried to keep an eye on both of them while his wife was in the water. He felt a need to relieve himself and left the scene. When he returned, Little Mai had disappeared. He became frantic, and searched for her for many hours without any success. Devastated and heartbroken, he eventually brought the boat back to shore and swore never to go to the sea again. Eight months later, Big Rock married another young woman. Wanting to cut his ties to his past life, he abandoned Snow Flake to the care of her grandparents.

On the efforts of her Grandmother Fei Fei, who looked older than her sixty years, Snow Flake was sent to school at the age of six. When she was fifteen, another misfortune overtook the Yuan family. Grandfather Lu Ke's arthritis was getting worse every day until it was impossible for him to fish out at sea alone. In desperation, the elderly couple made the decision to take Snow Flake out of school to help support the family.

The sound of a high-powered engine awoke Snow Flake from her reverie. She noticed a luxury yacht approaching their fishing boat. It wasn't difficult for her to make out the name. She read *The Nine Dragons*. She called to her grandfather, who held onto the rail while watching the yacht approach. When it came closer, the stately vessel cut its engines, sending waves smacking against their small fishing boat.

Tow, the white-uniformed captain of the yacht, was in his early fifties with a middle-sized build and a tanned face. Leaning over the rail, he called out, "Ahoy, do you have fish for sale?"

With a wide grin showing a toothless mouth, Lu Ke replied, "Yes, sir." Quickly he opened the lid of the container and Snow Flake came with a net. Once she brought the fish out, it struggled to escape but she swiftly secured it.

Snow Flake became fascinated by the sun's reflection off the huge diamond ring worn by a man standing next to the captain along the brass railing. The man was in his sixties, dressed in a navy blue jacket and white pants, and he wore a captain's cap embroidered with gold braiding.

Sir Henry Shih, clean shaven, overweight, short and tanned, peered at them from behind tinted sunglasses. The sight of the young woman's face and fine figure caused his heart to pound. Posturing, Sir Henry gave Snow Flake his most charming smile as a sign of friendship. In return she smiled demurely at him. That jolted Sir Henry, who rose on his toes and indicated that he was pleased.

He whispered to Captain Tow, "Buy all their day's catch at ten times the market price plus five hundred dollars tip. Invite them aboard for some refreshments."

"Yes, Sir Henry," the captain responded.

Captain Tow called out, "I'll purchase all your fish. Would you please come aboard the yacht to receive your money?"

Grandfather Lu Ke and Snow Flake placed all the fish into sacks, and two crew members came aboard the small boat to collect them. Snow Flake followed her grandfather up the ladder of the big vessel. On board, Captain Tow counted out the money as he placed the bills in Grandfather Lu Ke's hand. The grinning man bowed deeply to the captain. It was Snow Flake's first time aboard a yacht. She was very impressed with the spotless appearance of wealth. After he asked their names, the captain introduced Lu Ke and Snow Flake to Sir Henry.

Sir Henry beamed at Snow Flake. "What a lovely name you have, dear. It sounds so charming and has a musical ring. Would you care to have some refreshments?"

"Yes, sir, if grandfather permits." Lu Ke nodded his head. Sir Henry snapped his fingers and a steward came to escort Snow Flake and Lu Ke to the dining cabin. The table was set with an overabundance of food. They were served by two stewards and a chef. After they cleaned their hands with hot towels, Snow Flake ate slowly to savor each bite, while sipping the fragrant tea. Lu Ke was served fish and white wine. This was an experience that Snow Flake wanted to cherish and remember so she could tell her grandmother and her friends.

In addition to the good food, the teenage girl was in complete awe of her surroundings. She especially enjoyed eating with ivory chopsticks and drinking from crystal glasses. After they finished the meal, the pair was escorted back to the deck. Seeing Snow Flake again, Sir Henry was dazzled by her smile.

Lu Ke thanked them for their hospitality. "The food was wonderful, sir. It was very kind of you to allow us to visit your yacht."

"Would you like to see more of the yacht?" Sir Henry asked Snow Flake.

"Yes, sir." A deck hand was immediately ordered to escort Snow Flake on a tour. While Snow Flake was absent, Sir Henry started a light-hearted conversation with Lu Ke. Suddenly he stopped talking, and his face grew serious and discontented.

Shaking his head, Sir Henry sighed, bemoaning his fate.

"Would you believe all my wives have produced only daughters? I employed Taoist priests to exorcise any evil ghosts that might have wandered into my house, but that didn't help. Soon I shall be beyond the age of raising children, and I don't want to adopt a son who isn't of my blood."

The men continued their chat for some time. Sir Henry asked Lu Ke where they lived, and during the long conversation, he inquired the young woman's age. Soon Snow Flake reappeared and Sir Henry's delight showed on his face. Her natural beauty and graceful body movements fascinated him. He held his breath. For him, seeing this young innocent girl was pure enchantment. Sir Henry recognized that she had a quality that set her apart from other females he had known. Calming his emotions, he thought to himself, "Snow Flake and I were destined to meet. She is the one who will give me a son." He saw in her face a mystical aura.

Sir Henry thought of the prestige he would get by flaunting this young beauty before his peers. "She will be an attraction that will cause men to envy me," he mused. Lu Ke scrutinized this rich man's eyes and saw that they displayed desire for the girl. Sir Henry pulled in his paunch while he stood up straight and then ordered another round of drinks. Standing next to her grandfather who was broadly smiling, Snow Flake wondered what the two men were talking about that could bring such happiness to her grandfather's face. Lu Ke thanked Sir Henry again for the hospitality and the parting gifts, including a large basket loaded with cooked beef, bread, Japanese apples, and two bottles of French wine.

Sir Henry was in a jubilant mood, sensing that God made this meeting with Snow Flake happen. Suddenly another thought entered his mind. Sir Henry's eyes turned to study the emotionless face of his captain and mentally questioned the man's loyalty to him. It had infuriated him when he discovered that his wife, Victoria, had bribed some of his employees to spy on him. The very idea that Captain Tow would sell him out was unthinkable. He relied upon the captain's discretion and sense of professionalism too much to enter into that kind of intrigue. As a boss, Sir Henry demanded nothing less than total loyalty from his subordinates, and they were well-paid for their service. Certainly he believed that the captain would not betray him. Snow Flake's image returned to his mind.

With confidence he stated out of the captain's hearing, "This one will give me a son."

Thirty-five years earlier, fresh out of college, Henry Shih became employed by Chao and Pan Limited. It was a well-paid job obtained through a recommendation from a college professor who was a distant cousin in the Chao Family. Mr. Pan sold his holdings to Mr. Chao, but the name of the firm was retained. Mr. Chao became CEO of the company and Chairman of the Board. Ever since Henry started to work at the firm, he projected an image of being humble, polite and hard-working, a respectful young man who supported his widowed mother. Combining a positive image with a sharp mind for business dealings, Henry's performance outshone his competitors within the firm. As a result, Mr. Chao singled him out as the rising star of his enterprise.

At a company party, Henry was introduced to Victoria, the eldest daughter of Mr. Chao. Having just graduated college, she had the healthy glow of youth and beauty. She was also an independent woman. Even at an early age she always knew what she wanted. From all the enterprising young men surrounding her, she selected Henry to be her future husband. She understood that, with Henry's driven desire to succeed, coupled with an easy-going disposition, charm and intelligence, she could use him to gain control of her father's fortune.

While Victoria was indulging her dream of a prestigious future, Henry was having fantasies of his own. He desired a rich and powerful wife, the daughter of the CEO of the firm. He wanted someone who would adore him, a mate who could be easily manipulated and who could assist him to reach the top. Power and money are strong aphrodisiacs that often build into sexual attraction. Victoria and Henry soon found themselves drawn into a strong need for each other. Neither was aware that their attraction to each other was based on pure illusion and the idealized image of the other person.

After a two-year courtship, they married with all the festivities that money can buy. Shortly after the wedding, Henry's charm, together with his talent for business dealing and money-making schemes, won over the entire Chao family as well as the board of directors of the company. Noticing Henry's mounting accomplishments, Mr. Chao gave him a free hand in using the company resources on money-making treaties.

Shortly after the honeymoon, it did not take long for conflicts to arise. Victoria discovered that Henry's ambition clashed with her plan to gain control of her father's empire. That displeased her. She also started to notice that Henry wasn't as easy to bend to her will as she thought. Mr. Chao died a few days before Henry and Victoria's twentieth wedding anniversary. According to his will, Henry succeeded him and became the new CEO.

With power and money in hand and a desire to improve his image, Henry started to donate a huge part of the corporate funds to charities specializing in humanitarian purposes. This, in turn, would help him gain the support of the general public and establish his social status as a kindly rich man and a philanthropist. At the same time, the ambitious man gradually eliminated his opponents to secure his kingdom.

Henry was recommended to the English crown to be knighted due to his good name, his generosity to the needy and the poor in the districts of Hong Kong, and his connection with the British Hong Kong public officials. The company was soon renamed 'The Sir Henry Shih Limited', a name of which he was inordinately proud.

Back on their small fishing boat, Lu Ke was excited as he showed Snow Flake the money which he received from the day's catch. It was much more then they usually earned in half a year. The sun was setting over the horizon as they made their way to the shore where they secured the boat. Snow Flake often glanced at her grandfather who appeared to be extremely happy, radiating an inner glow which showed on his face ever since they left the yacht. She became curious as to what had produced this mood and wondered how this would relate to her.

After supper, Snow Flake sat on the stone stairs outside the house while the old couple spoke in whispers in the kitchen. Suddenly, Grandmother Fei Fei's angry voice leaped through the closed door, followed by banging on the kitchen table. Snow Flake glanced at the open window and saw her irate grandmother vigorously shaking her head as she swept the money off the table. She then turned away from her husband to cover her face with her hands and began to sob. A downtrodden grandfather exited the house and joined Snow Flake who placed her arms around his shoulder.

"What did Sir Henry say to you?" the young woman asked hesitantly.

"He wants you to be his little wife."

"Why?" she inquired.

"Sir Henry desperately wants a son. He has seven daughters by different women. I'm supposed to speak to you about this. Sir Henry will be generous and, if you agree, he will set you up for life. I consented to have him come over to speak to you. Did I do wrong?" Lu Ke kept rubbing liniment on his hands to alleviate his pain. His face was gloomy.

"Bad health combined with poverty, has stripped away what pride I had left. I'm not a wicked man; all I want is what is best for you. Your grandmother thinks that I'm putting you up for sale. That's not true. We both love you and wish that you could have a better life than the one you now have. I know very well that someone without an education or money in this society can go nowhere."

The news hadn't come as a complete shock. She had heard corresponding tales from other girls. A few friends who lived nearby had told her about the Red Light District as well as the working conditions in the big cities. Many poor youngsters toiled long hours in factories and had very little to show for it. Her grandparents' life showed her how poverty could crush a person. Snow Flake's heart was broken. She rose, took her grandfather's hand, and led him back inside the house.

In the dimly lit kitchen, Snow Flake somberly spoke to her grandparents.

"There is nobody in this world but I who will look after you."

"When Grandfather is not able to fish, I have to do it. We cannot exist on my meager earnings because it is not steady. Look at yourselves. You are worn out from a lifetime of hardship. For the love you have been giving me, I ought to take care of you." Her grandmother was crying while her grandfather kept his hands under his armpits.

"When Sir Henry arrives, I shall talk to him. I want to make sure that you're financially secured. It's the only way for us to get out of this hellhole."

Snow Flake went over to hug both grandparents. She hoped they would understand the depth of her love for them.

"In the entire world, you're the ones who are most precious to me."

Soon after, the Yuan family moved to a house in the upper class section in Kowloon Hill. Her grandparents received a bank account containing more than enough money for the elderly couple to live on for the rest of their lives. Not only did Snow Flake return to school to continue her education and to prepare her to be presented to high society, Sir Henry hired tutors to teach her French, music, arts, dance, and official Mandarin.

Eager to learn, she absorbed the training like a young spirited mare.

Two years passed and on her eighteenth birthday, at Sir Henry request, Snow Flake moved into a house on Victoria Peak in Hong Kong.

In the house, there were three staff members at her disposal as well as a tutor to teach her social graces.

Judy, one of Snow Flake's personal assistants, a slender young woman with puppy dog eyes and an eager-to-please attitude, chaperoned Snow Flake. What was unknown to Snow Flake was that Judy was paid to report to Victoria on whatever occurred in her household during her daily activities.

When Sir Henry came for a short visit, he always wanted Snow Flake to know that he was taking valuable time out from his busy schedule to be with her. But it wasn't long before she discovered that Sir Henry was an insufferable bore and he only talked about money, deals, and power. No matter what assurances Sir Henry gave Snow Flake, she understood that mistresses were shadows in Chinese society. Financial compensation was the only insurance against the time when Sir Henry Shih grew tired of her. From time to time, Snow Flake would visit her grandparents to comfort them and receive emotional support. Her only solace was in knowing their days of poverty were over and that she had grown into an intelligent and independent woman.

Eight months after she became Sir Henry's little wife, Snow Flake told him that she was pregnant. Delighted, he immediately employed nurses around the clock to ensure no mishap would befall the unborn child or the mother. When the doctor gave the news that the unborn child would be a boy, Sir Henry could hardly contain his happiness. To the expectant father, it seemed like an interminable pregnancy. Eventually the birth moment finally arrived.

Sir Henry, along with his entire entourage, waited anxiously in the hospital after Snow Flake was rushed to the delivery room. Soon a healthy male child was delivered.

Learning that Snow Flake gave birth to a son, Victoria became livid with rage. Quickly she left her residence to visit Tin Hau Temple where she prayed that the child would become sick and die. She pleaded with the gods not to desert her and reminded them that she had donated large sums of money to this temple. Now it was up to them to pay her back.

Later that day, Victoria sat in her drawing room. Her heavy, round face made her appear like an owl. But that was not where the resemblance ended. Victoria took to adorning herself with expensive jewelry, as if to prove to herself that she was really a worthy human being. Like her distant husband, she became totally arrogant and self-absorbed.

She was waiting for her younger brother, Ung, to get out of his chair to light her cigarette. He was in his late forties, with a fat body and a dull face. Her late father had given him a job in the company twenty years ago. Ung had failed to live up to the family's high expectations, largely due to his weak character and lack of ambition. Disappointed, his father had chosen the next best thing for his son and placed him in an office with nothing to do. He soon became Victoria's whipping boy and running dog. After Ung dutifully lit her cigarette, Victoria demonstrated her displeasure by blowing smoke in his face. Whenever she was unhappy, the woman made sure that those around her were miserable. After two puffs, the cigarette was crushed in an ash tray. Victoria demanded a drink. Ung hurried to the bar to fulfill her command.

She tasted the drink. "Can't you even make a simple cocktail right?" Ung lowered his eyes and meekly stood by her. They easily fell into the routine behavior of mistress and slave.

In the hospital's baby ward, a nurse held up Sir Henry's son for inspection. The proud father tapped the window with his fingertips and emitted sounds of joy as he shouted, "It's my son!" He thought that he could now divorce Victoria and marry Snow Flake. He already had a name in mind for his son, Charles Albert Shih. Long before the boy was born, Henry had selected the name of English kings. Now he felt his life would be complete.

Victoria's Last Laugh

On the following day, the newspaper reported that Sir Henry's newest arrival was a boy. Accompanying the news was a rumor that Sir Henry was planning to divorce his wife of thirty years, so he could marry his new son's mother. The report added salt to the wound of haughty Victoria's bloated ego.

In the living room, hurling the newspaper to the carpet, she shrieked, "How dare that vile man bring shame upon my family and humiliate me in public!"

The turbulent nature of Victoria would never concede defeat. To gain an edge over her husband, she planned to hire the finest lawyers in the district of Hong Kong to assist in her divorce case. When Ung saw that his elder sister had calmed down, he suggested an alternate plan which delighted her. Victoria being Victoria, her hatred and jealousy fed her mind with a secret plan of her own that was even better than the one Ung had suggested.

Sir Henry moved out of the large estate he shared with Victoria one week later to be with his son and Snow Flake. The following day, Victoria met with Lawyer Lum in her drawing room with nobody else present. She was dressed regally, much like a queen preparing for court. The lawyer appraised his client's jewelry and the richly furnished interior of the house while he sat on a high-back chair. He concluded that Sir Henry's wife treated herself very well. From the tone of her voice, he gathered that this woman wanted her orders to be immediately executed. Victoria looked down her nose at the short middle-aged man. He was wearing thick glasses and sported a pencil thin mustache. His hair was arranged carefully to hide his bald spot.

Calmly he lit a cigar. Unaffected by Victoria's glare, he exuded self-confidence. The lawyer waited for the woman to speak her mind. He earned a reputation for defending high-profile criminals who could afford his high-priced service. He often acted as a go-between among the gangs in the area, negotiating shady dealing with a big return. In a round-about way, Victoria finally reached the point of this meeting. Lum was aware of the current happening with Sir Henry and Victoria. It had been front page news for the past few days.

"I want some people to be eliminated," she said.

The expression of the lawyer's face never changed. "Whom do you want killed, the woman or the child?"

"Both," came back the quick reply. "How much do you charge?"

Knowing the wealth of his client, Lum lifted five fingers. "That's five million of Hong Kong dollars."

Victoria nodded stoically. Lawyer Lum would take half of the payment up front. He requested a good faith retainer while the remainder would be paid when the job was done. Victoria rose, indicating that the meeting was over.

"Goodbye Mr. Lum. Remember that this meeting never occurred. Just let me know when the deed is done."

He nodded in assent.

"Send the cash to my office tomorrow morning. No check please." After he left Victoria's residence, Lum informed his associates to start gathering information about Sir Henry and his little wife's daily schedules and activities.

Two months later, on a Sunday evening in the Green Jade Night Club in Kowloon, Lawyer Lum conducted a meeting in a private dining room. He stated that someone wanted two people to be killed. Gascon, in his early forties, known as Red-Headed Devil, was a pitiless, cold-blooded killer. He came to the districts of Hong Kong seventeen years earlier from Ireland. Gascon was six feet two, handsome, with burning green eyes, and a thick head of flaming red hair. He was in command of the Blood Brother Gang. He calmly replied that the price depended upon the target.

Lum placed some food in his mouth and chewed slowly. "Sir Henry Shih's little wife, Snow Flake, and their newborn son, Charles Albert Shih."

Gascon elevated his head and peered at the ceiling, mentally deciding how much money to ask. It took thirty minutes of bargaining to settle on a price of two million Hong Kong Dollars in cash which would be delivered to his Golden Pagoda club in Hong Kong at 8:00 PM tomorrow night. Lum agreed.

"Time frame and location?" Gascon inquired.

"On November 15th, at 6 PM, Sir Henry will throw a grand party aboard his yacht docked in Hong Kong harbor to introduce his son, Charles Albert Shih, to the world. That is the time to strike."

After Lawyer Lum's departure, Gascon refilled his glass with French wine. Holding the glass up to the light, he said, "With the death of the woman and child, Mrs. Shih will get the last laugh on her husband from the comfort of a jail cell. The evidence we leave behind will point directly at her."

In her office, the night club owner, Green Jade, raised her eyes from an account ledger book as Gascon came to her desk and sat on the edge. She was in her late twenties, with a movie-star face and body. The voluptuous beauty's rich perfume stimulated him. Filled with desire, he wanted this woman now.

Green Jade read what was in his mind. Ouyang, a big and muscular bodyguard was standing behind her and lifted the hilt of his knife from the scabbard.

Gascon asked, “Are you free tonight?”

“No, I’m not,” she replied curtly.

“Could you change your schedule for me?”

“Mr. Gascon, for that, you have to speak to Takamura the Dandy, who is my date for tonight.” She realized she was rejecting him rudely, but she didn’t care. She detested this man.

“That Jap fag,” Gascon snorted. Takamura was the owner of the Gates of Hell Bar in Kowloon. He was also an exceptional fighter as well as a cold-blooded killer in his own right. He usually dressed in a white suit, bright red shirt, white shoes, and carried a black sword cane. Gascon knew better than to tangle with him. This man had killed many of the Blood Brother Gang’s members with his bare hands.

When Green Jade noticed the fire in Gascon’s eyes, she shivered. He pressed her again. “Can I see you some other time?” Standing tall, the bodyguard was ready to earn his pay.

“Some other time, when I’m free,” she replied, trying to mask the loathing in her voice. Thwarted, Gascon left Green Jade’s office, mad as hell.

Later that night, Gascon returned to his Golden Pagoda Club. Gavial, the second-in-command, and Sasin, the third-in-line in the Blood Brother Gang, were seated in Gascon’s office. They clasped their hands together in an Indian greeting when Gascon entered the room. Gavial, in his early forties, was considered to be the brains of the gang. The lightly-skinned native of Calcutta was five foot nine, thin, with a pock-marked face, and a highly styled coiffure. Thick lips gave him the appearance of pouting. Sasin, in his thirties, was dark-skinned, muscular, five feet eight, possessing a large head and dark snake-like eyes. He was the chief enforcer.

Gavial listened intensively while Gascon announced their new job. He absorbed the details with his ears opened and his eyes closed. Finally he spoke.

“As a rule, we leave nothing that could point to us.”

Gascon agreed. “Yes. What I want is to leave evidence that will point to Mrs. Victoria Shih, who is Sir Henry’s wife. That responsibility is yours, Gavial.”

After the meeting, Gavial was sitting at his usual table away from the bar and near the dance floor. He ignored the noise and concentrated upon the job at hand. A waiter brought him his usual drink. He envisioned potential variations of his plan to accomplish the task. Hours passed and gradually a concept grew in his mind. Eventually the ideas developed into a series of events.

Gavial's final plan involved two boats decked out with large banners hanging from the top masts and fireworks orchestrated to compliment Sir Henry's happy day. A half dozen of Gascon's men under disguise would be aboard Sir Henry's yacht before hand, waiting for a signal to take out the security guards on the yacht. Knowing that additional helpers would be needed to service the guests for that big event, he would arrange for their gang members to be recruited to work on the yacht on that day.

After the gangs took control the vessel, the young woman and her child would be transferred to one of the Blood Brother Gang's boats and killed. Later, a ransom note would be sent to the grieving father who would believe it was a kidnapping. An expert forger would write the note using Mrs. Shih's script which would be recognized by Sir Henry. Pleased with his plan, Gavial reached for his drink while peering at the scantily clad women on the dance floor. He nodded to one of them, a petite thing that seemed to be steadily looking at him while rotating her hips.

It was 10:00 AM on Monday morning as Sir Henry sat behind his huge desk in his office located on the top floor of the Shih Building in the central commercial district of Hong Kong. It had a panoramic view of the ocean and the island. He was on the phone ordering his lawyer to commence divorce proceedings and validate his new will. The newly signed document made Albert Charles Shih his sole heir under guardianship of Snow Flake. It bruised his ego that some journalists dared write coarse stories in their columns insinuating the child wasn't sired by him. Their names were added to his black list.

When the time was right, he would destroy them, one by one. Sir Henry was certain that it was Victoria's money which paid his attackers. Gloating, he pictured himself as the winner in this dispute. No longer would he be Victoria's comic foil. This male child was living proof of his virility, manhood, and absolute power.

He wanted to introduce Charles Albert to the world and to celebrate his hundredth day. Two weeks before the big event, invitations were sent out to the elite of the District of Hong Kong. The celebration was to be held on November 15th, 1966 at 6:00 PM, on his yacht which was docked in the Hong Kong Harbor. The yacht had been renamed from *The Nine Dragons* to *The Nine Dragons of Prince Charles Albert.*

At that big moment, Sir Henry, with Charles Albert in his arms, posed for the press aboard his yacht. Snow Flake and an amah were delegated to walk behind Sir Henry who wore a jacket embroidered with his big crest in gold thread. He dominated the scene like a peacock among chickens. Snow Flake presented a stunning picture in a long blue silk gown with a gold sleeveless duster. Her hair was piled high topped with a long decorative hairpin in true regal fashion. She appeared to be much older than her nineteen years.

Aboard the yacht, security was extremely tight. The tables were lavishly arranged with plenty of food and flowers. Waiters toted trays of liquid refreshments to be served to the guests. It was slowly getting dark. Weary and bored with this humdrum party, Snow Flake's thoughts turned towards her son. With too much to drink and flushed by the praise of his guests, Sir Henry was delighted. He stood and touched the child's cheek with his jeweled fingers. In the meantime, his security guards continuously circulated among the guests.

Two illuminated boats decorated with long red and gold banners were approaching the yacht. The people on the boats were firing off brilliant displays of rockets, cherry bombs, and strings of fire crackers. Several guests rushed to the side of the yacht, applauding to show their appreciation.

Gascon concealed his red hair under a black wig and darkened his face, hands, and neck with makeup. He wore a large pair of sunglasses to hide his true features. More banners, red in color, were unfurled; it was a signal to the Blood Brother Gang's members on the yacht to overcome the guards. When the boats had maneuvered next to the yacht, a long loud whistle was blown from the yacht. Heavily armed men poured forth from concealment on the Blood Brother Gang's boats toward the yacht. After they boarded Sir Henry's regal vessel, they gathered the fearful guests together.

Once his men had secured the area, Gascon proceeded to board the yacht himself. Gavial was the last one to board. He had darkened his skin and inserted cotton inside his mouth to give his face some roundness. It was decided that Sasin would stay on one of their boats to await the arrival of their new guests, baby Charles Albert Shih and his mother, Snow Flake. It was his responsibility to carry out the killings.

Sir Henry was unaware of the danger because of all the drinks he had consumed. When he noticed that he was surrounded by unfriendly and rough-looking strangers, however, he raised his voice. "What is the meaning of all this?"

Gascon viciously punched him in the face. "Shut up, old man!" Sir Henry staggered backward, bleeding from his mouth and nose. He still held his son in his arms as he struggled to stand on his feet.

Gavial forced Sir Henry to relinquish his hold of Charles Albert and immediately passed the baby to Gascon. Being forcible handled, Charles Albert wet his diaper. Feeling greatly insulted because the baby peed on his hand, Gascon reacted by tossing the baby overboard while the horror stricken guests watched. Gascon seized Snow Flake by her wrist while she tried to jump into the sea after her son. The petite woman fought hard against him, using the natural strength and courage of a mother desperately wanting to save her baby. Snow Flake broke free of Gascon's grip and managed to rake his face with her nails.

This act sexually aroused him and he ordered his men to bring the woman below, instead of killing her. At the same time, when Sir Henry saw his son thrown overboard, he used a father's instinct and forced himself to move forward to save his only son. Unperturbed, Gavial shot him in the head.

Gascon entered the cabin where Snow Flake was being restrained by two men. Touching his cheek, his fingers came away bloody. He responded by sucking the blood and making loud noises, as if he enjoyed the sensation. Gascon waved the men out of the cabin before he locked the door.

"My beauty, it's all in a day's work." Suddenly, he punched her viciously in the stomach. As she bent over, he proceeded to rip off her clothing and shoved her onto the bed. He laughed while she was crying from the pain.

"I am Gascon, the boss of the Blood Brother Gang! I am the king of the districts of Hong Kong! Why don't you admit that you want a real man like me, instead of that old fart?" Hearing the name Gascon, Snow Flake inked it in her brain and in the depth of her heart. Combat and submission was his idea of foreplay. Gascon thought of strangling the woman just when he was climaxing. While Gascon was busy undressing, Snow Flake touched her hair and found the long decorative hair pin still in place. She lay quietly and acted subdued on the bed. While he lowered his body to cover hers, Snow Flake moved her hands behind her head, quickly removed the pin and stabbed it into his left eye. The attack caught Gascon by surprise. Red hot pain shot through his body causing him to violently retreat from the woman.

On his feet, Gascon shook his head like an animal in an effort to dislodge the pin from his eye. His loud screams alarmed the men outside the cabin door. They began pounding on the locked partition and Snow Flake realized they'd break it down soon. Worried, about to be caught, Snow Flake sought a means of escape. She spied the fastened port window. With a mother's vengeance permeating her body, she unfastened the bolts that secured the window and opened it.

With a last look back, she saw Gascon leaning against a wall still screaming. She pulled herself through the porthole and dropped into the cold sea. Snow Flake swam under the water propelled by strong, rapid movements of her feet and shoulder muscles. Further and further into the dark sea she swam, before she dared to pause for a rest and look back at the yacht. She began to swim toward the shore, but was caught in a strong undercurrent which carried her out further into sea.

Gavial and his men managed to break the locked cabin door. Inside, they found Gascon pounding on the walls with his fists and a tasseled hair pin protruding from his left eye. The woman was nowhere in sight, but an open port window told the story. Gavial shouted, "Bring the woman back! Do whatever is necessary to find her!"

Gavial ordered his men to spread out and look overboard. At the same time he ordered a boat which was headed by Sasin to circle around the yacht and look for a woman in the water. Meanwhile, Gascon's men assisted him back to the deck.

When Gascon noticed some of the guests were staring at him, his blood began to boil and he was filled with rage. He roared, "Kill every living thing on board and set the yacht on fire."

His men opened fire into the crowd above, and shots were also fired below decks. It didn't take long. Soon, all lay dead, including those who worked on the yacht. Blood was everywhere. Gascon was foaming at the mouth and his veins bulged in his neck as was aided onto his vessel. Gavial ordered the men to pour gasoline on the deck and over the bodies. Before boarding his own boat, he threw a lit match onto the pool of gasoline.

His crew quickly separated their ships from the doomed yacht, which soon became an inferno. Once ashore, Gascon was taken to a doctor. Sasin conducted his boat to continue the search for Snow Flake.

Adrift in the dark sea for hours, Snow Flake lost all awareness of time. Suddenly, a very bright light appeared on the sea. It took a while for her to realize that it was the yacht on fire. She felt hopeless and exhausted, swimming in the cold, icy waters surrounded by the vast darkness all around her. Snow Flake acknowledged a growing fear as well. She was certain that the killer would be looking for her and the knot in the pit of her stomach grew. Unexpectedly, something bumped against her back. It turned out to be a wooden beam about ten feet long. Hooking an arm around it for support, she allowed the waves to push her farther from the frightening scene behind her. She was grateful the piece of wood had not been a shark.

The sea and stars were witnesses to her torment, but they were indifferent to her loss. The same stars had seen many ships and men sink below the waves. The single powerful force that kept her going was the hope of one day facing her son's murderer. The scene of his death was clearly etched in her mind, and it drove her to seek revenge.

The next morning, November 16th, Victoria sat in her study, waiting for Lawyer Lum to report that the deed had been done and collect the second half of the payment, which amounted to two and a half million Hong Kong dollars in cash. Soon a maid arrived and announced that she had a visitor. To Victoria's surprise, her guest was not Lum but Detective Hom from the British Hong Kong Royal Police. He said he was investigating the case of the fire on her husband's yacht the previous night and the deaths of all aboard. When she heard him say that everyone onboard was dead, her first reaction was to laugh uncontrollably. She quickly became aware, however, of the disastrous situation her action had caused for herself. With the death of her husband, she would lose his royal title and drop out of the high society life which she had enjoyed for so long. The worst part of all was the thought that she could end up in prison for murder. She started to cry loudly and soon fainted. When she was brought to the hospital, doctors declared her dead from a heart attack.

Snow Flake Now Called "Shirley"

The hot sun and the strong current combined to work against Snow Flake. From her position in the sea, she could only take an educated guess where the land lay. She had no idea how far away she was from the shore. The waves broke over her, carrying her up and down in the swells. She picked a direction and pushed the beam towards where she believed the shore might be. Continuous exertion, no matter how small, took its toll. Snow Flake's muscles were aching and beginning to cramp but, driven on by her strong will, the young woman persisted to move on.

From sunrise to sunset, a day passed slowly and Snow Flake was feeling hunger pains. She also was thirsty and very tired. Finally, exhaustion caused her to succumb to sleep. Subconsciously, her arms locked around the beam. In her dreams she was eating and drinking in the port, but mouthfuls of salty water awakened her. Snow Flake became disoriented but her will to live kept her going.

On the third day, still clinging to the wooden beam, she became extremely dehydrated and she began hallucinating. By mid-morning, she was at the edge of losing consciousness. The low sound of engines didn't register in her mind and she was unaware of the approaching boat.

Standing at the rail on deck, men were calling out and pointing at the sea where they saw an arm clinging to a wooden beam. Lao Tung was sixty-three years old, with a husky, muscular definition. He was of medium height and had a weather-beaten face. Lao Tung was the master of the vessel and directed the helmsman to slow down because he wanted to see if anyone was alive. The first thing that caught his eyes was the hand holding onto the beam. It had a diamond ring which was reflecting sunlight.

He asked himself what the hell someone doing in the water so far away from the land. We saw no sign of a shipwreck. He ordered his men to lower a net from the boom to bring the person aboard.

When Snow Flake was laid on the deck, she suddenly became aware that she was on something solid and that there were men around her. Although incoherent and dazed, she still was consumed by rage and prepared to fight to the death. San Lin, in his early thirties, a medium-sized man with small head and weak face, went to grab the woman and was immediately bowled over by a series of vicious punches. The woman scratched his face with her nails. Hurt, frightened and panicking, he ran behind King, a large man.

Looking for sympathy, San Lin made a great show of touching his face and showing everyone that he was bleeding.

"Look what she has done to me!" he whined.

Snow Flake spied some clubs on the rail and, not knowing the men's intentions, quickly picked one up. She was like a coiled serpent. King walked towards her and feigned a move in her direction. Snow Flake ran at him. King, in his late twenties, tall and stocky, lost his nerve and hurriedly moved away, retreating behind his gang. They all laughed at him.

Yu, one of the group's best fighters, was slightly over twenty years old with a short but strong body. When he stepped forward, Snow Flake charged in his direction. Yu kicked the club out of her hand and dropped her to the deck with a punch. No sooner did she hit the deck, when she was on her feet again, on the attack. Down she went under a blow from his fist. The scene was repeated several times.

Lao Tung observed all the incredulous action. He thought that this woman was really something. He looked at her, haggard, water-logged, and exhausted. Yet she didn't know when to quit. What fired her up?

Her whole body was hurting but Snow Flake ignored the pain. She was still full of fight so again she arose and continued to stand her ground against these strange men. Lao Tung foresaw that, with the proper training, she could be an asset to his crew. This time he studied the features of her face. He liked what he saw in her and said to the men, "Yu, that's enough! This woman is mine!"

Obeying his uncle, Yu backed away from her. Gasping for breath, Snow Flake turned to glare at Lao Tung. One more time, she retrieved a club and held it ready for use. Lao Tung approached her and said, "Sea Devil, put that club down and come with me."

Without a warning, Snow Flake made an effort to spring at him. He applied a lock to Snow Flake's arm and applied some pressure. To his surprise, the young woman endured the pain and, didn't release the club. He swung her around, lifted her off her feet, and dropped her on her back.

King, who had fled from the woman, asked, "Sir, is this the woman whom the Blood Brother Gang's members are seeking?"

"Fool, does she look like a prostitute who stole Gascon's watch and money? This one would tear him apart, piece by piece. The woman Gascon is seeking is already on shore. This Sea Devil was washed or thrown overboard from a boat. If you believe the red-headed devil's men, then the woman is yours."

He sniveled, "She will kill me."

"You are a real Jelly Brain."

Suddenly, Snow Flake was on her feet and swinging at Lao Tung again. He applied a lock to her arm and, using pressure, forced her down on the deck. King picked up a club and came over to brain her, but was stopped by Lao Tung who dragged Snow Flake into his cabin and shut the door behind him.

Upon being released in the cabin and spying a knife on the table, Snow Flake made an effort to grab it.

This action amused Lao Tung who said, "I never encountered a woman as wild as you. You don't even know when you're beaten. That is what I like about you."

Snow Flake went for him again. He threw her down so many times that he lost count. Finally Lao Tung flattened her with a punch. The old man watched the woman lying on her back, making an effort to rise. He asked himself, "Who is this wild woman and why are her eyes projecting fire and madness?"

While he persisted to observe her, Snow Flake searched the cabin for an exit and a weapon.

Lao Tung raised his voice. "Sea Devil, do you have a name?"

She chose the English equivalent of her Chinese name. "Shirley."

"Shirley what?"

"Just Shirley. If you don't release me, I'll kill you."

He nodded his head while looking at her. "I believe you. I like a woman who isn't afraid to fight on men's terms. Since you can't beat me, this is what I want you to do. First, remove all of your jewelry and give them to me. These stones can get you killed. Secondly, get out of those wet clothes. You will find dry clothing in the chest by my bunk."

Snow Flake removed her jewelry and placed them on the table. Quickly Lao Tung applied a wrist lock forcing her face to the table. She felt her hair being twisted into a tight knot but no sound escaped from her lips. Lao Tung sheared the hair close to the scalp with his knife. He cast her cut hair into a garbage can before easing his hold on her.

"Shirley, what is your family's name?"

She shrugged her shoulders, answered, "Call me anything you like."

"I'm going outside. Change yourself. There is food in the refrigerator. I shall return in a half hour."

Outside the cabin, the crew gathered to talk among themselves about the strange woman. Lao Tung emerged from the cabin and called all hands on deck. He gave them an ultimatum.

"Do not talk to outsiders about this woman. I will break anyone who disobeys me. Is that clear?" The men then went about their respective chores.

Yu was scanning the horizon on the lookout for the ship they were supposed to contact. It was a rust bucket of a cargo ship, loaded with relics from the Philippines destined for the black market in Hong Kong and Kowloon. Lao Tung mused, "I wish my crew was as tough as Shirley and possessed her guts."

He returned to the cabin to find Shirley seated at the table sipping tea from a cup. When he saw that her breast was pushing out from the shirt, he roared, "Has the sea washed away all the grey cells from your brain? The Blood Brother Gang's members are searching the sea for a woman. I want you dressed like a man in loose clothing. Do it now!"

He kicked open the chest and pulled out more pants, shirts and overcoats. While she put some over-sized clothing on again, she observed him from the corner of her eye. He was mixing something in a glass bowl that smelled awful. "Girl, come here!"

Snow Flake still felt pain from all the fighting and Lao Tung's punches. She reluctantly came towards him.

Looking at her eye-to-eye, Lao Tung said, "Devil Woman, that won't do. Put on enough clothing to give your body bulk." She followed his orders and that pleased him.

"Sit in this chair and show me your hands." Snow Flake sat, glaring rebelliously. Lao Tung cut her fingernails very short. He pointed to the glass bowl on the table. "I am expecting visitors. You will apply this mix on your exposed skin." He left the cabin.

Snow Flake sat on the deck with her back against the cabin door. Together with the effects of hot sun and too many layers of clothes, she was sweating. Waves of fatigue overcame her and she fell into a deep sleep. Swirls of violence and unfocused emotion rapidly consumed her sleep. Snow Flake relived bits and pieces of the recent tragedy but couldn't seem to put them all together. Distressed, she wove them into a nightmare where she was being beaten and clubbed by faceless men.

From a safe distance, San Lin was mesmerized by the woman's changing facial expressions. The sun made the scratches on his face sting. This female wasn't like any woman that he had ever met, and she terrified him. He pointed out to his gang that tears were coming from the sleeping woman's eyes.

Lao Tung's nephew, Yu, sternly scolded the men. "Dog Shits, is there no work on this ship for you but to watch that Devil Woman?"

San Lin replied, "This woman will cause us a lot of grief. Let's cast her overboard."

Yu slapped the top of his head very hard, saying, “Imbecile! Even if she is a sea monster, you dare not touch her. Lao Tung will kill you!” The fear of the old master was enough for the men to leave the woman alone.

Under Lao Tung's Wing

As the mid-day sun progressed towards late afternoon, Lao Tung's vessel made their return journey to their small island, laden with black market contraband. Suddenly, King shouted from his post, "A ship is coming!"

Lao Tung gave his men an order. "Arm yourselves!" He spied Shirley who was in deep sleep, and shook her awake.

"Girl, get inside my cabin and remain there!" He handed her a pistol. "Do you know how to use it?"

Dazed from sleep, she felt the weight of the gun in her hand and automatically replied, "Yes."

He shoved her inside his cabin and stated, "If anyone but me enters, kill the son of a bitch!"

The boat came near and stopped within twelve feet of Lao Tung's vessel. It was one of Gascon's ships.

Sasin shouted, "Ahoy, Lao Tung, we are looking for a young woman who escaped from our boat." Before Lao Tung could reply, Sasin ordered one of his men to board Lao Tung's boat to search it.

When the man landed on the deck, Lao Tung pointed a shotgun at him and fired. He hit Sasin's man in the chest and the stricken thug fell backwards.

"I gave no permission to board my boat. If you are looking for a woman, there are plenty of them ashore. If you send another of your rats to my boat, I'll sink you!"

Spreading his arms wide, Sasin replied, "We are seeking no trouble with you, Brother Lao Tung." Sasin ordered his boat to be moved away from Lao Tung's. The man's defiance enraged Sasin and he vowed that some day he would make the old butcher suffer for this insult. When Sasin's boat was out of sight, Lao Tung ordered a man to throw the body overboard and washed the blood off the deck.

Yu approached Lao Tung, "Uncle, have you considered what kind of trouble this woman will bring us?"

Lao Tung raised his voice, exclaiming, "You are not using your head or eyes! Believe me, boy, that woman can be trained to be a first-class fighter. If this was the army, she would be the general." Yu bowed to his uncle and walked away. He couldn't see anything in the woman but trouble.

At the cabin door, Lao Tung shouted, "Shirley, I'm coming in." When he entered the cabin, he found her sitting on the bunk with the pistol in both hands, aimed squarely at his chest. From this distance she couldn't miss. Calmly he went to the table and filled two glasses of whiskey.

"Devil Woman, put down the gun." To his amazement she obeyed. "My name is Lao Tung. We are a gang of smugglers called the Sons of the Sea. Do you have a family to go back to?"

She shrugged her shoulders. If this man was treacherous, her grandfather and grandmother would be in danger.

"How did you get into the sea?" He received compressed lips and a blank stare.

"Those trinkets you wore on your fingers are very expensive." Still there was no response from her. "The man from that boat sought a woman in the water. He goes by name Sasin, third-in-command of the Blood Brother Gang." Lao Tung noticed that her eyes dilated to pin points, flashing hatred, but he couldn't make the connection between this woman and Sasin.

Pushing a glass of wine towards her, she grabbed it with both hands and drank the entire contents without making a face. The fiery liquid burned her stomach and made her feel nauseous but she dared not to show it. She turned the two names 'The Blood Brother Gang' and 'Sasin' over and over in her mind and etched them into her memory.

When Lao Tung saw the blank expression on her face, he was puzzled. Was Shirley a lunatic or merely suffering from exposure?

"You will sleep in this cabin on the floor because this old man needs the comfort of a bed." He handed her some blankets and then sat down on his mattress.

She made her bed on the floor and closed her eyes. She thought to herself that the devil who leads the Blood Brother Gang's boat is searching for me. "He is the one I want to kill. Someday I'll even the score. Now I must remain silent for this man could be lying to me to gain my confidence. I'll say nothing; otherwise my grandparents could be harmed." Mental and physical exhaustion soon lulled her to sleep. Within a few hours, they had arrived back at their small island that served as home base for the pirate gang.

Ko Nan, the leader of the Sons of the Sea, was in his early forties, tall, well-built, very handsome, well-mannered, and a good communicator. He listened attentively while Lao Tung told him the story of finding Shirley in the water. Lao Tung omitted the part about Shirley's diamonds, lest his boss wish to possess them for himself. When Lao Tung claimed this woman as his own, Ko Nan was filled with curiosity. He couldn't slight Lao Tung, the Kung Fu Master of the Sons of the Sea. He was a trusted second-in-command and a good friend of his late father, Luen Hing Nan. Ko Nan's resemblance to his father was the main reason he was chosen as leader after his father was killed. He emulated his father's winning personality and kept the group's command structure intact.

Immediately, he granted the old man's request. Ko Nan's eyebrows knitted together in deep thought as Lao Tung walked away. He couldn't refuse Lao Tung request after the old man made the claim of this woman being his. What irked him was that the old man had taken the decision out of his hands, without asking him beforehand.

Lao Tung's son, Fung Tung, was in his late thirties, taller and muscular like his father. He bluntly asked, "Father, why do you want to keep that young woman?"

"This woman will make a first-class fighter. I want her entered in your kung fu class."

Fung Tung was vigorously shaking his head. This open affront ignited Lao Tung's temper.

"She will be taught how to fight, if not by you, then by me!"

"From what the others tell me, this woman is a Sea Devil."

"Maybe she is and maybe she isn't. Only time will tell what she is."

The small island occupied by the Sons of the Sea was three miles wide by five miles long. At the north end was a slope which rose five hundred feet above sea level. Behind the white sandy beach was a tall reed marsh. On the opposite side was a stone wall two meters high with numerous gun holes situated halfway up. Beyond the wall was a cluster of old wooden and brick houses where the gang and their families lived. They shared the island with some local fishermen who sold them the day's catch for a reasonable price. Further back was a single path dug out of the slope. The narrow, winding route led to a large man-made cave.

Walking on the sandy beach, Snow Flake lamented as tears streamed down her cheeks.

Questions swam in her mind. When shall I ever see my grandparents again? I have no idea where I am. I don't know whether Lao Tung is a good guy or a bad one. What will happen once they learn that Shirley is just the Chinese pronunciation of 'Snow Flake,' the late Sir Henry's little wife? What will Lao Tung do?

Sensing that someone was following her, she turned her head to face four teenage boys. They were Chopstick, his twin brother Kim, and his two friends. Both Chopstick and Kim were seventeen, standing five foot six inches with husky bodies. Chopstick was good looking, while Kim had a mouth too big for his face. They were sons of Fung Tung and grandsons of Lao Tung.

Chopstick jumped when a rock hit his foot and looked around for his attacker. A girl named Ginger stood nearby. Her eyes were exuding mischief and her hand was full of stones.

"Touch her and your grandfather will skin you alive," Ginger warned.

Kim retorted "What is so special about that woman?"

Ginger replied, "Ask your grandfather, Dog Meat."

Fifteen year old Ginger had a slight built, large, dark expressive eyes, and a happy face. She directed her attention to Shirley. "Come with me. They wouldn't dare harm you. Chopstick is jealous because his grandfather is going to teach you Kung Fu."

One of the boys said to his companions, "Let's go to my house." They left hesitantly.

Once the boys were gone, Ginger grinned broadly and dropped the rocks. "My name is Ginger Sang. Mama is a witch and has the knowledge to cure the sick. Mama said your soul was damaged at sea." Without waiting for a reply, she asked, "How did you get in the sea? Did your boat capsize?" She waited for a reply but didn't receive any.

Worn out from her ordeal, Shirley went to bed sinking into a deep sleep. In her dream, she felt something touching her feet. She reacted by pulling her feet under the covers. It was Lao Tung who had given her feet a light tap with a stick.

"Open your eyes and eat your breakfast. See me outside and don't keep me waiting." Then he left the house.

Quickly, she dressed and went to the kitchen. On the table there was a large bowl of rice covered with pieces of fish and vegetables. After stuffing herself, she went outside the house. She saw Lao Tung resting in a chair with his feet on a knapsack. Without looking at her, he pointed to the floor.

"Take this and follow me," he growled.

Shirley discovered that the sack on the floor was filled with stones. The added weight plus her fatigue made her lag behind Lao Tung. She hurried to catch up with him. They walked towards a path leading upwards to a cave.

At the entrance to the cavern, Lao Tung removed the knapsack from her shoulders and placed it against the wall. Inside the wide cave, she watched the old man slowly perform a series of forms. Shirley followed his movements as best as she could. He performed the entire sequence and when it reached the end, he began again and she followed. Soon sweat soaked her clothing and face blinding her eyes. Lao Tung watched her for any sign of strain. During a break, she was given a drink of water and told to consume all of it and not mind the bitter taste.

When the break was over, he began again. This time he gave her a rag to use as a sweat band. She mimicked each of his body motions but felt that she was losing something in certain positions. When night fell, they descended from the cave. Her entire body was aching and sore, but she knew that her life depended on obeying Lao Tung's orders.

Upon reaching the house, she saw a huge vat of water in the middle of the large room filled with steam rising from it. As she was watching and wondering, Lao Tung walked past her into his room. Moments later he came out carrying an arm full of sealed bottles which he emptied into the large vat.

He said, "After eating, get into this vat and soak yourself up to your neck. Ginger will be here to make sure you don't fall asleep and drown. Don't get out until I come back!" He left the house.

Immersed in the awful smelling, warm concoction, she was surprised to find its soothing effect alleviating her sore muscles. Carrying a small bottle, Ginger entered the house and playfully splashed Shirley's face with water from the vat.

"This medicinal bath will strengthen your internal organs and muscles. It's Mama's herbal therapy. You are to drink the herbal brew in this bottle. If you refuse, I'll call Lao Tung and he will force it down your throat."

With her mischievous eyes twinkling, Ginger vigorously made a display of shaking the bottle. She handed it to Shirley, who sampled the brew, noting that it didn't taste too bad. When the brew was in her stomach she felt herself getting very hot. The internal heat caused her to perspire heavily and turned her complexion scarlet. She fought against the panicky feeling and wanted to get out of the vat. But soon, tiredness took hold of her and she was shutting her eyes.

Alarmed, Ginger shouted and pulled at her hair. "Don't fall asleep!"

The harsh shouting jolted her awake. Seeing Shirley fighting to keep her eyes opened, Ginger clapped her hands gleefully and laughed. She took a cup full of the brew from the vat and poured it over Shirley's head. Ginger then placed a plank across the vat for Shirley to rest her chin. She was playfully touching Shirley's nose.

"Lao Tung wouldn't pay if I allowed you to drown."

Over the next four months everyday without a break, Shirley continued her training. When Lao Tung was on a job, she would have to practice on her own under Ginger's watchful eyes. Shirley practiced the Panther form. Through constant repetition, with her eyes closed, she could visualize herself going from one position into the next. Gradually, she grew stronger. Carrying the stone laden knapsack each day, she was able to run from Lao Tung's house to the cave without stopping. It became a daily ritual. In addition to practicing the form, Lao Tung made her hurl the stones from the knapsack at a slender reed stuck on the cave's floor. She soon became proficient at hitting the reed using either hand. From push- ups to handstands, Shirley's strength soon enabled her to scale a rope as fast as a monkey.

Under Lao Tung's tutelage, her fighting skill rapidly progressed. During a break one day in late April, Lao Tung said, "One Dollar will meet you at the house tomorrow morning. You will go with him to the cave to practice."

Abruptly, he left. Seeing that Lao Tung didn't return after her routine practice was finished, she exited the cave.

Outside, Ginger was sitting on the ground throwing pebbles into a cup. There was a water canteen by her side. Flexing her muscles, Shirley performed the Panther Form again. While in motion, the mischievous Ginger threw small pebbles at her.

"I'm being paid to spy on you by Lao Tung."

"Go away Little Flea. I don't need your eyes on me." Ginger tossed a hand full of stones at her. Shirley evaded some of them. Exhilarated, Ginger laughed heartily until her sides ached. She snapped her finger to a rhythm.

Shirley asked, "Who is One Dollar?"

Ginger's fists struck at the air. "He's an accomplished fighter and skillful at throwing knives. I asked Mama why you never smile and why your face is so fierce while you are practicing. Mama said that your heart is filled with hatred. Is that true? Whom do you hate?" When there was no reply, she continued, "Mama also said that you and I are bound by fate."

"I thought your mother was only into herbs."

"Mama was born with a gift to communicate with her spirit guide. I don't have that gift."

One Dollar, a man in his mid-twenties standing five foot nine, with a heavily muscular body, gazed at Shirley as she performed the Panther Form. He often stopped her to correct a hand, leg, or body position. Just before the noon hour, he spoke for the first time since he brought her to the cave in the morning.

"Teacher asked me to spar with you. Now you can take a break and eat some lunch. Don't eat too much."

One Dollar said to Ginger, "Get two thick sticks and throw them at me."

"No, I'm afraid that you'll hurt me."

"Little Con Artist, you aren't afraid of the devil himself."

Ginger slowly rose to her feet looking around for some thick sticks. When she returned, she quickly hurled the sticks at One Dollar's head. His hands flashed behind his neck where there were two knives in a case which he carried on his back. The knives flew and penetrated the sticks in mid-air.

Looking at Shirley, he stated, "Lao Tung wants you to be able to duplicate what I just did. In return, teacher will promote me as instructor in his class. I'll work with you around the clock if necessary, until you are proficient at that feat. But first you need to learn other exercises and movements. When you are ready, we shall start with a straw dummy for you to practice throwing knives."

On the first day of their practice, they didn't leave the cave until it was dark. In spite of One Dollar energetically sparring with her, she still came out of the contest bruised all over but was not seriously injured.

One afternoon, One Dollar and Shirley squared off at the entry of the cave. She was knocked off balance and fell. Quickly rising on one knee, she charged at him. The results were the same. Ginger clapped her hands whenever Shirley was thrown to the ground.

Standing over Shirley, One Dollar shouted, "You're not a raging bull. You must sink into your roots, empty your chest of tension, calm your breathing, listen, watch, and feel your opponent's movements."

Later, when they circled each other again, he commented, "Very good. Now I'll come at you. You block my punches and kicks then counter with punches and kicks of your own."

There were times, after hours of practicing, Shirley's arms felt like lead. When One Dollar's punches struck her forearm, they weren't strong enough to injure her. During her break, he would slowly perform the entire Panther Form. She was attentive to watch each detail of his movements.

One Dollar wanted to teach Shirley how to handle unpredictable opponents and to ensure that she would be ready to practice throwing knives. Towards the end of the fourth week, One Dollar brought two thin sticks about eighteen inches long. When she attacked him with the sticks, he blocked them and countered with strikes of his own. During their routine practice, he suddenly sank to the ground, picked up two small rocks and hurled them at her. They struck her forearm, causing her to drop the sticks.

Six weeks passed. One morning, when they met in the cave, One Dollar said, "I told you on the first day of my training you, will practice the throwing knives with a dummy. Last night I constructed a dummy of grass and reeds. Tomorrow, you will start to work on the knife-throwing until you master it."

She cried out in anger, "When do I sleep?"

"Much later! Fighting isn't a game. It's a matter of life or death."

Ginger clapped her hands and rolled on the floor laughing. Annoyed, One Dollar scolded her.

"Stop that teasing and leave the woman alone. She is doing well." The praise from One Dollar was encouraging and it spurred Shirley's determination to master throwing knives.

A year had passed since Shirley entered Lao Tung's house on the small island. Physically she was transformed from a toy girl to an iron woman and a skilled fighter. Her unevenly cut hair and her flaming eyes gave her a wild appearance. Ginger, her constant companion, entertained her with many tales, some true and others not.

When Ginger had free time, she and Otto, Ko Nan's only son, would often stroll along the beach. On rare occasions, when Shirley's training day ended early, Ginger would ask Shirley to join them. On the beach, Ginger had an enjoyable time. Exhibiting youthful energy, she would dance to the water's edge and splash her feet in the incoming surf. Ginger liked to twirl long while veils in her hand as she danced. Sometimes, she would kick sand in the air absently and looked at her friend sitting on the sand. Otto would hold her hand and dance with her on the sand and in the water.

An Invitation

One week before the Chinese New Year, Ko Nan, the leader of the Sons of the Sea, received a peace offer from the leader of the Blood Brother Gang, Gascon. It was in the form of an invitation to a party which would be held at The Golden Pagoda Club in Hong Kong. The invitation read as follows: 'Come to celebrate the Chinese New Year with us to establish a venture for the mutual benefits of the Sons of the Sea and the Blood Brother Gang. We can co-exist in the name of peace and prosperity.'

The date was set for Chinese New Year's Eve at 7 PM. Approving of the idea, Ko Nan responded that his group would attend the party.

Lao Tung, who never trusted the Red-Headed Devil, urged the men to go armed. He warned Ko Nan that inter-gang parties were vehicles for an ambush.

Ko Nan touched his shoulder in a friendly manner saying, "We will be cautious."

All the gang members were to attend the party. Left behind on the island were the elderly men and women, and the youngsters. In a festive mood, the men cheerfully prepared to attend the party.

On the day of the party, around 5 PM, the men gathered on the beach. Ko Nan said, "This party represents peace and prosperity for the two gangs. It will not become a brawl. Old grievances towards the Blood Brother Gang will be forgotten. Tonight we shall dine in style for a great future, but don't drink to excess."

When it was time to depart, Lao Tung touched his concealed weapons. Ko Nan signaled the men to board the boats and soon they pulled away from the docks.

After the people who stayed behind had eaten their New Year's Eve dinner, it grew dark outside. Thick gray clouds were hiding the stars and moon, casting dense shadows over the island. Ginger was home grinding herbs for her mother. Several older boys, gathered in packs, were horsing around on the beach, Kim and Chopstick took their turn in mock fighting. The other boys sat around watching and laughed. Otto laid on the sand chewing on a reed. The youth was seventeen years of age, with a sun-burned complexion, and a stocky build. He had an oval face and deep set eyes. Otto dreamed of the time when he would fill his father's shoes and perform daring deeds. Later, the boys followed Otto to Ko Nan's house to sleep for the night.

Ever since Lao Tung and One Dollar worked her to the point of exhaustion every day, Shirley rarely had reoccurring nightmares about her son's death. Tonight however, she awoke at midnight feeling thirsty. After drinking some water, she decided to go out for a walk on the beach before returning to sleep. The ghosts of her past suddenly surfaced and they began to haunt her. The throwing knives which had been given to her by Lao Tung were in crisscross cases behind her neck. They were there ever since Lao Tung gave her a beating for being caught without them. Now she wore them like a second skin.

After aimlessly walking around the beach, she entered the reeds. Invisible among the tall swaying plants, Shirley sat cross legged and shut her eyes only to open them when low murmurs reached her. Not wanting company, she remained motionless in the reeds. Although it was night, she made out two indistinct figures running across the beach and followed their progress with her eyes. When she saw them pause to look about and then move on, she became suspicious. Now the figures reached the stone wall and ran towards her right to the edge of the reeds. They were close enough that Shirley could clearly see them.

A male voice said "All is quiet. Let's signal to the others to land." Shirley listened, hoping to see if they would identify themselves.

The same voice continued, "Little Shau … signal now."

"Didn't Sasin tell us to check and make certain that all were asleep?"

"Fool, can't you see that all the houses are dark?" The other man, cowed by the forcefulness voice, gave the signal by pressing the switch on a flashlight pointed seaward.

Little Shau replied, "It's done. Let's wait here..."

When Shirley heard the name 'Sasin', she realized the peril to the sleeping people on the island. She withdrew her knives, arose from the reed and said, "Hello."

The men looked into the reeds to determine where the voice came from. Before they thought to raise their weapons, her flying knives struck the two men, killing them instantly. Toting their rifles, she ran to Ko Nan's house where, some of the boys were sleeping that night.

Bursting through the door, she tripped over Chopstick and Kim who were sleeping on the floor. Annoyed, Shirley kicked Chopstick's feet. He opened one eye.

She said angrily, "Get up, we need to fight!"

When Chopstick recognized her, he replied by turning over on his stomach. "Shirley, get out of here! Has your moon cycle affected your brain?"

When Kim giggled, she kicked him very hard in his rear. Deliberately he kept his eyes closed. When she laid the rifle barrels across the nape of his neck, he screamed, awakening everybody in the house.

They sat up looking at the weapons in her hands.

"Where did you get the rifles?"

"From the men I killed on the beach by the reeds. I overheard them signaling for someone to come ashore. They are from the Blood Brother Gang! I heard them mention the name Sasin."

Otto was on his feet making round motions with his finger circling his temple. Chopstick said, "Shirley is crazy."

Otto stated, "Crazy or not, show me the dead men."

The boys spread out, following Shirley to the reeds. They stared at the dead men. They didn't recognize any of them.

One boy asked, "What are they doing here?"

Otto began to issue orders. "Chopstick, Kim, Little Tiger, Fish Eyes, Baby Ox, go to the back room to get weapons and alert everyone on the island." With guns in their hands, the boys quickly scattered.

Alarmed by the news, the women silently gathered their small children and animals and, helping their elders walk, retreating to the cave.

Hearing the news of the fight, most of the boys and some of the girls, including Ginger, left their houses and came to Ko Nan's house. The girls were standing by Shirley. Otto ordered the girls to leave for the cave as well. When they saw Shirley was armed for the fight, they picked up weapons too, refusing to leave.

Shirley nodded her agreement. "We need everyone who can pull a trigger."

Addressing Ginger, Otto asked, "Can you kill a man?"

Grim-faced, Ginger answered, "If it means them or my mother, I can do it."

"They don't know we are prepared for the attack." Shirley continued, "Or how many we are. Let's not show them our full strength. The girls will hide in the reeds with me. You boys seek protection from behind the stone wall. We'll have them in a cross fire."

Otto was furious with Shirley who seemed to be taking command out of his hands. "Who are you to be giving orders?"

"Shall we fight among ourselves or against a common enemy?"

A flush spread across his face as he angrily stated, "When this is over, I shall seek you out for an accounting."

"Anytime. You know where to find me."

Otto's maternal grandfather, Hoi Bing, an overweight man in his seventies, was an ex-spy and former army officer. He refused to go to the cave. He felt that it was his duty, as the only adult man with fighting experience, to guide the youngsters in a situation like this, even though he could hardly move due to poor health. He shoved Otto away from Shirley. "Accept good ideas from wherever they come. Let's not show our number to the enemy. Let's confuse them." Knowing his grandson had more ego than brains, he continued, "Shirley will control the firing of the rifles by whistles: One long sound, we all fire. Two short whistles, the girls and I will fire. Three short whistles means only the boys should fire. Now let's conceal ourselves."

Disgruntled when his own grandfather sided with Shirley, Otto was filled with resentment.

He stormed off while shouting, "How could a woman who isn't one of us issue battle commands?"

All was calm, but ten minutes later two boats reached the shoreline. Men leaped over the sides of the boat into the water, and they ran towards the beach, spreading out in an irregular line on the sand, as they advanced in the direction of houses. In the darkness, Sasin could make out that the stone wall was on his left and the swaying reeds on his right. He became angry when he couldn't locate his two scouts who were supposed to give them cover. The silence of the small island gave the men a sense of a quick victory as they increased their pace.

In the reeds, Ginger, remained down within sight of Shirley. Hoi Bing crawled on the ground touching every girl and whispering a number in the firing order. He had a weapon as well, even though he was severely rheumatic. Each girl had a rifle in her hand. They were waiting for Shirley's signal to fire. Crouching behind the stone wall and watching the approaching attackers, the boys were ready for the battle.

Filled with anticipation of the fight, Otto was elated with this opportunity to display his leadership qualities. He pictured himself spearheading a smashing victory. Destiny had given him this opportunity for high achievement. He thought up a brilliant plan which was to divide his force into two groups, one behind the stone wall and the other behind the houses in case they had to retreat. Otto, pleased with his insight into generalship, mused that soon the gang would look up to him as a future chief and commander of the younger generation of the Sons of the Sea.

Shirley, who never removed her eyes from the advancing enemy, spoke in a low voice to Ginger who was on her right side, "Some of us will die. You go to the cave if you want."

Ginger stubbornly declared, "Never…"

"Ok, Little Flea, but remember to keep your head down when the shooting begins."

She replied, "You aren't one of us, and you should to go to the cave."

"Kiss my ass, Little Gnat." Shirley heard Ginger's soft giggle.

Sasin's full complement of men was fifty feet away from the stone wall. With the thought of obtaining a great deal of loot, they broke into a run. The dark-skinned man felt uneasy as his men raced ahead of him. He thought it was too calm. He asked himself why the dogs weren't barking. Where were our scouts?

Sasin said to his men, "Don't leave anyone alive." The men would obey his order without question. Dozens of his men ran headlong to attack.

Fear suddenly gripped Otto as he saw the attackers' faces and the heavy weapons they carried. He wanted to prevent them from getting any closer and let out a long loud whistle. Immediately, both the girls in the reeds and the boys behind the stone wall fired a volley.

Sasin's men were caught in crossfire. More than ten of them were down. They were out in the open while their opponents were concealed somewhere up ahead. His men could not pinpoint the exact locations where the firing originated, so they had no choice but to continue charging in the same direction. Sasin urged his men on. Since the shots came from two separate positions, they hesitated. The men slowly advanced forward before stopping and falling back. Soon another long loud whistle was heard. Both the girls and the boys fired again, and more of Sasin's men went down. This was repeated several times, and more of the Blood Brother Gang's members fell under the withering crossfire.

Noticing that his men were looking to retreat back to their boats instead of returning fire, Sasin screamed at them to charge the reeds. But it was too late; they were caught in a hail of bullets and more of them were down. Some of them were shot in the back while running for the boats and fell into the sea. The wounded screamed for help and tried to crawl away back towards shore. Those who did not make it either dropped on the sand or dropped in the water, dead.

Baptism in Sasin's Blood

Sasin, an experienced fighter, attempted to force the defenders to reveal their position. He set his rifle down and removed the sword strapped to his back. He hurled the sword in the air and it stuck in the white sand, thirty feet away from the stone wall. He cupped his hands over his mouth.

"I am Sasin, the third-in-command of the Blood Brother Gang. Is there anyone among you who will fight me one on one?"

Chopstick dropped his rifle, leaped over the stone wall and ran forward, yelling, "I'll fight you!"

When Shirley heard the names of 'the Blood Brother Gang' and 'Sasin', her temper flared. Thunderstruck, she watched Chopstick emerge from behind the wall with two short sticks protruding in his belt. She thought the young idiot had fallen for the oldest trick in the books. Sasin confidently rose as he ran forward to engage the newcomer. With a series of punches and kicks, Chopstick failed to block his opponent as Sasin toyed with him. From Shirley's observation, she concluded that Chopstick was no match for this veteran.

In the dark, staring at the dark-skinned man fighting Chopstick, and hearing his laugh, a memory was awakened in Shirley. He was the one who led a boat to search for her in the ocean and sent a man to come aboard Lao Tung's boat. A sudden hatred erupted inside her. Retaliation, always foremost in her mind, surfaced in a white-hot rage.

She set down her rifle, touched the knives strapped to her back, and ran forward from the reeds crying, "Stay put! I'm going to help Chopstick kill the beast." In the darkness, Ginger couldn't see Shirley's contorted face or the wildness in her eyes.

Just as Sasin decided to finish off Chopstick, he was caught off-guard by a piercing 'Ki Ai'. He paused and Chopstick took the opportunity to hit Sasin's face with his fist. Shirley dove for the two sticks that had been knocked out of Chopstick's hands. When she came to her feet, she swung the sticks at Sasin's knees. He evaded the strikes by backing away from her then advanced forward quickly, kicking at her body but she didn't release her weapons.

Sasin suddenly turned to grab Chopstick by the throat and squeezed. At that moment, Shirley dropped the sticks and extracted a knife from the sheath. From seven feet away, the young woman hurled the blade at her opponent, striking Sasin's forearm. Released from the death grip, Chopstick fell to the ground and gasped for air. Backing away from his advancing attacker, Sasin pulled the knife out of his forearm, and quickly bound the wound with his head bandanna.

He shouted. "Come to your death!"

Shirley came feet first crashing against Sasin's chest. The impact floored him as he swiftly rolled forward to a standing position. He struck at her face and missed. She countered with punches and kicks. Even though she was outweighed and Sasin had a longer reach, he was forced to back off.

Looking around for a weapon, Sasin eyes rested upon a pistol on the ground. He ran to retrieve it. Shirley, lighter and faster than her adversary, went in hot pursuit and withdrew the sword from the sand. At the same time, he reached the gun and the feel of it in his hand gave him a sense of triumph.

Consumed by hatred and fueled by vengeance for her son, Shirley's strength increased. She swung the sword as Sasin turned to face her, ready to fire. The sharp blade severed Sasin's right arm above the elbow, sending the gun and bleeding arm to fall heavily on the sand. Numbed by pain and in shock, Sasin staggered to remain on his feet while desperately struggling to clear his brain. With red eyes blazing white hot rage, Shirley let out a blood-curdling snarl. Swinging the bloodied sword in her hands, she separated Sasin's head from his shoulders.

Warm blood spurting out of Sasin's body and drenched Shirley, filling her open mouth. She spit out the vile liquid. Barely able to breathe, she retrieved the head and raised it high in the air. She punched at the sky with the sword in her other hand. Her trophies were displayed to Heaven. Her shrieking 'Ki Ai' filled the air.

Horrified by the sight of this blood-soaked woman who exhibited Sasin's head for all to see, Otto cringed from fright and covered his face with his forearm. As long as he lived, he would never forget that piercing scream or the sight of the woman standing over her kill.

Terror stricken, subdued, and unable to close his eyes, Otto muttered, "Shirley is some kind of Sea-Devil bathing herself in her victim's blood. Her fighting skill isn't normal. She behaves like some wild thing that had risen from the sea."

Chopstick was awed by the sight, and as he got to his feet, he hoarsely muttered, "Devil or God, I'll proclaim her my Guardian Angel and forever my sister."

The fighting continued around her but, in the grip of madness, Shirley was unable to release either the sword or the severed head. Standing in the open, she was oblivious to the bullets that struck the sand around her. Hoi

Bing, the old soldier, was aware that the death of Shirley would turn the tide against them. He hobbled as fast as he could move on his weakened legs, ignoring the bullets, and threw himself at Shirley, knocking her off her feet. The bullets meant for Shirley tore into his body.

The sight of Shirley lying prone and unmoving under Hoi Bing's body filled Ginger with fury. She put six clips of ammo in her waistband and let out a long whistle, rose and fired while advancing towards her adversary. This act energized all the girls to follow Ginger's lead. They marched forward, releasing a deadly stream of bullets. As the boys behind the stone wall continued their shooting, several other youths behind the row of houses rushed out to the wall and fired directly at their enemy. With the loss of their leader and horrible visions of their own men dying all around them, the remaining gang members threw down their weapons and fled towards their boat. They moved like demons, shoving the boat back to the water and starting its engine. They did not waste a moment in their effort to get off the shore. Sadly, they even left their wounded in the sea to die.

Kim assisted Chopstick to stand. Slowly, Chopstick walked and spoke in a whisper, "If my sister is alive, bring her to the cave because she is wounded."

Ginger was at his side, wild-eyed, enraged, and full of fight. She aimed her rifle at Chopstick's chest. "If Shirley dies, I swear to God that you will share the same grave, but at her feet." Little Ox dropped to his knees and pried open Shirley's finger to remove the sword and head from her grip. Kim lifted Shirley and carried her to the cave. He was followed by three boys, who passed Sasin's headless body and spit on it. Little Fish, afraid of the head with its eyes staring at him, ran away.

Finally, Otto pulled himself together and led a group of youth to count the dead.

Thirty-seven bodies on the sand belonged to the Blood Brother Gang. The bodies in the water they did not count. They only lost one man, Otto's grandfather, Hoi Bing. There was blood on Otto's arms and face from fragments of a rock struck by gunfire. When he saw his friends looking at his wound, he decided to demonstrate his courage by not making very much of it. To his credit, he was generous with praise for Shirley.

Otto stood near Sasin's headless body and boasted, "When I'm commander, I'll make Shirley my advisor and second-in-command." Later, Otto backed away from the group, walked into the darkness and turned to look out at the sea. Embedded within his brain was the bloody face of the Sea

Devil. Her scream made his soul cringe. Secretly, Otto prayed that Shirley would die from her injury.

In the cave, the frightened elders, children, and women were waiting quietly for news from the beach. They were worried about their loved ones who were outside fighting the war. Suddenly, the shooting ceased for a few minutes but quickly started all over again. It seemed to go on for a long time. The tempo of the fighting finally diminished until it became very quiet. This added to the uneasiness they felt. Gradually, some of boys and the girls arrived at the cave. They were greeted by their fearful mothers or grandparents who held them tight in their protective arms and comforted them with warm kisses.

All the while, the teens breathlessly described Shirley's fight with the dark faced one and their victory. A high-pitched whistle pierced the air. Summer Flower recognized it was her daughter's whistle.

Ginger was shouting, "Mama, we won, we won! But Shirley is hurt!"

Summer Flower ran to Ginger and shook her, "Why weren't you here where you belonged?"

Still clutching her rifle, Ginger fell to her knees. She replied, "I could not let them kill you, Mama. I would die protecting you." Summer Flower embraced Ginger against her body and sobbed. She was trembling from relief. A scream came from one of the women when she saw Kim carrying the blood-soaked body of Shirley.

A girl shouted, "Shirley killed the dark-faced one!" One more time, the saga of Shirley's battle was repeated.

In the cave, Summer Flower ordered Kim to set her down on a wooden bench. Immediately she proceeded to open Shirley's clothing to check her wounds. She ordered Kim to bring her a pail of water with a clean towel.

Ginger squatted down while watching. With a quiver in her voice, she spoke rapidly.

"The dark faced one was strangling Chopstick and Shirley saved his life. He was stupid to fight someone so big. After all, he is still a boy."

After checking her body, Summer Flower checked Shirley's pulse and the lump on her forehead. She concluded that Shirley would live. During the course of her examination, Summer Flower noticed stretch marks on Shirley's abdomen. She reminded herself that Shirley was found in the sea far from land. How did she get into the sea? What kind of past did she have? These stretch marks are from giving birth, she realized.

Ginger couldn't stop talking. "Shirley displayed great courage fighting against the dark-faced one to save Chopstick. People may call her a Sea Devil, but she is also a heroine." Summer Flower told her daughter to hush. The girl put her arm around her mother's neck and kissed her. Tenderly, Summer Flower touched her daughter's face.

Later, Chopstick entered the cave to look for Shirley. Upon seeing her with Summer Flower, he asked, "Mrs. Sang, how is my guardian angel?"

Ginger's sweet innocent face changed and her eyes projected daggers of anger. She yelled, "Brainless idiot! Get down on your knees! She saved your worthless life!"

Summer Flower restrained her daughter and said, "Can't you see that he is injured? Bring me some bruise medicine from my sack."

When troubling thoughts wouldn't go away, Ginger questioned her mother, "Mama, why is Shirley unlike other girls?"

Summer Flower affectionately stroked her daughter's head. "Shirley has been touched by a sea god. Once that happens, a person is never the same. Not all sea gods are evil. Some are good. Her future deeds will be like bright stars shining in the night sky. If there ever is danger, seek Shirley, she will protect you. Why are you still holding that rifle?"

The innocent eyes looked at her mother's face. "I want to protect Shirley's body until her spirit returns. Mama, could being baptized in evil blood, affect one's soul?"

Summer Flower kissed her child's forehead. "Fear not for your friend. A sea heroine lodges within her body. The force within her is very powerful making it difficult for evil to enter."

Otto was still piqued by the sight of the head in Shirley hand, but came to see if Shirley was dead. He carried her throwing knives and made a show of wiping them clean before dropping them beside Shirley's sleeping body.

Trying not to overplay the part, he asked, "How is Shirley, Mrs. Sang?"

"Resting..."

The answer disappointed him. Otto muttered, "I'm glad to hear it." Reluctant to reveal his deeper emotions, the young man would never admit to the fact that this woman terrified him. He would keep his secret deep inside himself.

"Can you look at my arm?" he asked, holding it out for examination.

Ginger saw the caked blood. "Does it hurt?"

Sharks Appear in the Water

It was the commencement of daybreak. The sky was brightening as the Sons of the Sea Gang returned from the peace party. The two gang leaders had signed a peace agreement amidst cheers. One Dollar was on the port side of the boat looking off into the distance. He was thinking about his pregnant wife. The others were either sleeping or singing in groups. When One Dollar noticed that there were an abundance of sharks in the water, he mentioned it to Yu, who shook himself to keep awake. He yawned slowly and looked at where One Dollar was pointing.

"Right. There are too many fins in the water," Yu agreed. The need for sleep had dulled his sense of caution.

One Dollar went for the binoculars. "The sharks seem to be in a feeding frenzy."

Yu saw Lao Tung on deck and shouted over to him.

"Uncle, come over here and have a look at the water near our beach." Lao Tung focused the binoculars on the sharks, then on their island.

His face became grim as he yelled, "Full speed ahead, and arm yourselves! " The men brought out their weapons from the cabin.

When the boats finally reached the dock, Lao Tung took the lead, racing across the bloody sand with the others close behind him, spreading out. They were alert for any danger. When they approached the stone wall, Lao Tung whistled. Immediately he was answered by some of the armed boys and girls who arose from behind the stone wall. They were holding rifles and looked at him expectantly.

Lao Tung asked them, "What had happened while we were away?"

Everyone began to talk at the same time, describing the battle and Shirley's heroic deed. Listening to the story, a smile curled around Lao Tung's lips. Ko Nan arrived with the second wave of men and soon they all heard the story about what had happened. Spotting his son, Otto, Ko Nan placed his arm around the boy's shoulder and went off for a short walk. Otto explained what he had done with his command. Later, after Ko Nan heard more details about the battle, he became angry with his son. The boy had missed the opportunity to display leadership and he became aware that Otto's lack of good judgment and guts might someday come back to haunt him.

A small dog called Woody was in the arms of a little boy sitting outside the cave. Suddenly the animal raised his head and growled. The boy held on tight to the dog's collar because he was ready to attack. One Dollar was running ahead of Lao Tung as the rest of the men followed. He shouted, "Ah

Lan! Ah Lan!" A pregnant young woman hurried out of the cave. There was a broad smile on her face and tears in her eyes.

"One Dollar! One Dollar! I'm here!" Both ran to each other embracing and kissing.

When Lao Tung viewed the headless body and the severed head lying on the ground, he recognized the head as Sasin's. It angered him that Ko Nan failed to heed his warning about this peace nonsense with the Blood Brother Gang. He saw that the agreement was pure balderdash. It was only a piece of paper and not a binding deal forever. There was no honor among thieves. Gascon couldn't be trusted to start with. He thought to himself, "Why had Ko Nan been so blind to the fact and didn't use common sense?"

Inside the cave, he looked around. "Where is Shirley?" he asked a group of women nearby the entrance. Someone pointed to a prone form lying on a wooden bench. He walked over to the sleeping figure and, dropping to his knees, placed an ear against her chest. Summer Flower eyed him critically.

"Old man, what have you been doing to this young woman that made her homicidal? Her injury is superficial. I have given her something to make her sleep."

He ignored the question. Swelling with pride, he lifted Shirley in his arms. He felt exhilarated.

"A little over a year's training, and this Sea Devil knocked Sasin's head off. Everyone said that I brought in only trouble, and this Sea Devil would be an embarrassment to the gang. She has proven me right all along." He exited the cave and carried Shirley towards his house. Lao Tung became aware of Ginger walking behind him and carrying a rifle.

"Little girls shouldn't be playing with guns," the old man said. "Fighting is for men, not women."

"Shirley is a woman and she fought better than any of the men. We killed over thirty of the enemy with only minor losses."

Lao Tung carefully placed Shirley on the bed. Ginger filled him in on the night's adventures.

"Sasin, the dark man, pounded away at her but Shirley kept fighting. She fought to save Chopstick's life."

Lao Tung listened to the girl's chatter as he examined Shirley's bruised face and the lump on her forehead. Rhythmically she breathed in her seemingly peaceful sleep. Chopstick silently entered the house. His face and neck were swollen with purple marks.

"Grandfather, I have come to pay my respect to my sister."

"Boy, you have courage but no common sense. A cub doesn't fight a full grown lion."

For Ko Nan, this instance couldn't have come at a worse time. He resented Lao Tung for being right in warning him about the Blood Brother Gang. He felt he had lost face and pride. He would need to work hard to regain them again. The villagers went about removing all signs of the battle. They wanted revenge. Ko Nan's own gang, led by Lao Tung, wanted revenge for the assault on their island, the death of his old friend, Hoi Bing, and the injuries to several children. In the meantime, the excited children wouldn't stop talking about the battle and their new heroine, Shirley.

Ko Nan belittled his son for his shortsightedness. Once, the boy had been the apple of his eye but now he was treated with scorn. Otto couldn't convey to his father how the battle unnerved him or how terrorized he was by Shirley.

A Brother of the Sons of the Sea

To honor the dead and to comfort the living, the next day the Sons of the Sea held a cookout in the afternoon and everyone on the island was invited.

Shirley awoke hungry and felt sore. Upon sitting up, she experienced dizziness because of Summer Flower's pain-killing medicine. She had no recollection of Hoi Bing's collision with her. She couldn't recall anything about the fight. It seemed like a dream that was quickly forgotten on waking. She felt the lump on her head and it pained her. The young woman slowly rose to her feet and went over to look at her face in the mirror. She made a grimace at her reflection and then proceeded to wash, pee, and get dressed.

The sounds of dogs barking mixed with music made her wonder. Shirley walked toward the direction of the noise. When the women saw her, they nodded in her direction. Seeing a food line where people were waiting to be served, she stood at the end of the line. Hunger pains squeezed her stomach.

When One Dollar walked by and saw her on the food line, he immediately escorted her to the front. With a feeling of pride, he loudly asserted, "Who will serve Shirley food?"

Her eyes widened as the serving woman provided a big bowl with rice, to which was added pieces of chicken, fish, meat, and vegetables. A second woman set a bowl of hot soup in One Dollar's hand. He would hold it for her. She followed One Dollar to a table. A seat was made for her to sit next to Lao Tung. While she concentrated on eating the men passed around a bottle of spirits.

Ko Nan, looking handsome and dignified in his new clothes, rose slowly and asked for silence. He stood and looked directly at Shirley.

"Brother Shirley, we welcome you as a Brother of the Sons of the Sea."

Warmly he smiled at her, as everyone voiced their approvals. She couldn't believe her ears. The title 'Brother' belonged solely to the fighting men.

Quickly, Chopstick and Kim came to stand behind her. Chopstick stated, "Brother Shirley, I'll always fight by your side. We are family now."

She was silently taking it all in. After Chopstick drank from the bottles being passed around, he passed it to the new woman warrior. She wiped the mouth of the bottle and took a drink.

Yu, with a broad smile on his face, commented, "Shirley, be careful! That stuff you are drinking will knock your tits off."

Lao Tung was very pleased that Shirley was accepted into their ranks. She earned that honor for saving the women and children from certain death. And her accomplishments gave her a good standing with the Sons of the Sea. Nevertheless, he was disappointed that Ko Nan fell short of giving her the full credit which she deserved.

Shirley was feeling the effects of the alcohol now and it didn't take long for her mind to get disoriented. She slid off the bench onto the sand. When she couldn't get up, Lao Tung asked One Dollar to carry her home. Ginger followed them.

"Why did you let Shirley get drunk?"

"It's alright to get drunk when you are among brothers. She earned her place. More than some others I could name," One Dollar said.

Shirley awoke and started to rise, only to experience everything spinning around the small room. Her head throbbed. In spite of her condition, she forced herself to wash, brush her teeth and dress. From the position of the sun's rays entering the house, she knew that she overslept. Running outside, she found Lao Tung sitting on a chair with his leg dangling over the armrest of the chair. In his hand was a bottle of wine, from which he was drinking.

"Sorry, Sifu, I've overslept." He was amused. This was the first time that the sign of madness wasn't in her eyes.

"You are not going to the cave until you are fully recovered, but that doesn't mean you're not to practice. Do everything slowly without straining yourself."

While he was drinking, he mulled things over in his mind. In all this time, he couldn't get her to freely talk about how she got into the sea where they found her. She never mentioned a family name. In spite of their kindness and friendship, she still didn't trust anyone. He took a long drink from the bottle and swallowed it to clear his throat.

"You must be wondering how we make our living and why we live on this little island. We weren't smugglers or pirates to begin with. After the communists took over the mainland China, Chiang Kai Shek's central intelligence chief ordered us to stay there to work undercover. We were to spy on the communists for Taiwan, 'the Republic of China', which was ruled by the Kuomintang party led by Chiang Kai Shek and his followers. Our duties were to collect information on Red China's political and military activities, and to act as insiders to support the Kuomintang's return to mainland China later. We were highly trained intelligence officers and soldiers; we had fought against the Japanese first and then the communists. The year was 1949. We believed our leader would regain power and return to the mainland China within a short period of time."

"One year later, the Korean War began. The communist regime was getting bigger and stronger while Taiwan became weaker and weaker. When we lost our contact with Taiwan as well as our financial resources, we were bewildered. Gradually, one by one, our men were caught and executed by the communists. The remaining sixty decided to escape from the mainland China." Lao Tung stopped talking to refresh himself with another long drink.

"Luen Hing Nan was the highest ranking officer among us. He commanded a boat. We made our escape just hours before the communists could reach us. Some lucky ones brought their families with them and some of us left without saying goodbye to our love ones. Upon reaching Hong Kong, we made contact with the Kuomintang official there. They branded us as traitors. We did nothing wrong. We simply obeyed orders from our leader. All the promises given to us were broken by the Kuomintang. Half our group chose to live in Hong Kong as refugees, while the rest of us sailed out to the sea. Finding asylum was no easy task. Feeling hopeless and angry, we landed on this small fishing island. There, the poor villagers and fishermen welcomed us with open arms. Since then, we ceased being soldiers and spies. To make a living, we took on smuggling and piracy." Shirley, sensing his pain, lowered her eyes. She found herself strangely moved by Lao Tung's recital of his life experience.

Lao Tung continued. "After years of struggling, we had to have some establishment here. For essentials of living, we built a dock and houses, and repaired the old stone ones. We brought in electrical generators and later had phone lines installed. Gradually, the original residents—the majority of them are fishermen—and their families had mingled with us. Eventually the younger fishermen had given up their fishing and joined the Sons of the Sea while the older ones remained on the island, living on our resources. Some of the young women married our gang members or our daughters married some of the young fishermen. The people living on this small island became one big happy family. That is what you see today! Believe it or not, we have a doctor here; she is Ginger's mother."

During the following six months, Shirley, Kim, and Chopstick worked out together, both inside and outside the cave. From time to time, ether Lao Tung or One Dollar would come to check their progress.

Ko Nan was under constant pressure from the majority of the people on the island, including members and non-members of the Sons of the Sea, to punish the Blood Brother Gang. Gavial explained to Ko Nan that his gang had

had no part in the raid on that New Year's Eve night. He said it happened because Lao Tung made Sasin lose face by killing his man. The attack was Sasin's own idea; it was done without Gascon's consent. Ko Nan accepted the explanation.

However, Lao Tung refused to buy that excuse lightly, he bitterly told Ko Nan, "Gavial is lying! None of the Blood Brother Gang's member would dare to act without Gascon's permission. I can see Sasin wanting revenge, but how about the other seventy odd men? Gavial can't explain them away! Besides, right now they have been facing a major setback, a loss of fighting men. If we don't retaliate now, not only we lose the opportunity but the other gangs in the District of Hong Kong will see us as paper tigers."

Tsung Chun was in his fifties, strongly built and tall, a renowned fighter, and the third in command of the Sons of the Sea. He was eager to take over the leadership from Ko Nan. "Lao Tung is right. I side with Lao Tung. Gavial was white-washing the attack at the very time when you signed a peace agreement. I see it as a well-planned and premeditated action."

In the back of his mind, Ko Nan really wanted the memory of the raid to fade away. But the voices of Tsung Chun, Lao Tung, their combined followers, plus the rest of the islanders wouldn't allow him to forget or ignore it. Since Gavial was the brains of the Blood Brother Gang and the second in command, instead of fighting the Brood Brother Gang face to face, the Sons of Sea would, therefore, target Gavial as the first to be killed. A failure on Lao Tung's part would serve to weaken his standing in the Sons of Sea Gang. Success, on the other hand will diminish the force of the Blood Brother Gang that serves Ko Nan's ambition to be the greatest shark in the Districts of Hong Kong. For this purpose, he agreed on the action to eliminate Gavial.

San Lin, a supporter of Ko Nan, was an avid gambler and was encouraged by Ko Nan to circulate false rumors about Lao Tung. He spoke to others how old and out-of-date Lao Tung was. The men backing Ko Nan expected he would consolidate his power in the gang and eliminate his rivals. In the meantime, Ko Nan secretly offered Iron Hand, Tsung Chun's nephew, money and an upgraded position in the gang, if he would spy on his uncle for him. Short on brains and eager for recognition, glory and fast money, Iron Hand agreed.

Ko Nan was aware that a victory over the Blood Brother Gang would elevate his own position in the region's underworld. He thought killing Gavial, one of the most influential men among his rivals, would be a good way to start. He would be steps closer to reaching his ambition.

While Lao Tung and Tsung Chun were busy with the preparations for revenge, Ko Nan opened discussions with Chief Goo of the Seven Oceans Gang to establish an alliance to challenge the Blood Brothers. The rumor on the street was that the Blood Brother Gang was talking peace but, at the same time, quietly eliminating the smaller gangs in the region.

To get the police force on their side, Chief Goo suggested that they should put some police officials on the payroll. When Ko Nan assented, Chief Goo proposed that they also annex territory belonging to weaker gangs and initiate themselves into dealing drugs. He declared that, with the profit from the latter venture, they could pay for police protection and still have a surplus left over. Chief Goo's smile indicated greed. However, Ko Nan's eyes weren't seeing a partner; he was looking at a dead man.

When Lao Tung and Tsung Chun learned of Ko Nan's intention of territory expanding and the drug trading, they were disheartened. Lao Tung stated, "Expansion is going to create enemies and, besides, since when is Chief Goo to be trusted?"

"Drug money is not worth the risk," Tsung Chun added.

With a smile on his face, Ko Nan's sugar coated words drew pictures that fighting men understood. Avarice tipped the scale in Ko Nan's favor, as the majority of the Sons of the Sea sided with him.

The Truth

Since the Sir Henry incident, Gavial had grown both in size and in his pocket book. After Sasin's death, he increased the number of his bodyguards to five men. As an extra precaution, he constantly wore a bullet-proof vest. Two of his newly hired bodyguards were a Cuban named Julio La Casa, a prize-winning karate fighter, and Obanda, imported from Japan's Yakuza.

It had been a year since the raid on Ko Nan's island and Lao Tung now set the revenge plan in motion. Yu and One Dollar had shadowed Gavial for months, familiarizing themselves with his habits and daily routines. The plan was to kill Gavial after he emerged from his limo but before he entered the Black Rose Brothel. The establishment was operated by Black Rose, and located down a narrow alley in the red light section of Hong Kong. According to a source, Gavial would visit there almost every night.

Yu was assigned to blow the rear tires and Motai would take care of the limo's engine. Motai was in his late twenties, of medium size with a strong body. He had good features and was one of Lao Tung's best fighters. A group under Yu would ensure that none escaped from the alley or entered the brothel. Lao Tung stressed that there were to be no living witnesses to the attack.

Shirley was ready to do her part in the assault. From pictures that Lao Tung had passed around, even his face had been changed from the night on Nov. 15 1966, but she still recognized Gavial as the one who handed her son, Charles Albert, to Gascon. This was the opportunity she had waited so long for. It was 9 PM when Lao Tung sat with his team in a van parked in the alley nearby the Black Rose Brothel. Shirley, Motai, One Dollar, Yu, Tsung Chun, Iron Hand and ten more men were awaiting Lao Tung's signal.

At 10 PM, a black limousine entered the alley and stopped at the entrance to the Black Rose brothel. Five men emerged and formed a protective semicircle around the car's rear door. Julio was continuously looking around. When he was satisfied it was safe, he knocked on the car's rear window. Gavial emerged, quickly surrounded by bodyguards. As the group approached the back door to the brothel, Iron Hand suddenly peppered the bodyguards from his hiding position. It caught Gavial's men by surprise.

Immediately, Gavial calculated that he couldn't safely make the brothel door so he turned back towards the limo. Just at that moment, shots were fired at the limo tires and engine disabling the car. One Dollar lay down a steady stream of gunfire into Gavial's bodyguards. Shirley positioned herself to intercept anyone who attempted to flee. Motai shot a man who was charging Shirley from her blind side. Aware that the car was useless, Julio dragged Gavial toward a street he knew should be opened. Obanda followed closely behind them. It was Lao Tung's gunfire that brought Julio to the ground where he died.

With everyone's attention focused on Gavial, Iron Hand, acting upon direct orders from Ko Nan, shot and killed Tsung Chun, eliminating one of his commander's rivals.

During the heat of the battle, Obanda shoved Gavial ahead of him while they ran, with Shirley in pursuit. Coming into range, she hurled her knife at Obanda, piercing his neck. He fell heavily upon the pavement. Without a bodyguard, a fearful Gavial continued to run. Soon he was fatigued and panting for breath.

Gavial turned to face his assailant, raising both arms up in a gesture of surrender. Soaked with sweat and gasping for breath, he said between pants, "I'll go peacefully. Any amount you desire will be paid."

Shirley replied, "There isn't enough money in the world to pay for your life! Remember Charles Albert Shih, the baby you handed to the red-headed devil? That baby was mine!"

Fear was replaced by panic as Gavial desperately turned his head searched for a way out of the alley.

Without a hope of getting past the woman, he pleaded. "Have mercy."

"Mercy! She screamed at him. "Did you show mercy for my son and the people on the yacht? I want vengeance!" Knowing that his death was imminent, Gavial speared two fingers at her eyes. Shirley grabbed the fingers and broke them. The pain sent Gavial to his knees. She struck at his throat with her knife until his eyes bulged. His hoarse cry was drowned out by the blood filling his throat. He didn't want to die. She stabbed his neck again with such force that the blade came out the other side. She continuously stabbed the body with all her strength until Lao Tung came to pull her away. He was puzzled by the excessive viciousness.

"Woman from hell, I'll see you back at the house!"

On her way to the boat, Shirley passed by a temple. She stopped to pray for her son's soul. The aroma of incense filled the hall. She told the child's spirit, "Revenge was close at hand. Total retribution would be most sweet."

When she confronted Lao Tung inside his house, he suddenly lashed out with a kick. The impact sent her upwards and she landed on her back.

He stood over her. "Why did you mutilate Gavial's body? Speak or die here."

Their eyes locked together. “I can’t die until I have killed Gascon.”

He folded his arms across his chest. “Tell me about yourself and you had better tell the truth!”

“I was the late Sir Henry Shih’s fifth little wife. My name is Snow Flake Yuan and we had a son, Charles Albert Shih, the first male heir in Sir Henry’s line. On my son’s hundredth day celebration, the Blood Brother Gang’s members attacked the yacht. It was Gavial who took my son from Sir Henry Shih’s arms. He then handed my son to Gascon, who threw him overboard. Gavial shot Sir Henry in the head. This all occurred in front of my eyes,” she sobbed reliving the scene “Later, Gascon attempted to rape me. That’s when I took his eye with my hair pin. I made my escape through a window of the cabin of the yacht and jumped into the sea where you found me. They also set the yacht on fire. I saw the yacht become a ball of flame while I was trying to swim toward the shore.”

“What proof do you have that corroborates your story?”

“I’m the only living proof.”

“Do you have any relatives?”

“My grandparents...”

“We shall visit them tomorrow. Get your ass off the floor and clean yourself up.”

At noon the next day, Shirley was dressed in feminine finery, accessorized with sunglasses and a wig. She stood alongside Lao Tung in front of the iron gate of her grandparent’s house. Dressed in a suit and tie, Lao Tung rung the bell. A woman emerged from the house and came over to the iron gate.

“Sir, can I help you?’

“Yes, does the Lu Ke Yuan family live here?”

“The Yuans used to live here. They are dead now.” The woman then closed the door as she went inside the house.

A dumpy woman from across the street called to them. “Are you related to the Yuan family? They were such a nice couple.”

Lao Tung replied, “No, they are related to a friend of my daughter.”

They walked across the street towards the woman. Her mouth was moving rapidly, spitting out words as fast as she could move her lips.

“The old man died over a year ago after a stroke. His wife was despondent and alone. A few months later, she became ill and committed suicide at his grave. It was such a pity. The police were looking for their relatives. I don’t know the outcome.”

Shirley's face was ashen. The woman was shaking her head. "They were really nice people and devoted to each other."

Lao Tung thanked the woman for the information.

While walking away, he took Shirley's arm and whispered, "I believe your story. Control yourself. Let's quietly leave this place."

On the bus, Lao Tung lowered his voice and scolded Shirley.

"I know it's a shock. They were your only living relatives. However, you must clear your mind and think. The Blood Brother Gang's members are searching everywhere for a trail leading to Gavial's killers. Keep your wits about you." Lao Tung peered at the faces of the people as they sat on the bus. He saw that they were reading newspapers or looking out of the windows. A few stops later, Shirley felt Lao Tung putting pressure on her arm.

He whispered to her, "We'll get off here."

In the House of Chung restaurant, Shirley sat across from Lao Tung. She had no appetite for food. While Lao Tung was eating, he often glanced at her. A group of young men entered the restaurant looking for trouble. They made loud noises before sitting at an empty table. Zen Chan, a tall, skinny youth, eyed every woman in the place. When he noticed Shirley, he rose and walked over to Lao Tung's table.

"Woman, come over with me and serve us!" When Shirley ignored him, he angrily shouted, "Do you want us to hurt this old man?"

Lao Tung replied forcefully, "Get the fuck out of my sight!" The youth attempted to kick him but Lao Tung caught the leg and punched his shin, breaking the bone. A howl of pain erased the smiles on all his friends' faces. The old man stood and declared, "This old man will give you a lesson you'll never forget!"

Wanting to avenge the insult to their friend, the group attacked Lao Tung as a pack of wolves would go after helpless sheep. Lao Tung knocked them all unconscious with quick punches. He snapped his fingers at Shirley, beckoning her to follow him out of the restaurant.

Ko Nan was relieved that Tsung Chun was dead; removing another rival suited his purpose. While everyone thought that Tsung Chun's death was unfortunate, only he and Iron Hand knew the truth. He gave Lao Tung and Tsung Chun full credit for the killing of Gavial, the second in command of the Blood Brother Gang.

One afternoon, during her break from practice, Shirley walked on the beach. Heart-wrenching scenes flashed before her eyes. It was constantly replayed in her mind—the loss of her son and her grandparents. Finally she sat on the dry sand and pounded it with her fist.

Ginger came to Shirley. She was disturbed by the painful expressions on her friend's face.

"Are you alright?" Ginger asked.

"Will you ever stop asking me questions?"

Undaunted Ginger replied, "How can I learn anything if I don't ask questions?"

Shirley stretched out on the sand looking up at the sky. Ginger came closer.

"Otto said that he wants to marry me when I'm of age. Mama said that I shouldn't marry him because he has a weak face and a short chin which represents a short life." She went on and on, but Shirley heard nothing. She was completely lost in her own world of sadness.

Ever since Gavial's death, Gascon had became extremely cautious. All his efforts to uncover those who killed Gavial and his henchmen came to a dead end. This made him feel very uneasy. Compounding his present problem was the British Hong Kong Royal Police. Sergeant William Chu had him brought into the station for questioning about drug deals and recent murders in the region.

Gascon arrived with his lawyer, Lou Keung. Controlling his temper and peering at the ceiling, he allowed Lou Keung to do all the talking. Sergeant Chu portrayed him as a ridiculous figure in the Hong Kong underworld, brushing aside Gascon's accusations that the Sons of the Sea killed Gavial. Instead, Chu showed him pictures of dead women, asking, "Do you know them? Do you know who killed them?" Sergeant Chu looked into Gascon's eyes, searching for the truth. "When will your next shipment arrive?"

Lawyer Lou Keung answered for him, "My client's a businessman, not a criminal. How could he know who killed them? And there is no next shipment, because my client does not know anything about drugs."

Hours later, Gascon was out on the street. He chided his lawyer for not filing a complaint against Sergeant Chu for character assassination.

Lou Keung asserted, "The sergeant is only doing his duty."

Gascon received orders from the Blood Brother Gang's governing body in India to retain his floundering position. He proceeded to recruit more men while awaiting the arrival of his new second-in-command from India. One of his recruits was Peter Hsu, a relative of San Lin's wife. The man was given the assignment of introducing San Lin to Indian hashish. He accomplished this order by paying for the drugs that San Lin used. Soon after, he was addicted to it.

Due to his gambling habit, San Lin worked all the angles to make extra cash. Recently he had been caught by Lao Tung stealing from their consignment. That act should have been his death warrant, but Ko Nan thought he could still be of some use and exiled him temporarily instead of killing him. Saving his life made San Lin indebted to Ko Nan.

Gascon questioned Peter Hsu as to what he had learned concerning the killing of Gavial. The young man said, "San Lin had mentioned that Ko Nan was satisfied with Gavial's explanation for Sasin's raid. He accepted our assurance that it was provoked by Sasin being angry with Lao Yung for killing his man." This pleased Gascon. The "Redhead" had his own theories about Gavial's murder, believing smaller gangs were attempting to muscle in on his holdings. One particular person came to mind—Takamura the Dandy. However he had quickly ruled him out. Takamura, owner of the Gates of Hell Bar, didn't need others to kill the few men who guarded Gavial.

From some informants, Gascon learned that Lao Tung, in the company of a young woman, was in the area around the time of Gavial's death. Peter Hsu stated that Lao Tung got into a fight with some Blood Brother Gang's members over a woman. Gascon thought to himself, "That's not like Lao Tung's style! So, it's unlikely the Sons of the Sea's members were involved in Gavial's killing. There is always the possibility that the real perpetrator organized a team to take out Gavial. Then it could have been someone within the Blood Brother Gang itself who was jealous of Gavial's influential position and sought to replace him."

Shirley Goes after Gascon's Head

It was November 15th, three years ago to the day when Gascon threw her son, Charles Albert Shih, overboard. In the morning, Ginger did not see Shirley in the cave. She searched for her friend in their usual hangouts, but her efforts proved futile. The girl went to Lao Tung's house and no one was home. There, on a table in the kitchen, she found a note. It was addressed to Lao Tung, written in Shirley's hand, and stated she was going to Hong Kong after Gascon's head.

With the note in her hand, Ginger raced out of the house to look for Lao Tung who was practicing Kung Fu with members of the Sons of the Sea in a clearing behind his house.

She went over to him, showed him the note, and whispered, "Shirley has gone to Hong Kong after Gascon's head." The words brought a scowl to his face. Usually Lao Tung was quick to be anger and just as quick to be cool down, but this news made him silently fume.

"That young woman will age me before my time!" He addressed his students, "Come with me." He approached Ko Nan and pulled him aside. "A private matter has arisen and I must attend to it."

Lao Tung ordered his men to go to Hong Kong to search for Shirley. He then went into his house, and reached for the phone.

He muttered, "Didn't that wild woman learn not to throw away her life?" Lighting a match, he burned Shirley's note.

On the phone he spoke rapidly. "William, One Dollar will deliver a picture of a young woman to you. Please find her for me." Still irritated, he cursed to himself. "Why didn't that hard-headed woman consult me first?" Suddenly a thought popped into his head. He dialed another number.

The ringing went on for a minute before someone answered. "Takamura, this is Lao Tung…"

In Hong Kong, heavily padded with a stocking cap pulled over her face, Shirley waited five consecutive nights in a dark doorway, opposite the Golden Pagoda Club. Her gang brothers had mentioned the place belonged to Gascon. She was burning to complete her vendetta, and the waiting did nothing to appease her anxiety. Observing all the dressed up patrons walking into the club, she recalled the times when she and Sir Henry dined in such places. On the sixth night, she changed her lookout position to the rear of the club and found that luck had followed her. As she was waiting around the street corner, three limos came down the block, spaced a short distance between themselves, and headed towards the rear entrance of the club.

After all the cars were parked, the bodyguards emerged. To Shirley, it seemed to be a lifetime before Gascon appeared. When finally he did, the bodyguards quickly surrounded him. Touching her knives for reassurance, Shirley raced from the dark shadow towards the group. The alert guards immediately spotted her. Quickly, eight of his bodyguards shoved Gascon inside the night club while the remaining ten battled the sudden intruder in the dark ally.

Armed with guns, Lao Tung's men began to wonder why Shirley was going after Gascon all alone. In addition to Chopstick and Motai, four more of Lao Tung's men arrived at the Golden Pagoda club grounds. When they were alerted by the sound of fighting coming from the rear of the nightclub, they ran to investigate.

Motai shouted, "Look! There is your crazy sister! She is taking on the entire Blood Brother Gang. We must open an escape route for her, or else Shirley is a goner." They fired at Gascon's men, who turned to meet their new attackers. Now bullets were flying and coming from two directions at once. Gascon's men broke off their attack on Shirley and retreated behind the limos. Two long whistles followed by a quick third one pierced the air. It was a signal for Shirley to know that she wasn't alone. She fought her way through the thinning ranks and made her escape.

Shirley covered three miles in her sweat soaked clothing. She discarded the knit cap, and the extra clothing in a garbage can down the street. Later she entered a clothing store, purchasing a light red nylon jacket, blue stretch pants and a pair of high heel shoes. Being a brother of the Sons of the Sea entitled her to a share in their profits. The cash was squirreled away for a time like this one. Further down the street in a public rest room, she changed her clothing. With a thought of getting off the street, Shirley checked into a small hotel. The next morning, she was on the move again, riding buses through the town.

Gascon was furious. Blind with rage, his eyes bulging and the veins throbbing in his neck, the leader of the Blood Brother Gang vandalized his office after being informed the assailants had escaped.

He ranted and raved, "Comb this fucking region and beat any informer who knows nothing or won't talk. I don't care how many you kill but don't return without concrete information."

Sergeant William Chu was off-duty drinking in a bar. On the table lay a picture of Shirley, the young woman Lao Tung wanted him to find. William was in his early thirties, and stood five foot eleven. His build was thin but wiry. William's martial arts skill and positive attitude had earned him plenty of respect on the street. Even though he and Lao Tung were on different sides of the law, they were good friends who treated each other like father and son. Years ago, Lao Tung saved his life when, as a rookie, William was caught in a cross fire between rival gangs. Since that time, they had forged a special friendship which spanned many years.

It was through Lao Tung that William had met Takamura the Dandy. There was something in their characters that drew the three men together. Not only were they drinking and eating buddies, but Takamura's suggestions often helped William Chu untangle many difficult cases. Now, William had this particular woman whom Lao Tung asked him to look for on his mind.

"What's so special about this woman, Shirley, whom Lao Tung wants me to find for him? But since Lao Tung asked, a favor is a favor." Placing the picture back in his pocket, William committed the woman's features to memory and left the bar. The hunt was on.

In a room of a hotel in Hong Kong, Lao Tung paced the floor like an anxious father awaiting the appearance of his wayward child who had being absent for many days. One Dollar, Chopstick and Motai came to his room.

One Dollar addressed his teacher. "The police are everywhere. While we were on the street, we were picked up and taken to the police station for interrogation."

Chopstick added, "Motai and I got Shirley out of the trap unharmed, but she passed us on the run."

Lao Tung pounded the top of the table. None had ever seen him so angry.

"She apparently made her escape but to where?" Both men were silent. He peered at Motai who merely hunched his shoulders and shook his head.

Lao Tung exploded, "Did you see which way the Sea Devil was heading?"

"Only as she flew past me without saying a word."

"Why didn't you stick to her like fly paper?"

"You didn't tell us to act as her nursemaid. It would have been dangerous if we were seen together."

Lao Tung was ranting, "She is behaving wildly and not thinking rationally. It's imperative that we find her before it is too late!"

In an effort to keep off the street, Shirley purchased a ticket for a movie theater. As she sat in the small seat, she was thinking on how to finish her plan of revenge. There must be a way that I can kill the red-headed devil! Suddenly her attention was drawn to the action on the screen. The picture was a spaghetti western made in America. It mesmerized her the way the gunfighter quickly and accurate fired his weapon. The scene inflamed her imagination. She contemplated if she could learn how to shoot like the man in the movie, I could kill Gascon no matter how many bodyguards surrounded him. When the movie was over, she stood up and calmly walked outside. She was pleased because she found a way to murder the red-headed bastard. Shirley spent another night in a different hotel.

After showing Shirley's picture to numerous hotel clerks, William finally received a nod. When Shirley emerged from the hotel in the morning, William immediately recognized her. Without attracting attention, the police sergeant trailed her on foot. When he saw Shirley enter a restaurant, he stood outside peering within, pretending that he was looking at the menu on the front window. In the meantime his partner parked the car nearby.

Inside the restaurant, Shirley was sipping her tea while her restless eyes were in motion. When the policeman entered and stared at everyone's face, she became uneasy. She lowered her arm, touching a knife hidden in her pocket and obscured by a table cloth. William sat down opposite her and placed both his hands on the table.

He smiled at her. "Good morning. Could I see your ID, please?"

"Are you a cop?"

William turned to the waiter, "Soup of the day, shrimp with lobster sauce, sesame chicken, and a bottle of red wine."

She leaned towards him with the knife in her hand touching his genitals.

Still smiling, he ordered, "Lean back in your seat. I would like to think that because of my good looks, your hot, excited hand is touching my genitals and not the tip of your knife. Lao Tung wants you home. I have your picture in my pocket."

When she heard Lao Tung's name, she sat back in her seat, returning the knife to her pocket. The waiter brought the food and set two plates on the table with chopsticks and poured out the wine in two glasses. William dropped the picture on the table where she could see it.

"I'm Sergeant William Chu of the British Hong Kong Royal police, a friend of Lao Tung. You may call me William."

After a glance at the picture she shoved it towards him. "There is a resemblance, but it's not me."

"This is good wine. Shirley, do you have a story to tell?"

"Doesn't everyone?"

"Do you want to tell me your story? I'm a good listener."

"Why should I trust you?" This put a damper on their conversation. They ate slowly until the meal was finished.

William called for the check, said, "Shirley, come with me."

"Why should I go with you? You haven't shown me your ID? How do I know that what you told me is the truth?"

"That's a good point, but I won't answer that until you call me William."

"Why play cat and mouse? I'm not Shirley."

"Fine. Prove it to me." He extended his left hand.

"I left my ID in the hotel." He eyed her purse next to her elbow. He removed his ID from his jacket pocket and held it open before her. She gave it a quick look.

He rose from the table, saying, "I'll escort you back to your hotel. Perhaps you will be able to locate your ID."

William held the front door open for her as she stepped past him onto the street. When the policeman noticed her tense body language, he knew that she was going to make a break. Quickly he pinned her arms behind her back and pressed her body against a wall. Within seconds, she was cuffed. He extracted her knives from her pocket and moved her towards their police car. His partner opened the rear door and ushered her inside.

William sat next to her. "Sorry about the inconvenience but One Dollar had warned me how dangerous you could be in close quarters. I can't take the chance of having any one injured. Relax. We are going to the docks to find your friends."

William was studying her face and saw the hostility in her eyes. She appeared crazy enough to try to fight her way out of the car.

Softly, he said to her, "If you attempt to attack anyone, I'll resort to chaining your hands and feet to these floor rings. You have my word, we won't harm you."

As they approached the pier, they saw two vessels moored alongside. She recognized them and knew that the Sons of the Sea's members were here. The car stopped and the rear window rolled down. William called to Fung Tung who was standing among a group. He swiftly approached the car. William got out and pointed to the woman in the rear seat. Fung Tung bent over to look inside the car. A broad grin appeared on his face. He turned to William and nodded. William brought the woman out and removed her handcuffs.

Fung Tung made a big show of circling her while eying her up and down. She stood there and ignored him.

Fung Tung said, "It's a good thing father isn't here. He is mad enough to make you swim behind the vessel back to the island." He looked at her flashy appearance and smiled. "Let me say that you look like a million dollars. Are you ok?"

Her face remained expressionless. "I'm fine. Who is that policeman?"

"He's father's good friend." She stood there quietly while Fung Tung turned to thank William.

"You acted wisely handcuffing that one. With her hands free, there is no telling what damage she could have done." William paid no attention to what Fung Tung was saying. He found himself highly attracted to this woman. It was more than a casual interest. He wanted to see her again.

Shirley and her companions boarded one of the vessels, and the lines were slipped off the mooring. The engine started, and the vessel moved away from the dock. On the boat, at the order from Fung Tung, she was surrounded by the gang until Captain Yao led her to the cabin.

"I don't want to anger Lao Tung any more than you have already done. Stay here until we arrive at the island."

Shirley Meets Takamura

From the dock, carrying her high heel shoes, one in each hand, Shirley walked to Lao Tung's house. There, she found him seated on a stool in the middle of the kitchen. His flaming eyes bored into her. He had been drinking his red wine.

"Where are your brains? Are the cells out to lunch? Is your thirst for revenge so powerful that it obliterates your rational thinking?" His voice took on a sharp edge as he continued speaking, "Now, have you learned that revenge isn't like a quick fuck? It involves a great deal of planning and preparation!"

Shirley interjected, "If I can be taught how to shoot like an expert in the American western movies, I can kill Gascon, no matter how many men guard him." He fell silent while absorbing her remarks, giving no clue as to what was in his mind. Occasionally he nodded his head. Although he knew what needed to be done, he toyed with her to teach her a lesson. She stood in front of him for ten minutes before he waved her to leave.

Shirley remained standing on the porch, commenting to herself, "At least Lao Tung hasn't kicked my ass." Inside the house, Lao Tung was on the phone talking with Takamura to discuss Shirley's situation.

Suddenly she heard her teacher shout, "Come inside!" Shirley reentered the house and found her teacher in a better humor. Lao Tung was drinking red wine from a bottle.

"Sunday, we will go to Kowloon. There you will meet Takamura the Dandy, who will take you under his wing. Today is Monday. During this week, he and I shall put our heads together and devise a plan on how to successfully avenge your son."

Shirley was relieved that the Old Dragon was going to send her to learn precision shooting. On Saturday night, Lao Tung was on the phone with Takamura and it was decided that Takamura would pick up Shirley at 11AM the next day, in the alley behind his girlfriend's apartment building in Kowloon.

In the car, Shirley studied the man sitting next to her. He wore a white suit, bright red shirt open at the neck, red socks, white shoes and a panama hat. The man was tall with a strong, good-looking face, black hair, and long, well-manicured fingers. He wore a heavy gold chain around his neck which reflected under the sun light. She guessed he was in his early thirties.

He commented, “Lao Tung is getting soft in his old age. Had you been my student and acted so foolish on your own, I would have tied you to a tree and beaten you.”

Instantly, she disliked this man. His nickname, “the Dandy,” rolled around in her head. Then it came to her who he was. He was the infamous proprietor of The Gates of Hell Bar. This Japanese fighter easily outclassed her. She heard the name Takamura from One Dollar and Yu. They had often spoken about Takamura’s fighting skill. He would kill his challengers with his bare hands and his fierce reputation established his position in the Districts of Hong Kong. They concluded that, without an equal, he was the most skillful fighter in the entire region and beyond. She wondered why Lao Tung placed her in this killer’s hands.

That afternoon, Shirley stood beside Takamura in a high class French restaurant, waiting for the maitre d’ to escort them into a private dining room. The Japanese man had brought her here to carefully study her.

Takamura thought the woman seemed to belong in this classy setting. Why had Lao Tung told him that she was a wild woman? Was the old man seeking another opinion of her? She had been described as very cunning with a fire burning inside her. The waiter came and spoke in French. Shirley ordered her meal in the same language.

The wheels in Takamura’s head turned while he watched her eat. “She is using the correct utensils and good table manners as she eats and sips her wine. Where did she learn French and correct table etiquette?” Now Takamura studied Shirley’s face in earnest.

“This woman has a strong face and good looks. She seems very smart yet has a background steeped in mystery. With patience and specialized training, she could develop into a fine mercenary. Lao Tung can also read faces. There were signs of power etched on her face along with a tendency to be headstrong.” He observed how she sat in the chair. “Who taught her to sit like that?”

After the meal, they walked together along Kowloon Bay, looking at the well-kept houses. She opened a discourse while holding onto his arm.

“Takamura San, I want to kill Gascon for my own reasons.”

He cut her short and changed the subject. “Woman, when Lao Tung asked me to help you I should have paused to consider his motives. By the way, where did you meet Sergeant Chu?”

“William?”

“Yes, that’s the rogue’s name.” He was grinning at her. “He likes you and I can’t blame him. You’re beautiful and appear to be smart. I warn you, don’t make a fool of him. He is my friend. He's been talking about you a great deal."

Shirley didn't reply. Takamura switched the subject again. "I am going to hire an instructor to teach you how to shoot. His price is $5,000 U.S. dollars. I shall pay him up front and later you will repay me ten times that amount."

"Takamura San, where am I to get that much money? Besides, what if I should die in the act of my revenge?"

He brushed that aside. "You will become a mercenary."

"Don't I have a say in matters of my life?"

"You are smart and headstrong. Your nature can't stand too many bosses, especially if they are men. I shall not tread upon your feelings."

On a street, Takamura walked ten feet away from her, then stood there and looked at a house. Shirley thought of William. She liked his warm, friendly smile yet her urgency for vengeance of her son's murder overshadowed everything else. She walked over and stood beside Takamura. They looked into each other's eyes.

* * *

Thirteen years earlier, at mountain Dojo in Japan, Yagako Ohara was the best student whom Grandmaster Shiro ever produced. He was far superior to all the other students, including Yoko, the grandmaster's son, who was jealous of Yagako's talent. The two became rivals.

Four years later, on his sixty-fifth birthday, the grandmaster let his students know that Yoko would receive his robe of authority when he retired. This injustice went against Yagako's lofty ambition and embittered him greatly.

One day during his midnight walks, Yagako came upon the master instructing his son. Shiro was teaching his son the secret kata of the Shiro family. Crouching behind a tree in the dark, Yagako absorbed the secret kata form and made it his own. Feeling betrayed, he decided to leave Grandmaster Shiro. However, he felt he needed a good reason to do so.

Six months later, when the master was relaxing on the porch painting a picture, Yagako approached him.

"Master, I have received an offer of a position from my uncle in Hong Kong where I shall be trained to operate a textile company." The statement was partially true. The uncle was only a minor manager in a clothing department store which was owned by a Chinese man in Hong Kong. In the store, Yagako would start as a salesperson.

The grandmaster gave him his blessing. Before leaving Japan for Hong Kong, Yagako and Yoko fought one final time, but it was hardly a contest. Triumphant, Yagako left Grandmaster and the mountain Dojo behind with his head held high.

In Hong Kong, Yagako was bored with his dreary sales job. Since he was a fast leaner, he used his spare time studying languages and reading literature. He enjoyed books of all kinds and from different countries. He was especially fond of detective stories. His problem-solving skills and quick thinking could make him a first class inspector or detective, if he chose to be one. On one summer's day, two years after he arrived on the island, a young Japanese sales representative came to the store on business. The visitor was eager for some adventure, so Yagako's boss instructed him to accompany the young Japanese on a night out on the islands.

The man insisted they go to the Gates of Hell Bar which was well-known in Japan. The bar was filled with people of all nationalities. When Yagako and his Japanese associate were drinking beer, a tall English seaman, with a large belly overhanging his belt, sat at the next table drinking with his mates. He saw the Japanese men and, picking up an empty bottle, rose to go to their table. Standing over the two of them, he said nothing. Suddenly, the Englishman smashed the bottle over the head of Yagako's guest. The blow sent him to the floor.

The Englishman started kicking him and shouted, "I'll kill the Japanese bastard!"

The word cut Yagako like a knife. Rising, he shoved the drunken Englishman away from his fallen friend.

He said, "Englishman, you have won. The fight is over."

The man, drunk and infuriated, attacked Yagako.

"Jap, I'll crush you like a bug!" He kept coming at the Japanese pair when suddenly nine more large men walked over and joined the action. Yagako slammed his fist into the Englishman's face. Quickly a free-for-all ensued in the bar and Yagako fought like a trapped tiger. When the melee was over, Yagako was the only one standing tall. However, he couldn't locate his companion, who had left in a hurry during the commotion. For the first time since he left Japan, Yagako felt like a man and he enjoyed it.

The door in the far end of the bar opened. A current of air brought the aroma of a rich perfume into the room. A small, elderly Chinese woman emerged. She stood slightly less than five feet tall, heavily made up, and dressed in clothing from the Manchu style worn by royalty in the Ching

Dynasty. She was escorted by two young girls, who supported her arms as she walked.

Lady Anne said, "Young man, you are the finest fighter I have seen in many years. What do you call yourself?"

He reached for a name. "Takamura...Takamura." It was the name of a famous Japanese baseball player whom he admired. He noticed that the woman was old but had retained some of her beautiful features.

"Takamura San, do me the honor of dining with me tonight."

He was led into her private quarters at the rear of the bar. Glancing at his surroundings, he recognized that every item in the room was from the Ching Dynasty. They were priceless. The young girls assisted her by holding her elbows as the elder woman sat down in a chair.

A little while later, she explained herself looking up at him. "I am called Lady Anne. I own the Gates of Hell Bar. My hired helpers were all subdued by you. I drink to your fantastic skill and courage."

Meanwhile, Lady Anne was studying her guest's face. "May I ask what brings you to this side of the world?"

"Escape from the past."

During the meal, Lady Anne often looked at her new companion.

"My life had always centered on intrigue, and it's a trait which I inherited from my Manchu blood and family court connections. In my younger days, I was a spy, arms merchant, and advisor to whoever paid the highest price. My youthful years were filled with glory and adventure. Growing into maturity I added the Gates of Hell Bar to my belongings. I graduated into smuggling and planning mercenary operations. I employed only the best fighters to defend what is mine. Tonight, you, Takamura San, defeated the best fighters in the entire region. Would you consider being my bodyguard for ten percent of the total gross of my operations?"

"I'm not interested in a small percentage of your gross from this bar." Lady Anne's mouth moved but she didn't make a sound. She was thinking.

"My side dealings produce huge profits." The money wasn't Yagako's main interest but it occurred to him that this place was an outlet to sharpen his martial skill and nurture his ambition.

"I don't work cheap, Lady Anne." With that, the negotiation went far into the morning hours with a final figure totaling 900,000 Hong Kong dollars a year. Content with her bargaining, she drank a final toast with him. He scrutinized her face and thought, here was a master of mind and money. I should study her methods and learn about the art of negotiating and dealing.

As time went by, Takamura became known as the Dandy, a term derived from the way he preferred to dress while he walked on the streets. He ruled the Gates of Hell Bar and some other businesses for Lady Anne, competing against all challengers while protecting her interests. This hot spot became a magnet which drew fighters who desired to display their talent seeking jobs in this region. Anyone who fought against Takamura would be defeated. For those who would never admit defeat, the fight lasted to the death. In addition his fight skill, there were many talents of Takamura seen only by a few people. He was a fast and eager learner, a voracious reader, a serious painter, a poet, and a deep thinker. To further broaden his interests, he mastered the art of stage make-up. Lady Anne, under Takamura's protection, freely continued to apply her money-making deals until her death.

From Lady Anne's will, Takamura discovered that her real name was Fire Lady Fu and her birthplace was Manchu in northeast China. It was also revealed that he was the sole heir to her vast fortune that included numerous legitimate and illegitimate businesses. He transferred large amounts of cash to an account in Japan under his real name. He sold some of his businesses to various investment houses throughout the world, but kept his hand in smuggling and mercenary services and the Gates of Hell Bar. It was due to Lady Anne's connections in purchasing antiques that he met Lao Tung. Instantly they liked each other and a deep friendship was formed. It was at that time the Blood Brother Gang emerged from a vicious war against the other gangs and became the most powerful gang in the Districts of Hong Kong, under the rule of Gascon.

According to Lady Anne's financial records, a large sum of money went to various charities, such as refugee camps, schools, orphanages, Hong Kong senior centers, animal rescue missions, art institutions, and medical research. Some money was donated to charity organizations in Taiwan. All the donations were made under the name of a third party, Kown Yen.

Takamura was curious about her past. It took him two years of investigative work to find out the true Lady Fire Fu. She was the first cousin of Yee Fu, the last king of the Ching Dynasty. During World War II, after the Japanese occupied the Districts of Hong Kong, she was sent to Kowloon as a spy by the central intelligence bureau of the Republic of China. Her mission was to obtain information about Japanese war activities for her country. Later, some of the information was sent to the United States, which was allied with Republic of China in the fight against Japan.

She established and operated the Gates of Hell Bar as a cover. After the communists took over mainland China, she continued her spy work on and off, unofficially, for the government of Taiwan. Throughout all the changes, her loyalty was always to her country, the Republic of China, now Taiwan. It took a tough woman to run her businesses, both legitimate and covert. Her courage, her unique character, her exciting, colorful and adventurous life story could have been made into a top selling movie – maybe a female version of the British spy James Bond, alias 007. Takamura San respected her kindness to all living things, her support of educational and cultural causes, and her loyalty to her country, from the depths of his heart. To keep her legacy alive, Takamura continued Lady Anne's charity works under the same name of Kown Yen, the Buddha of Mercy.

Shirley Becomes an Expert Shooter

Shirley stood behind Takamura while he rang a bell of a big house by the Kowloon Bay. A Chinese woman opened the door. "I'm Lily Gam. How can I help you, sir?"

"I would like to see Mr. Ahn Tran on business." She nodded and ushered them into the living room.

While Takamura was looking around the room, the Chinese woman asked, "May I have your name, sir?" He handed her a card with the name Takamura San.

"Please be seated. I'll be right back," Lily replied, before disappearing into the hallway of the house.

Takamura told Shirley to sit next to him. Within minutes the woman returned with Ahn Tran. He was in his late thirties, slight of build with an expressive face and intelligent eyes. He sported a broad mustache and a military style haircut. Smiling, he addressed his visitors in Chinese. "Who referred you to me?"

Takamura paused as he placed his cane on the expensive stone coffee table. His host said, "I have the finest jade collection in the Districts of Hong Kong."

Takamura interrupted him. "Major General Nguyen."

Ahn Tran glanced at Lily who was serving tea. He recognized the name of his commanding officer, wet his lips and added, "What can I do for you, Takamura San?"

"Let's get down to business," Takamura announced. "How much is your current fee for teaching someone how to shoot?" Ahn Tran's eyes went to the Chinese woman, seeking a sign.

Receiving none, he replied, "My business is only in Jade. I don't instruct in the use of firearms." Takamura removed his wallet, extracted 5,000 U.S dollars, waved them in the air, and set the bills on the table.

"I'm not connected with the police or any organization of the government. Perhaps my name is unfamiliar to you. I'm the owner of the Gates of Hell Bar."

Lily Gam's eyes flashed recognition. Ahn Tran said, "Your name means nothing to me."

The woman, however, came to collect the money. "Takamura San, Mr. Tran will teach the young woman how to shoot," she announced.

He replied with a nod of his head. "Since you're a professional," Takamura continued, "we abide by the rules. Under no circumstances you are to ask this woman her name. While she is staying here, be certain that nobody else sees her or has any contacts with her. Just teach her how to shoot."

Ahn Tran suddenly became very business-like. "It will take two months if she stays here during the entire period."

Takamura sprang to his feet and picked up his cane. "Two months to this day, I shall return to see the results."

He turned to Shirley. "I will leave you here. Learn well. See you in two months." She bowed to him.

Shirley lived in a room in the basement and ate her meals there. That arrangement was made by Takamura for her safety. She arose early each morning. The practice room was in the basement next to the room where Shirley was staying. It was soundproof. At the beginning, she was taught how to care for her weapon. Later, she was taught to fire with either hand. While shooting, she wore soundproof ear covering. Her first targets were stationary penny arcade figures on a track. When she became proficient, the targets became mobile.

Ahn Tran trained Shirley long hours. During her rest periods, he filled her head with an image of a leading man in a western movie and he used two guns at the same time to kill all the bad people in the story.

Before Takamura brought Shirley to Ahn Tran, the Dandy had learned that Ahn Tran was a jade dealer whose sideline was to teach individuals how to shoot for a high price. The background check on the ex-lieutenant colonel cost Takamura ten thousand Hong Kong dollars. Ahn Tran's distinguished career in the Vietnamese Army's branch of jungle warfare came to an end when he was injured. The small man had the distinction of being the best shooter in the army, and he was a gold medal winner at the Asian Olympic Games. Years later, he emerged in Kowloon where he met Lily Gam, a widow owning a residence where she rented out rooms. Ahn Tran's relationship with Lily Gam blossomed into a business venture. Because he was not particularly good at accounting, Ahn Tran left the financial end to Lily while he focused on his jade trade and sideline jobs.

Two months to the day later, Takamura returned to Ahn Tran's place. After the demonstration of Shirley's shooting skill, Ahn Tran, who was proud of his accomplishment, said, "She is good."

Takamura's eyes displayed discontent. Slowly he stated, "Perhaps I didn't make myself clear enough." He waved 5000 U.S. dollars. "Her rapid fire must have pinpoint accuracy against moving targets, and she must be able to use both hands to shoot at the same time. Can you accomplish that?"

Lily stared at Ahn Tran, who replied, "It will be done to your complete satisfaction." The money was place on a table.

William had been searching for Shirley and, not finding her with Lao Tung, asked for a meeting with Takamura. At the Tai Hing restaurant, William and Takamura behaved like contestants in a grand championship chess game.

"Takamura San, where are you hiding Shirley?"

"Just because you can't find the young woman doesn't mean I'm hiding her. William, old friend, there are other fish in the water besides Shirley."

The British Hong Kong royal policeman looked his adversary in the eye. "I sense your involvement in a shell game. All I want is to talk to her." With no response coming from his Japanese friend, William shook his fist at him. Takamura's fingers were brought together until they touched. Seeing that gesture, William realized he would get nothing out of him.

William shouted, "You egomaniac!" He rose to leave.

Takamura calmly replied, "Are you certain that Shirley wants to see you?"

"Tell me where I can find her."

The response was quick. "Sit down and finish your drink."

"Takamura San, you're a piece of shit!"

With his eyes twinkling at William, the man laughed. It confirmed William's judgment. Takamura knew how to get in touch with Shirley. Lao Tung had feigned ignorance when William had asked him the same question. Therefore the policeman concluded that Takamura and Lao Tung had teamed up to do something. He was willing to bet that Shirley's disappearance might be just a distraction. To what end, he couldn't surmise, but he knew it was only a matter of time before he ferreted out the truth.

Takamura was curious about her as well. He often wondered who she was. Where did she come from? Who taught her French and high class table manners? How did she get in the sea? That was where Lao Tung found her more than three years earlier.

"Why did Lao Tung talk to me about a plan to kill Gascon?" Takamura asked himself. "There's got to be a connection." The mystery intrigued him and began to occupy much of his thoughts.

Since Takamura's second visit, Ahn Tran pushed Shirley to excel. Their practices were longer and more difficult. He was adamant in his instructions. Years of shooting experience were compressed into four months. She practiced firing at rapidly moving targets. Her performance was above Ahn Tran's expectations. She memorized all of Ahn Tran's lectures, and could field strip her weapon blindfolded. Shirley's ability to quickly draw with both hands at the same time and rapidly fire with deadly accuracy improved. With a stop watch, he timed her response.

Ahn Tran said in a calm voice, "Draw and fire." When she did something wrong, his voice would slightly rise.

"Open your ears and eyes miss! Keep your mind focused on what you are doing!"

Two months had passed since Takamura's last visit and again he returned to collect Shirley. Takamura were standing beside Ahn Tran, watching Shirley demonstrating her skill of shooting with both hands at the same time. Takamura appeared to be pleased with what he saw.

"You have done well. Once we are gone, eliminate all traces that this woman was ever with you."

Ahn Tran replied, "Your words will be followed to the letter."

Before departing, Takamura handed Lily a thick envelope. Lily gave Ahn Tran an inquiring glance and passed the envelope to him. On returning to their living quarters, Ahn Tran kept weighing the sealed envelope in his hand.

He commented, "I'm not psychic or clairvoyant, but I tell you that things in the Districts of Hong Kong are going to heat up. That young woman's skill will be employed in a way I don't wish to mention."

In the living room, Lily took the envelope away from Ahn Tran and opened it. It contained 10,000 U.S dollars plus two first class tickets for a four week cruise on a luxury liner.

Peering at the tickets he stated, "Takamura San is a man of honor. When we return from our vacation, whatever he has planned will be old news."

A Fine Edge

One afternoon, Lao Tung came to call on his old friend. While relaxing in Takamura's apartment, they talked about both past and current topics. Finally, Takamura got around to a point that had been bothering him.

"I used a lot of legwork to gather bits of information about Shirley's past." When Lao Tung averted eye contact, it revealed that he knew more about the woman's past than that he was telling.

When Lao Tung remained silent, Takamura pressed on. "Even William got sidetracked, but he is actively looking for Shirley. Do you know that William often plies me with questions about her?" Lao Tung swirled the red wine in his glass.

"I should have never sought William's help to find Shirley."

"Can you prevent the rain from falling?"

"Damn you, you think too much!"

Takamura, shaking his head, declared, "And you, old friend, are guilty of burying your head in the sand. It isn't like you."

When he got no response from Lao Tung, he continued, "After Shirley kills the murderer of her son, she should be channeled to a different line of work. If not, Ko Nan will see her as his rival for Gascon's vacant position." Lao Tung was out of his chair and dropped back into it. He wondered how much Takamura knew about Shirley's past.

"On what basis can you draw this conclusion about Ko Nan?"

"We both know Ko Nan well. He's actively building the Sons of the Sea to fit his ambition using greed and the weaknesses of human nature. He understands that once Gascon is dead, the seat of the lead position in the underworld of the districts of Hong Kong becomes vacant. He plans to fill that vacancy. It would be a big mistake for you to become complacent." Takamura was hinting to Lao Tung to watch his back.

"Ko Nan is not his father, the honorable soldier, Luen Hing Nan."

One month later, a meeting took place in Kowloon at the apartment of Lao Tung's girlfriend, Blossom. Lao Tung sent her out shopping before his group arrived. Shirley, Chopstick, Yu, and Motai got down to the business at hand. Since Lao Tung was second in command of the Sons of the Sea, he first conferred with Ko Nan about the killing of Gascon. The eagerness didn't show on his face or in his eyes. Ko Nan understood that the killing of Gascon meant that, once it was accomplished, his next agenda to eliminate the Blood Brother Gang would be a piece of cake. His ambition to be the king of the entire underworld of the districts of Hong Kong would be reached. With that goal in mind, he willingly gave his consent.

Shirley was attentive while Lao Tung explained the plan. "Chopstick, Motai, and Shirley will be dressed as if you come from a rich family. Shirley will flirt with Gascon if she gets the chance in the night club. A Chinese jacket will cover your weapons. Motai's weapons will be strapped close to his body and his suit jacket will be tailored to hide the weapons. Chopstick will be at the bar wearing a raincoat with the gun inside his pocket A generous tip will obtain a table where Shirley can be seen by Gascon. Shirley, your appearance must be sexy enough to attract Gascon's attention." Lao Tung looked around the room to make sure he had their complete attention.

"If and when Shirley is invited to Gascon's table will be the time to kill him. Gascon never allows his bodyguards to sit with him at the same table. Chopstick, at the bar, will be Shirley's backup. While Shirley shoots Gascon at his table, Motai will get near the bodyguards' table and take them all out. Shirley, you will make your escape using the fire stairway which is behind the bar. Motai will find his own way out, if he doesn't take part in the action. If he does, he will follow Shirley out. Yu will be in the car waiting outside the rear door."

"What about me?" Chopstick asked.

"Chopstick, you will flee as a member of the panic stricken people. If you foul up this operation, there might never be another chance to kill the redhead." Lao Tung spread out the floor plan of the night club on a table.

"Since the Red-Headed Devil doesn't come to the night club on set days, everyone must be ready to act in an instant. Our informer will notify me when he is at the club."

At the end of the meeting, Lao Tung showed everyone a recent picture of the Red- Headed Devil.

The next day, Shirley, Motai, Yu and Chopstick gathered at a hotel three blocks away from the Golden Pagoda Club. They were waiting for Lao Tung's orders.

It had been more than three and half years ago since Snow Flake's son was thrown overboard by Gascon. It had been a long wait but she hoped that her patience would soon pay dividends.

At 9 PM, a caravan of three limos arrived at the Golden Pagoda Club carrying Gascon, Black Diamond, and other bodyguards. Immediately, Jade Pang alerted Lao Tung.

Shirley, dressed in a low-cut, light blue evening gown with a diamond necklace, checked her red jacket to ensure her weapons couldn't be seen.

Motai was dressed in a tailored suit and Chopstick wore a long, black raincoat. They were on their way to the Golden Pagoda club after Lao Tung gave them a final inspection.

Shirley, on Motai's arm, made a grand entrance. The head waiter fell all over them, as Motai royally tipped him for a table by the stage. With a cigar in his hand, Gascon was seated near the dance floor, talking to women who sat on both sides of him. Shirley opened her jacket to display the curvature of her breasts. Black Diamond, whose snake like eyes never rested, observed everyone in the place. Immediately he noticed the woman who just arrived with a friend. He couldn't take his eyes off the beautiful Chinese woman.

When the stage lights dimmed, the Emcee trotted out on the stage to begin the show. The comic, "Big Feet," warmed up the audience who applauded his clever monologue. The redhead was watching the comic with his good eye but soon his attention was directed to the Chinese woman seated at a table across from him. The beauty of the young woman excited him, and he pointed her out to Black Diamond.

Gascon said, "That one in blue."

Black Diamond signaled to another bodyguard with a hand wave, and they came over to him. He ordered them to invite the Chinese beauty to Gascon's table. After the show had concluded and the lights came back on, the bodyguard went to the table and spoke to the woman, who nodded acquiescence and remained seated.

Now, Gascon's attention was riveted on the Chinese woman again. While the Chinese beauty was walking across the stage to his table, he ordered the other women to leave. Chopstick's hands went inside his raincoat pocket to surround his weapon, while casually drifting along the bar to a point where he could clearly cover Shirley's back. Motai already had the gun in his hand. Motai and Chopstick counted the seconds it took Shirley to cover fifteen feet. A broad smile shone brightly on Shirley's face as she approached Gascon's table. Meanwhile a light misty rain hung in the air outside, damping everything.

In his girlfriend's apartment, Lao Tung was glancing at his watch. "It's about to happen," he said to himself.

At the Golden Pagoda Club, Gascon rose to his feet as the Chinese woman approached him. She stopped five feet away.

"I have this feeling that we have met before." He was smiling at the beautiful woman.

"Yes, we have," Snow Flake agreed. "Don't you remember me?"

"No my lovely, you're someone I could never forget. Have we met before?"

"The last time I saw you, I left my hair pin sticking in your eye."

Before the words had meaning to Gascon, she withdrew her guns and fired. The bullets penetrated Gascon's eye sockets, blowing his skull apart. At Shirley's first shot, Motai was on his feet firing at Black Diamond drilling holes in the center of his forehead. Then he fired another round at Gascon's other bodyguards as Chopstick shot at them from the bar about the same time. After all were dead, the pair followed Shirley, heading for the fire escape. Once down on the street, a car was waiting there to pick them up. The patrons picked themselves up from floor under the tables and ran out of the night club.

Long after they were gone, sirens filled the night air. Patrol cars came to a screeching halt in front of the Golden Pagoda Club. Inspector Wang walked into the night club with an armed circle of men behind him. He came over to check the bodies while his detectives rounded up the people in the club and took statements from them, one by one. Gascon and all of his eighteen bodyguards were dead. Each waiter gave different descriptions of the men and woman who did the shooting. All the shots were in the head. Immediately the Inspector became aware that this was a professional hit.

Shirley changed her clothing in the car, removed her makeup and rearranged her hair. She was still flushed from her revenge killing. She peered at herself in the car mirror.

"I have passed the last threshold. My goal has been accomplished. I have avenged my son's death." When the car stopped at a light, she got out of the car and hailed a cab. Once arriving at the Moonlight Hotel, she bathed and felt restlessness. Soon, she was again out on the street. Her watch read 11 PM. Shirley had been told to meet Lao Tung at the Gates of Hell Bar at 2:30 AM.

Wearing a yellow hooded raincoat, she looked at the store windows while strolling. Shirley ruminated that killing that beast hasn't restored her son's short life or even made her happy. Now she was devoid of any feelings. Sergeant Chu emerged from his car. His police trained eyes were searching the street. Immediately he recognized Shirley who was standing in front of a ladies apparel store. William's heart beat faster. He approached her and lightly touched her back.

Shirley instinctively moved her arms ready to fight.

"Good evening," he said calmly.

Seeing William, she smiled. "Good evening, Sergeant Chu. I don't hold a grudge, but you mustn't be seen with me. Your professional career is at stake." Under his steady gaze, she averted her eyes.

"In that case, you should come with me so we can have some privacy." He took her arm but she hesitated.

"Shirley if you resist me, I'll take you in for questioning."

A tantalizing look was on her face.

"What kind of questions will you ask me?" William's facial expressions resulted in her laughing, as he rolled his eyes.

"Hide and seek is over. Come with me."

This time she took his arm. "Where are you taking me?"

"Dancing..."

"What I need is fresh air, not a smoke filled night club."

"I know what you need. Come, you will like the place where we are going." He led her one block when she abruptly stopped. He brought his face so close to hers that she thought he was going to kiss her right here on the street. A minute later, he was escorting her to his car. Often he glanced at her while he was driving.

Several miles later, before he pulled into a parking lot near a building, she noticed the sign above the entrance marking the 'Police Academy Ball.' William ushered her inside the night club. Before crossing the dance floor, the music started. It was a disco hustle. He looked at her and they began to dance. She was following his lead. While on the dance floor, thoughts were swirling in her head. This is complete delicious madness. Who would be looking for the killer of Gascon at a police ball?

When the music stopped it changed to a slower temp. William opened his arms, and her body blended with his. Together, they swayed to the music. Soon the music stopped and William heard his name being called. He recognized the voice.

He offered his beautiful guest his arm and was pleased she took it readily. He brought her to a table where six people were seated and introduced them to her.

"This is Sergeant Wu, Inspector Lu, and his sisters Iris and Judy, Captain John Hung and his wife, my sister Jessica." Jessica looked at Shirley while displaying a warm, friendly smile.

The young lady wrinkled her nose at her brother.

"I want to talk to Shirley alone," Jessica said. "Why don't you take Captain Hung and the rest for a drink at the bar?"

William sat at the bar but kept an eye on Shirley. He was relieved to see the women laughing and touching each other's hand. He wondered why Lao Tung said that Shirley was a savage and too wild for civilized company. She certainly seems to know the social graces. Shirley peered at her watch and waved to William who came over as she rose.

"William, I must leave now. Thank you for bringing me here and introducing me to your charming sister."

Jessica answered, "William, you must bring Shirley around to see us soon."

Shirley smiled. "I'm sorry I can't stay longer, Jessica, but it is a delightful party and I'm pleased to have met you."

"Good night Shirley. Don't be a stranger at my house." Watching her brother and Shirley leave, she reflected that they seemed to be a good couple.

Waiting for Their Teacher

Shirley sat next to Chopstick and Motai at the Gates of Hell Bar, awaiting Lao Tung's arrival. The feelings of restlessness, frustration, and uncertainty irritated her. Killing Gascon hadn't relieved the hatred from her heart and mind. She was more confused than ever. Trying to deaden that confusion, she downed shot after shot. When Motai noticed the way Shirley was drinking, he removed the bottle from the table.

"That's enough."

Wild-eyed, she glared at him. "Don't tell me what to do, Dog Meat! I have enough bosses. If you butt in again, I'll kick your ass!"

"Woman, you are stinking drunk and looking for a fight. Why can't you be like other drunkards who would snore with their heads on the table? You're getting to be a real pain!"

Shirley had had it with this present company. Her blood-shot eyes scanned the bar looking for trouble.

At a table in the middle of the bar, a group of English seamen were drinking and talking loudly. Shirley arose and staggered over to them.

One seaman stood up, asking, "Would you like to drink with us to earn some money?"

Shirley retorted in English, "Robbers of China, I want to break your nose!" He winked at the men. They noticed that she was drunk.

She shouted louder, "I'll destroy you!"

A very tall man, weighing well over three hundred pounds, rose to his feet and towered over her. His face was bright red and his breath was terrible. "Bitch, fuck off. Can't you see we are drinking?"

Shirley's punch landed on his jaw. He collapsed like a dead log. With their mouths open, the others looked at their mate who was spread out on the floor.

Dressed in a light blue pants, pale yellow shirt, and white and black shoes, Takamura had been observing the scene from his own table. Motai and Chopstick watched the one-sided battle like spectators in a prize fight. They passed the bottle between them, while Shirley put all her opponents on the floor, one by one. She staggered to another table where there were three Afghans staring at her.

One spoke in broken English, "Woman, we are all killers!" Pulling out his knives he struck one against the other. Without hesitation she smashed his face. Blood flowed from his nose as the others quickly drew their daggers.

Chopstick shouted to the men seated at a table across from him. "Bet a thousand Hong Kong dollars that Shirley will cream them!" Shirley advanced, eying the men. One made a move and tried to slash her arm. Shirley kicked the dagger out of his hand and sent a second kick against his leg. A third kick to the face knocked him off his feet. In the heat of battle, she was ready to kill. Fragments of their features blended in her mind with that of Sasin. Hatred was fueled within her blood.

With a knife in her hand, she shouted, "I'll carve your name across your face!" At that moment, she was stopped by Takamura.

Shirley glared at him. "Fuck you too, Jap!" Now Chopstick and Motai were worried. They knew the Japanese man who stood in front of her was the best fighter in the districts of Hong Kong and had a reputation of taking nobody's bullshit. All her attempts to stab him were fruitless. The crowd leaned forward expecting to see that the Jap would kill the woman.

To everyone's surprise, he held firm. In an authoritative voice, he said, "Stop driving away my paying customers. Lao Tung asked you to wait for him here, not make a nuisance of yourself." She hurled the dagger at the wall. Takamura understood that her actions were a way of purging hatred, sorrow, and pain in her heart. He shooed her away with finger motions.

However, the urge to fight had not left Snow Flake. On her way back to her table she saw two Caucasians with a gargantuan black man. The young black man, enthralled by the beautiful woman, gave her a broad smile and rose to his feet. Takamura thought either this young man is fearless or he is a complete fool because he is not paying attention to her warning signs.

"You are in the presence of an aroused lioness," the bar owner muttered under his breath.

"Miss, you are very beautiful when you are angry." The punch to his midsection came so quick that the smile was wiped off his face. The young man, Peter, dropped to the ground and rolled over on his back.

Jamal was on his feet saying in French, "Young woman, he means you no harm." Jamal stood six-three, with a three hundred pound frame, and a hairstyle that made his head appear flat. Shirley's kick against his chest sent him backward. On his feet, he smiled at her and brushed the footprint off his jacket with a huge hand, "You're very good. I'll show you how a man plays with a woman."

She measured his height against hers with a hand gesture. Shirley's next punch caught the side of his face. Jamal grabbed her hand. In a fluid motion, she ducked under his outstretched arm and threw him over her shoulder.

Jamal's body slammed against the cold, hard floor. The friendly smile vanished from his face as he felt the cold steel against his throat.

"If you kill him," Takamura spoke to the girl harshly, "I'll make you carry this bull's carcass over your shoulder clear across Kowloon!"

Looking at Jamal on the floor, he pointed at Shirley, "Sit down and behave yourself!" Reluctantly, she put away her knife.

Lao Tung appeared during the commotion. "Little girl, why are you fighting everyone? Didn't Chopstick tell you to wait for me here?" As he moved closer and smelled her breath, he knew she was drunk.

Muttering a reply, she pointed broadly at those men, whom she had fought. "I fought them because they are bigger than me. Besides, I don't like their faces." Lao Tung's own face came inches away from Shirley's. Softly he said, "I know how you feel."

She screamed at him. "Nobody knows how I feel!'

"Motai, Chopstick, hold her up."

With a finger, Lao Tung stabbed her solar plexus. They caught her as she was about to fall. Chopstick placed the unconscious girl over his shoulder.

A Russian sailor asked if he could pat her ass for luck. Motai pointed a gun at his head, "Just one touch and your luck runs out!" Frightened, the man turned away from them.

Lao Tung went over to Jamal as he rose to his feet and roared at the African. The big man didn't understand Chinese. Jamal turned to Takamura for an explanation. Lao Tung kicked Jamal's chest. He landed on his back. Before he could rise, Takamura put a foot on him.

Looking at the big man he said in French, "Stay put. Otherwise, Lao Tung will kill you."

From his own experience, Takamura understood Lao Tung wouldn't stand for anybody harming his students and his friends.

"Old friend, Shirley was bored while waiting for you. She just fought to pass the time. You ought to teach her better manners. More and more the girl acts like you." Takamura places his arm around his friend's shoulders.

The old man responded, "Shirley is basically alright, but a little too rough around the edges. She does need to be socialized. I have trained her to do nothing but fight." Lao Tung threw up his hands and left the bar with his companions.

Jamal approached Takamura. "Thank you, sir, but what did the old man say?"

"He said how could a big ox like you pick on a little girl who hasn't gotten rid of her milk teeth?" He thought what he had seen was unbelievable.

"If that femme is a child," Jamal said with astonishment, "I'll pay for your dinner and I'm known to be tight with money. Where can I find Takamura San? We were sent here by Major Abduk, the Scar, to see him on business."

"What does the Scar want from me?"

"We are seeking employment."

"Come back before the noon hour on Friday."

A New Assignment

Jin Hu was a self-made millionaire who lived alone in Hong Kong. He was in his late sixties, with a large, heavyset body. Estranged from his family member for years, he desperately wanted to bring them under his control once more. His only son, Ping Hu, had been living in Singapore with his wife, Red Lantern, and their young son, Yee Hu.

Unfortunately, Ping Hu died in a skiing accident while on vacation in Austria two years earlier. Ever since then, Jin Hu had been attempting to get his daughter-in-law to relinquish guardianship of his grandson to him. His biggest worry was that she should remarry and change the boy's last name to her new husband's. If that happened, his family line would end forever and his own life would be finished as well.

First he tried to buy his daughter-in-law's consent and when that did not work he attempted to use his underworld connections to threaten her and her family. This created the opposite effect.

Six months ago, he suddenly received a letter from her with a picture of his grandson. This was the first time he saw what his grandson looked like. The letter stated that Red Lantern would finally allow her son to live with Jin Hu in Hong Kong provided he paid her a settlement of $10 million US dollars. The funds, she stated, must be a cashier check from the Charted Bank Hong Kong and payable to her. The cashier check must be delivered in her hand at the time Jin Hu picks up the boy. The location of the exchange would be the Hu village, Gansu Province, in China.

Jin Hu was eager to see his grandson and wanted to go in person, but he knew that was impossible. He had killed a communist official twenty years ago and would be arrested on the spot if he tried to re-enter the country again. He decided to consult with his lawyer and friend, Bei, who had advised him to seek out a meeting with Takamura.

On a windy golf course near the Hong Kong race track, Takamura and Jin Hu teed off on the long fifth hole. While Jin Hu drove the golf ball into the air, he said, "I have been in touch with my daughter-in-law in Red China about bringing my grandson to Hong Kong to live with me. For personal reasons, I can't enter that country. Therefore I'm seeking an agent to act on my behalf. I'm willing to pay a hundred thousand US dollars to anyone who will go to Red China and bring back my grandson, Yee Hu, to Hong Kong."

"Not enough money," Takamura replied as he set his own ball onto the tee and stepped back to survey the straightaway. Jin Hu watched Takamura.

"How much is enough?"

"Three million US dollars sounds about right." The bargaining proceeded and was finally concluded at the eighth hole for two million US dollars.

Takamura stated, "The payment must be up front and in cash."

Jin Hu didn't agree, but he suggested they meet again to continue their discussion.

Takamura continued his legwork on Jin Hu. He had learned from various sources that a harsh rivalry existing between Red Lantern Hu and her father-in-law. Takamura pondered what had caused this sudden change of heart. Does Red Lantern need money? After a prolonged down and dirty tug-of-war with Jin Hu, why had she chosen Red China as the location for the exchange? He removed a samurai sword hanging on his wall. He tested the sword's weight in his hand. But sword play wasn't on his mind. Bringing the boy out of communist China would be a challenge, but should I succeed, the experience will make the ordeal worthwhile.

Takamura visited more people who were familiar with Jin Hu's background. He learned that many sources called him the Old Fox. He was given that name due to his reputation for cheating his employees and the people whom he had dealings with. The rich man took delight in squeezing those who were depending upon him for their livelihood. He was known for reneging on agreements he made. The poor people couldn't fight back because the law was on his side. If he felt good that day, he would pay a fraction of the money or give none at all.

Takamura continued to dig into his background and what he found was even more troubling. Jin Hu had disinherited his son, Ping Hu, after he eloped with Red Lantern to live in Singapore years ago. Apparently, Jin Hu had had some other young woman in mind for his son. It was clear from the onset that his headstrong daughter-in-law was difficult to manage. However, Jin Hu's wife threw a wrench into his manipulations. The woman also had assets of her own and used them to support the newlyweds. Upon her death, she passed her fortune into Red Lantern's able hands.

Thus, the beautiful Red Lantern enabled her husband to maintain a lavish lifestyle for himself and his family. While many commented that Red Lantern loved her husband and was a good mother, others thought that she was self-centered and vain.

After lots of legwork and money spent, Takamura obtained the piece of information he was most interested in. One year ago, when the Beijing Chinese Opera group performed in Singapore, a young handsome Kung-Fu actor named Li Wang was introduced to Red Lantern. As they became familiar with each other, she discovered he came from the same village in

Gansu province, China as her father-in-law. Li Wang's father used to work on Jin Hu's land before the communists took over mainland China. Soon Red Lantern and Li Wang became lovers. On his departure from Singapore, he invited her to visit him at his village in China. Since Jin Hu was very influential in Hong Kong, Red Lantern opted to stay with Li Wang in China, far from her father-in-law's interference. With the help of communist officials and Li Wang's connections, Red Lantern did well for herself in her newly adopted country, the Peoples Republic of China.

During their second meeting at the Lee Normand restaurant, Takamura accepted the job. Jin Hu left his grandson's picture on the table, paid Takamura half of the agreed price in cash, and rose from table haughtily.

"When Yee Hu is in my hands, I'll pay the remainder of the money in cash as per our agreement."

Takamura wasn't going to be personally involved in this affair. With consent from Lao Tung, he decided to make Shirley the lead agent. He selected some others of Lao Tung's people to help her in this assignment. In Takamura's mind, this operation would be the chance to distance Shirley from Ko Nan, and would serve as notice that she was now an independent agent.

Ever since Gascon's assassination, a nervous Ko Nan saw Shirley as a rival. Takamura and Lao Tung had so far protected their star student from Ko Nan's heavy hand and he knew enough not to move against her...at least for now. Since the police were actively searching for Gascon's assailants, the time was right to absent Shirley from this area. Furthermore, Takamura was interested in how Shirley would handle the given situation. The main drawback was Shirley's headstrong attitude. It is crucial that she should follow his plan to the letter, he thought. However, he was uncertain that she would do that.

A few days later, around noon, a "Closed" sign was hung outside the Gates of Hell Bar. Eight people sat around a table. They included Takamura, Motai, Shirley, Chopstick, Ricky, Crazy Mary, Jerry and Tom. Takamura, sitting at the head of the table, vaguely outlined the job. A team would travel five thousand miles into the middle part of Red China to bring back a little boy. To ensure the success of the operation, fourteen additional men would be added to the group.

"Going to Communist China could be dangerous," he asserted, "so anyone who changes his mind can leave right now. For those who remain, I'll allow nobody to endanger this operation. Subtracting all the expenses, the remainder will be split. Ten percent off the top goes to me, five percent goes to Shirley who will lead, and an equal share for the rest of you. I shall supply everything you need and I will pay the guide, the fourteen extra men and any extra expenses. Any questions?"

Shirley spoke up first. "Since we don't want to draw attention, I would prefer to exclude the whites and Africans."

Takamura raised his voice to an octave. "You'll take everyone I select!" Staring her down, he turned to the rest of the people. "Any more questions?"

Shirley threw her hands. "It's your game, Takamura San."

Tom was in his thirties, with a tall, muscular frame, and red hair. He had established a name for himself in the districts. He wondered why they needed so many heads for a simple grab operation. What was the catch? He cleared his throat and addressed his boss.

"Takamura San, why do we need so many men?"

"That is my business. Do as you are told and I'll pay you." Tom peered at his companions who didn't hesitate to nod their heads. They all had learned that the Dandy's word equaled money in the bank.

Crazy Mary, a good-figured woman in her early twenties who had once called Ireland her home, was fair of skin, with short red hair and freckles across her round face. She was currently making a living as a street fighter in Kowloon. The woman leapt to her feet, her eyes red with anger. "I take no orders from a woman I can beat!"

Takamura shouted her down. "You will take orders from the one I designated."

"In a pig's eye!"

Takamura leapt quickly out of his chair as Crazy Mary extracted her weapon from her holster. He kicked the gun out of her hand and landed a punch to her solar plexus. The large woman sailed across the room. He went behind the bar, removed a broad sword, and stood over Crazy Mary who lay dazed. Helplessly she looked up at him.

He roared, "Will you obey Shirley or not?" All eyes were on the Irish woman who was biting her lips. She nodded her consent.

"There can only be one boss. It's better to remove any obstacles that would hinder the success before it's too late. You are all professionals. I have selected a Chinese man whose named is Chen as the guide to lead you into Red China."

Pointing to Crazy Mary who was still on the floor, he addressed Shirley. "Take this woman with you. She will certainly need a doctor. If she dies, dump the body into the sea."

Shirley took an instant to dislike Crazy Mary and said, “Chopstick, Motai, take that cheap baggage to our hotel and get a Chinese doctor.” Filled with anger because of Takamura’s orders, she continued with more directives.

“Motai, do not leave her pistol behind as someone will surely steal it.” Her eyes burned into Takamura. Chopstick carried the woman out of the door. Motai did as he was told. Still angry, Shirley stormed out of the bar.

Later, Tom, Ricky, and Jerry went to their hotel room. They ordered dinner from room service and discussed the situation while eating. Both Ricky and Jerry were in their late twenties and of African descent. All three belonged to a small group called the English Bulldog Gang in England, working as fighters for hire. They had come to Hong Kong to try their luck

“Shirley was correct that the risks would be increased by taking so many people into Red China,” Ricky commented.

Jerry agreed. “I also can’t figure out why this operation needs so many hands plus some sore thumbs.”

Tom replied, “I don’t see the need for so much manpower either. Shirley is a top-notch fighter. Let’s see if she makes the grade while covering her ass.”

Ricky reached for the bottle and poured himself a stiff drink.

“Fifty thousand U.S Dollars is my only incentive. We can’t back out. See what happened to Crazy Mary? I thought the Jap was going to kill her. Let’s see something exciting in town while we are here.”

Tom was certain that Takamura knew what he was doing. The man had a reputation for always coming home with the cash.

Crazy Mary lay on the bed in her hotel room. She was pale and sweaty, and her breathing was labored. Motai sat in a wooden chair closely watching her while Chopstick stood behind him.

“Do you think she will die? She doesn’t look too good.”

Shirley, still angry, started to remove Crazy Mary’s blouse.

“Help me raise her. I want to look at her back. If there is a large purple mark than she is in very big trouble.”

Chopstick ran to help Shirley. “This woman has large boobs and a fine figure.”

“Any woman who has big breasts, a narrow waist, and full round hips will catch Chopstick’s eye,” exclaimed Motai.

Shirley examined the girl’s back. “She has more luck than brains. There is no mark.”

Chopstick gently lowered her body back down on the bed. Shirley was annoyed at the attention Chopstick was giving the foreign woman, because his eyes never left her. She shoved him away from Crazy Mary.

"Go get a Chinese doctor or someone who knows external medicine before I shoot you and this bitch." Moving without haste to annoy her, Chopstick strolled out of the room. Crazy Mary stirred and tried to raise herself up, but fell backwards on her bed. They eyed each other warily.

"If you walk out of this room you'll be dead before night fall. Takamura has a million eyes plus a long reach. I have sent for someone to get a doctor. Is your name really Crazy Mary?"

"Call me what you like," was her weak reply.

"As of today you earned a new name. Discard the crazy for lunatic."

Crazy Mary was able to get out of bed after two weeks. She was always cursing in Gaelic, and confinement made her more difficult to deal with. Shirley was under the impression that Crazy Mary wanted a rematch with Takamura. Chopstick kept warning Crazy Mary to calm down and not get into a fight with anyone. Meanwhile, Shirley was in a constant state of agitation due to Takamura's arrangements.

She walked around her room pondering, "There are more than enough bodies needed for this type of task. What is Takamura holding back?" Suddenly an idea came to her; conceal the majority of the team until it's time to return to Hong Kong. All that are needed are three Chinese...Chopstick, Chen, and I. We'll be taken for a family while we are traveling in Red China and we will return with the child.

Shirley went back to the Gates of Hell Bar to confer with Takamura. She was totally unaware that he was conducting a test of her ability to solve a problem. It pleased Takamura that she not only identified the flaw, but she knew how to correct it. After she explained her idea, she was elated when he nodded his approval. She was set to listen to his explanation.

"The extra people are necessary to counter Jin Hu's double-dealing scheme when the time for the final payment arrives. Being forewarned of the danger you will face is a great advantage." In the back of Takamura's mind loomed a contingency plan that would prevent Jin Hu ever short-changing anyone again.

One week before the departure date, using his money and connections, Takamura prepared the travel documents for the group who would enter Red China. On paper, Chopstick, Chen, and Shirley were brothers and sister who planned to visit relatives in Red China and the rest were regular travelers to China.

Gathering and Seeking

Jack Eng was in his late fifties, a middle-sized, scholarly-looking man with thick glasses on his nose. He was a reporter who wrote a gossip column about the rich and famous as well as the gangsters in a Hong Kong newspaper. He was highly educated and wise. He knew all the dirt on famous people living in the Districts of Hong Kong. His experience with digging up stories generated contacts at all levels of society, including the underworld. Jack became the unofficial private detective and source of information to many people. With a generous reward bulging in Takamura's pocket, Jack was going to tell him what was new.

In Takamura's private room in the Gates of Hell Bar, Jack leaned forward and whispered, "Ko Nan is rapidly filling Gascon's empty shoes. He has been crushing not only what is left of the Blood Brother Gang, but all his rivals. Takamura San, why don't you consolidate the remaining gangs under you? Ko Nan wouldn't dare go up against you."

Takamura was silent. Bringing his fingertips together, he spoke to himself, "I have no ambition to rule any gangs, except the Gates of Hell Bar. Ko Nan will not be an overnight success. He needs the cooperation of Lao Tung. Without it, he stands upon shaky ground. Let him waste his strength in foolish folly."

"You should thank me for sending you those sets of literature classics," Jack boasted.

"What for? The more I read, the more I discover that how little I know."

Takamura gathered data from various sources which enabled him to compile a clear picture of the current situation and what the future might bring. Lao Tung had been complaining of his disappointment with the direction the Sons of the Sea were taking, especially drug trafficking, and was earnestly thinking of retirement. He even suggested to his students that it might be time to leave the Sons of the Sea and to switch to legitimate businesses. This kind of talking caused a split within the gang and that greatly annoyed Ko Nan.

Takamura turned his attention to his friend, William, who was eagerly searching for Shirley. He was aware that William had the tendency to be compulsive. Takamura was undecided about how much information should be given to his friend about the woman. He was certain that William would discover the information by himself if fate determined they should meet.

Recently, Ko Nan gathered the high-ranking men of the Sons of the Sea for a meeting. He enthusiastically described his vision for their future. He was voicing what each person only imagined and wished to accomplish. This wasn't a lotus eater's dream. Rather, it represented a real chance to pet the dragon. Avarice was reflected in the men's eyes as they pictured the spoils within their reach, if only they extended their strong hands.

It was clear to Ko Nan that Lao Tung and his followers opposed his view.

He graciously proclaimed, "Those who wish to leave, let them go now on good terms. To those who wish to remain my brothers, join me in this venture into a bottomless sea of wealth."

Lao Tung walked out of the meeting and Fung Tung, Yu, and some of his students followed. Fish Eyes whispered to the man next to him after the old man left.

"He is out of touch with the modern ideas. This is what happens when you get old and your mind and eyes are closed. What we have here is a strong leader and a bright future."

Otto, following his father's script, declared, "With Gascon dead, the field is wide-open. We must grab the brass ring or be buried along with the Blood Brother Gang. With your support, my father, your chief, will fill Gascon's shoes in the Districts of Hong Kong. The Sons of the Sea will be prospering beyond your wildest dreams." Ko Nan knew his dream to be the king of this region was one step away from fulfillment.

William arranged to have supper with Takamura at the Peony Pavilion, a Beijing cuisine restaurant. He was determined to obtain some answers from his friend about Shirley. It was obvious that his failure to locate Shirley was due to Takamura's manipulations. She was being moved around like a piece on his chess board. He concluded that if Shirley was being hidden, there was enough reason to believe that she might be implicated in Gascon's murder. The description in the police reports stated that a young Chinese woman was the key assassin. The very idea that Shirley might be the killer infuriated him. He went as far as to blame Lao Tung for her involvement with the killing, and Takamura for being the brains behind the hit. William was outraged.

"Why would the old pirate and the Jap make a cold-blooded murderer out of Shirley? It doesn't make any sense."

At the restaurant, William demanded that Takamura tell him the truth about Shirley, but the man remained silent. In disgust, William threw his napkin on the table and stormed out of the restaurant. Takamura's temper flared. He thought of going after William and confronting him. However, he knew that if he wanted to retain William's friendship, he had to compromise. He couldn't tell him everything outright about the woman, but he could provide enough clues to lead the policeman to the truth.

One week later, while William was eating lunch with two policemen at Peony Pavilion, Takamura entered and walked over to their table. He looked down at William.

"Are we friends or not?"

The two policemen rose, leaving William at the table alone. William stared at him and said nothing at first, but suddenly the hardness left his eyes.

"Please forgive me, Takamura San, for being very rude to you last week. I was very angry and upset."

"Never mind the apology. After we eat, let's go outside for a walk."

The two friends walked several blocks before Takamura spoke.

"Is your mind open and receptive or not?"

"Speak. You have my full attention."

"Gascon's death was by Shirley's hand. It was the result of revenge."

"Did the animal kill her sister or her father?"

"Worse than that, my friend. It goes back more than three years ago. Keep in mind that Lao Tung rescued Shirley from the sea."

"What is the rest of the story?"

"Since you're a policeman, use this lead I have given you to find out for yourself."

"Takamura San, why don't you save me legwork?"

"William, it isn't in your nature to draw conclusions based upon other's information. I will tell you this much. She is somewhere else on a job to repay me. Don't ask me what it is."

"Ok, I'll nose around." They shook hands and each went their own way. Takamura felt that his friend should lose no time in starting his mission.

William buried himself in the library newspaper room absorbing every murder case that happened three years ago. The results of his findings were narrowed to three cases. There was the story of Sir Henry's yacht massacre, and there were pictures of Sir Henry and other's aboard the yacht. It was chalked up to a botched robbery. Another covered the death of a young wife whose name was Ana Hong by the hand of a stranger. It was a bloody story about rape and murder. The last one was of a young woman, Fen Shaw, who came from Southern China to Hong Kong. Unable to get a job, she ended up working on the streets. She was reported missing by a cousin and later found with her throat cut.

After weeks of legwork, William was ready to probe Takamura again. In a dark mood, he ate his breakfast at a sidewalk stand. On the move, he noticed someone was shadowing him. With a policeman's memory for faces, he came up with a name, Little Wah Hop of the Blood Brother Gang. In his late twenties, with small build and a weak face, the out-of-date gangster had little nerve but a constant need for cash. He was one of the Takamura's paid informers.

Across the street, Little Wah Hop was waiting for Sergeant William Chu to leave the food stand. Takamura had given him enough money to flee Hong Kong because the Sons of the Sea had put a price on his head. When William walked into an alley, he followed him.

Coming face to face with the policeman, Little Wah Hop said, "Sir, could I have a word with you?" William roughly shoved him against the wall and frisked him. He found the man was clean.

Turning him around, William said, "What have you got to say for yourself?"

"Take me to the airport and I'll tell something which will greatly interest you."

"Ok, but if you try to pull a fast one, I'll break you apart."

During that ride, he began telling a story. "The date was November 15, 1966. I was on a boat with Sasin, Gavial and Gascon. The Blood Brother Gang was paid to hit Sir Henry's little wife, Snow Flake, and her son, Charles Albert. Gavial had worked out a detailed plan that would make it look like a kidnapping. He was put in charge to carry out the plan, but at the last minute, Gascon decided to come. At the very start of the operation, everything went south. Gavial took the child from Sir Henry's arms and gave him to Gascon. For some reason Gascon threw the baby into the sea. When Sir Henry and Snow Flake tried to save their son, Gavial shot Sir Henry in the head. "

Wah Hop grew quiet but William sensed there was more. The little man looked him in the eye with a mischievous grin.

"Later, Gascon got hot for Snow Flake. The madman took her into a cabin and all he got was a hair pin stuck in his eye. She escaped into the sea. In frustration, Gascon had everyone onboard killed and the yacht burned. This is the truth." William pulled the car to the curb in front of the terminal at the airport. Wah Hop got out and hurried through the revolving doors.

William drove directly to the Sing Tao newspaper building in Hong Kong and he sought Mr. Yeh who was a reporter there for more than twenty years. They spoke for over an hour and William followed up their conversation with more legwork. From the retired Captain Lung Hsu, he got the name of 'Snow Flake Yuan' as the little wife of Sir Henry Shih. He also learned where Snow Flake used to live with her grandparents and the house where her grandparents lived until their death.

That evening in his apartment, William arranged the facts in his head. Snow Flake killed Gascon to avenge the death of her son. Wah Hop didn't come to me with the story for no reason. It smelled of Takamura's fine hand. The egomaniac knew everything, but made me find out for myself. Wah Hop was telling the truth, because he would never lie to an unforgiving Takamura or to me.

"Snow Flake showed courage by slaying Gascon," he thought. "Ultimately she saved the lives of many people who otherwise would have died by the Red-Headed Devil's hand."

Strolling along the sunny street, Takamura was pleased William had finally learned the story of Snow Flake's revenge. Just before entering the park, he was stopped by a middle-aged man who was known around the streets as Pork. The small-time gangster, who was in his late fifties, was frequently on the prowl for a quick buck. The Japanese man was slightly annoyed with the interruption of his daily walk.

Pork addressed him in a hoarse voice. "Good day, Takamura San. Would you be interested in buying two of the most beautiful young Chinese women in the world?" He began to sweat as Takamura's cold eyes scrutinized him.

Quickly he said, "Min Liu brought them out of Red China to work off their passage. To collect his money, he put these girls on sale to the highest bidder."

Takamura was ready to brush him off with a blow from his cane, but decided to see if the man was telling the truth.

"Pork, you may escort me there."

Pork flagged down a cab. Lack of money often makes the timid act bold. Inside the cab, the street thug sat as far away from Takamura as he could. Pork feared making eye contact with the Dandy, whose face had become hard and stoic.

They got out of the cab at an alley in a run-down section of Kowloon. The Dandy noticed a man in his early sixties, with a small build and a street-wise look on his face. Min Liu waved his arm and two young, frightened Chinese women emerged from the back seat of an old car parked nearby. They walked slowly to a wooden platform in the middle of the alley. Takamura noticed their similarity. Pork was right. These women were something special. Takamura walked up to the wooden platform. He looked at Min Liu and addressed him.

"Name your price for these women."

Two rough looking men came from behind Min Liu and placed themselves between Takamura and the women. One man made a mistake of touching Takamura's white suit jacket, leaving a smudge. Takamura took this act as an insult and immediately avenged himself. With a punch, he smashed the man's jaw, sending him flying off the small platform. The second man attacked Takamura with a knife but it didn't take long for him to break the thug's arm with a loud snap. Takamura picked up the dropped knife and slashed the man's leg. Blood poured from the man's open wound. He screamed in agony holding his leg.

Frightened, Min Liu attempted to restore order, "Sir, please, can't we talk?"

"I am Takamura. Pork, come over here now!" Pork came by the wooden platform and bowed to Takamura, all the while casting his rheumy eyes at Min Liu.

"Takamura San, how may I assist you?" Min Liu's mind connected the name with the owner of the Gates of Hell Bar. Sweating from fright, he mopped his brow with a dirty handkerchief. The young women were holding onto each other. They were trembling.

Min Liu broke the silence. "The price is 150,000 Hong Kong Dollars."

"Come tonight to the Gates of Hell Bar for your money." Min Liu's attitude changed to that of all business. He knew he would get his money. Takamura gave Pork a big bill for his services. Pork bowed to him many times and continued even when he had already gotten into a cab.

In the car, Takamura asked the frightened Chinese young women their names. The one with a small mole at the corner of her mouth said, "I'm Po Ling Chen and this is my cousin, Mai Gee Yao."

Both were about five foot seven inches tall and 120 pounds, with square faces, liquid dark eyes, and exquisite bodies. It was evident to him that they left Red China to find work here. The next item on Takamura's agenda was to take them to buy a new wardrobe.

He told the cab driver that he would hire him for the day.

Pleased, the driver replied, "I'm your man, sir."

"Drive to the Soho department store and wait for us there."

Hours later, with a trunk full of bags of purchases, the cab arrived at Gates of Hell Bar. The driver carried their bags inside and received his biggest payment of the year.

Takamura's residence was located behind the bar. Inside the building, his servant, Little Moon, took them into an apartment. Po Ling and Mai Gee walked on the soft floor, as if they were in a dream. Their new home wasn't a brothel; it was a rich man's living quarters. That night they slept together, exhausted, like the dead. The next day, a middle-aged female arrived to teach the young women English and how to eat with western utensils. Later, another woman came to arrange their hair and paint their nails. Days later, there were trips to the dentist to have their teeth checked and visits to doctors for a physical.

After being there for one month, they boldly asked Takamura for money.

"We came here because of the promise of work. Our parents are having a tough time supporting our grandparents and themselves in Red China."

Takamura went to his desk in his study, opened the top drawer and handed them each some cash. They thanked him many times. Little Moon escorted the young women to a post office where they bought cashier checks and mailed them to their parents in Red China.

The girls spent their days in the apartment studying English and helping Little Moon with the cleaning and cooking. They also enjoyed reading the books that lined an entire wall in the study. Little Moon was very kind to them. She became their closest friend. She became a mentor for the girls and helped them speak Cantonese. There was laugher in the apartment. Sometimes during the late afternoons, they would accompany Takamura on his daily stroll. The young women chatting like little girls in high school.

One day at breakfast, Takamura spoke to the young women. "Since you are here without resident cards, I shall obtain them for you and provide you with jobs, if you choose to be on your own." The women peered at each other.

Po Ling replied, "Speaking for both of us, Takamura San, you are very kind and overly generous to us. We have been discussing the situation between ourselves and our conclusion is that we prefer to remain with you, so that we can repay you for sparing us from a life of shame."

The Way to Red China

Without knowing Jin Hu and Takamura were watching, Shirley gathered her group of twenty-two, excluding the operators, on a boat in Hong Kong Harbor an hour before their departure. The swiftly moving ship made good time in reaching their landing point on the coast of Shandong. The boat was dock at the port of Gindao.

They went ashore and found a hotel near the train station. In her room, Shirley addressed her people. "Chopstick, Chen, and I will travel to the village in Gansu province by train and on foot to get the boy. It would be dangerous enough for us to travel there even in a small group. Use the time to get yourselves in top condition and act like regular travelers in this city. I'll leave Motai in command. We should be away for a week. You will stay here for this time. If we are gone longer than that, Motai will lead you to board the ship to take you back to Hong Kong."

The three of them boarded the train the following morning. The trio kept to themselves and didn't mingle with other passengers. Shirley tried not to think of William. The more she attempted to erase him from her mind, the stronger his image grew. Takamura's superior attitude vexed her. She saw him as a sharp-minded person with a warped sense of humor and a big ego. She tried very hard to understand the common ground that made Lao Tung, William, and Takamura good friends.

During the long march along the dirt road leading into the Hu village, they came upon an old man carrying a bale of sticks. Shirley and Chen became apprehensive as the stranger approached. He might alert the ever-watchful eyes of the communist officials in the village. It was essential that their papers pass any inspection.

Boldly, Chen went over to the old man and asked him if he knew where Red Lantern Hu lived.

With eyebrows knitted together, the old man blew his nose with his fingers. He replied, "You are in luck. All the party members are away in the city. Follow me."

That remark made them suspicious. The old man was talking too brazenly to strangers. They remained on alert as the man led them down a narrow, stone-covered road.

The old man stopped in front of a house and pointed a bony finger in its direction. He then left the three strangers behind without saying goodbye. Immediately, the door opened and Red Lantern invited them in. She matched the description they were told – five foot five inches tall, slender and beautiful. Inside the house, standing behind Red Lantern, was a tall, handsome man in his early thirties. He introduced himself to Shirley and her companions.

"I am Li Wang, Red Lantern's husband." To Shirley's disappointment, there was no seven year old boy in sight. Tension was in the air.

To break the ice, Red Lantern said to Shirley, "Do you have the cashier's check?"

Shirley removed an envelope from her zippered pocket and held it in her hand. "Where is Yee Hu?"

"Let us see the check first and when everything checks out, you will see Yee Hu." Li Wang replied.

Shirley handed Red Lantern the envelope and watched her open it carefully. Both husband and wife verified the signature against another document LI Wang held in his left hand. They looked at it for what seemed like a long time. Finally Red Lantern said, "Everything is in order. You will have dinner and stay the night here. I will have Yee Hu ready for your departure tomorrow morning."

As promised, the child was ready for the trip before the sun had risen over the eastern horizon the next day, dressed in simple peasant clothing. Li Wang provided Shirley with travel papers for the boy. The child hardly spoke to anyone including his mother and step-father. Most of the time, he just peered out the window. Neither of his parents seemed to show any emotion at their son's departure. Snow Flake thought that the situation was very odd, but concluded that if Jin Hu was satisfied and paid the money, that was all that mattered.

Upon their arrival back in Hong Kong, the group went to the Waterfall Hotel for a night of rest. Shirley met with Takamura in another hotel nearby. Shirley reported their situation and said that Yee Hu and the rest were close at hand. She said the trip was uneventful but she had a nagging question.

"May I now ask, again? What was the need for so many men for such a small job?"

Sarcastically he replied, "I'm pleased that you saw it and wisely you took two men for this job. In reality, only Chen was needed. The reason for a large force, I repeat, was to make a show to Jin Hu, who would think that this operation would be difficult and therefore it would be expensive. His idea of being fair is to pay one cent on the dollar for services rendered. The final part of this operation will be the most dangerous. Your skill with guns and the knowledge of his intentions will give your group the edge. If, by some ill fate, the child is taken away from you before the final payment is in my hand, I'll personally hold you responsible for all the lost money! I repeat, Jin Hu is a known skinflint and a cheat. While you were away fetching his grandson, the Fox was busy hiring five times the number of bodyguards he usually has on hand. It is a clear indicator that he is up to his old tricks. The drop-off point is at his estate. Now you need to keep your mind focused on what will happen once the boy is delivered to Jin Hu's house."

Shirley glared at him without saying a word.

Takamura continued, "Must I keep repeating myself so there is no mistake? If you fail to overcome the Fox's trap, your part of the operation will be zero and I'll triple the money due me." He grinned at her.

Shirley was filled with anger. "You could easily handle Jin Hu yourself. Why force me to...?"

Takamura wanted to gauge her ability to think under stress.

"Clear your mind. Concentrate upon the task at hand. Come tomorrow to the Gates of Hell Bar around 9 AM. I have sent for Mr. Wang, who will teach you how to spot counterfeit currency. Secondly, I want you and your people to wear soft body armor and carry concealed weapons in addition to your guns when you enter the Fox's Den. Control the situation from the start. Do you have any questions?"

With a look of distaste on her face she shook her head. "No, sir."

"To make the Old Fox wait, I will notify Jin Hu that the delivery day will be on Wednesday at 9 PM. The weaponry will be delivered to your hotel on Tuesday night. William is searching everywhere for you. Try to remain hidden until this operation is complete. Don't underestimate William's ability to find you. He is a very clever detective." Shirley's heart pounded at the mention of William's name.

She wondered why Takamura was always playing head games with her. "Why doesn't he trust me or see me as an equal? I hope someday we can have an open conversation about all these underlying and hidden agendas of his."

On Wednesday morning after breakfast, Shirley gathered her team in her room. She alerted them about the final phase of the operation. She told them that not only would they all be armed and wearing body armor, they would also be carrying concealed weapons.

At 9 PM, when they arrived at Hu Jin's spacious residence, they were greeted by several armed guards. Shirley entered the house with Tom, Ricky, Jerry, Motai, Chopstick, and Crazy Mary who held the boy's hand. Jin Hu welcomed them. At the sight of his grandchild, Yee Hu, the man was jubilant and the boy was very happy too.

Jin Hu coughed as a signal to his men in the next room. Suddenly Shirley and her companions found themselves surrounded by more than twenty, tough, armed Chinese men in addition to the bodyguards. While they pointed their weapons at Shirley and her people, Jin Hu asserted, "Thank you for bringing my grandchild to me. Your services are no longer required. Drop your weapons and go in peace, or die here for all I care."

When Crazy Mary first voluntarily handed a guard her gun, Shirley raged at her, "They bought you, bitch! You double-crossed us!"

Itching to see a fight between the women, a guard smiled. "That's right, she is one of us."

Shirley rushed and grabbed Crazy Mary who reached for one of the two guns concealed in Shirley's jacket. Deciding it was now or never, Crazy Mary turned to fire repetitively at the guards. Shirley took the other concealed gun and also fired. During the shooting, Tom was shot in the face and went down hard. Shirley shot the men surrounding Jerry who, in turn, ripped the shotgun out of a guard's hands before he could use it again and returned fire. Ricky was hit in the right forearm but continued firing.

Meanwhile, Motai was firing rapidly to cover Shirley. Down went more men until Shirley was shot in the right shoulder. She dropped to the floor but recovered quickly. She reloaded, switched the gun to her left hand, and continued firing. Chopstick covered Crazy Mary who welcomed the feel of his back against hers. Jerry also covered Shirley. When the firing ceased, Jin Hu's men were all dead.

Jin Hu screamed in fright. "Don't kill me! I'll give you the money. It's in the wall safe."

Motai put a gun to his head. "Old Fox, if you attempt any more tricks, both the child and you will die."

Jin Hu opened his safe and stepped back. Chopstick removed all the money from the compartment and placed it on a table. Shirley examined the bills then gave the okay sign.

Motai said, "Shirley, there's more than ten million US dollars."

"Take it all for our trouble! Let the Old Fox live. Motai and Chopstick, deliver the money to Takamura San at the Gates of the Hell Bar."

They all were certain that nobody in his right mind would run away with the money, because whoever did that, would not die of old age.

You Will Be the Death of Me

Shirley awoke in a hospital room. Lao Tung was sitting on a chair with his feet on the bed. She didn't know how long she was there or when he arrived. Lao Tung noticed that Shirley was stirring and masked most of his thoughts.

"Woman, one of these days you'll be the death of me. Why didn't you take charge the moment you entered Jin Hu's house?"

"Why must I accept all the blame? I didn't shoot myself."

Lao Tung mimicked her voice. "'I didn't shoot myself.' You didn't follow orders either, Sea Devil! What happened to the body armor Takamura gave you to wear?"

The reason she did not wear the soft body armor was that she gave hers to Crazy Mary. Shirley found out Mary could not fit the one she was given and opted to give up her own to help her teammate.

Shirley didn't reply, sensing she was being held responsible for the dead. Crazy Mary walked into the room dressed in western attire. Chopstick strode in behind her wearing a blue suit, tie and white shirt.

Crazy Mary stated, "It's about time you woke up. How is the wing?"

Lao Tung grunted, "Who is the foreign hooker and why is she holding hands with my grandson in front of people?" Crazy Mary didn't need to understand the dialect to see Chopstick's face redden. It was apparent that the old man was talking about her. Chopstick turned his head put a finger to his lips, indicating to Crazy Mary to shut her mouth.

Shirley asked Lao Tung if everyone had been paid.

"Yes, with a big bonus. Even the widow was given her husband's share. Yours is in your bank account. Here is your bank book. Takamura opened it for you. He was very generous with Jin Hu's money to everyone who was on this job."

While Lao Tung was talking, Shirley caught Chopstick's eye and gestured him to take Crazy Mary and leave the room. When they were gone, the irascible Lao Tung displayed his temper by kicking over a chair. It was obvious that the old man wasn't pleased at seeing a possible relationship between Chopstick and Crazy Mary.

The following afternoon at the hospital, Chopstick and Crazy Mary were standing by Shirley's bed. Carrying flowers, William entered the room. Upon seeing a stranger who looked like a policeman, Crazy Mary reached for her pistol. William saw the foreign woman's hand movement, dropped the flowers, and beat her to the draw.

Shirley excitedly shouted, "William, leave her be! But if you must pull the trigger, aim for her head. There you will cause the least amount of damage!" William cautiously holstered his weapon and picked up the flowers. He handed them to Shirley.

"These are for you. Who is the foreign woman?"

"Crazy Mary."

"What is she doing here?"

"Stop acting like a policeman and put these flowers in a vase." Chopstick hastily ushered Crazy Mary out of the room.

"How is your shoulder?"

"It's coming along just fine." He held her hand and gave it a squeeze.

"Yesterday I was at Jin Hu's estate. He wanted to press murder charges against you and Takamura San. During our conversation, I pointed out that he was the cause of the unfortunate incident. I said to him if he continues to seek redress within the law, his dirty laundry will come out at the trial and he will be exposed before the public. He will be the biggest loser of all. When he shouted that you and Takamura are thieves, I replied that a thief steals from a thief. It's the hazard of the trade. I hinted to him that insulting Takamura San might result in him seeking his own kind of justice. The bottom line was that he saw that his only way out was to drop all the charges. Now that you are a free woman, in that respect, when can we go dancing?"

"William, if a commitment is on your mind, forget about it. I owe Lao Tung my life, plus I'm up to my ears in debt to Takamura San. Also I have blood on my hands from my acts of vengeance. All this will keep us apart."

William smiled at her. Filled with confidence, he replied, "I'll seek your freedom." She almost screamed, but clamped her mouth shut. She didn't want him to fight with Lao Tung or Takamura. It could be a deadly game. She also didn't want William's police career to be jeopardized because he was seeing her. Being with William had given her a new feeling, a good sensation, a kind of feeling she had never had before. In her heart, she knew she would die rather than see William harmed.

That very night at closing time, William stormed into the Gates of Hell Bar with an angry look on his face. Takamura correctly interpreted the reason for his friend showing up and invited him into his private quarters. Once inside, William vehemently demanded that he set Shirley free from bondage. The tone of William's voice annoyed the Dandy. When he saw his friend assume a combat stance, he reacted to the threat by compressing his hands into fist.

Taking a deep breath, William lowered his hands and decided to try a different approach. "Takamura San, forgive me for my arrogance."

"William, do you know the meaning of friendship?"

"I'm still learning, my friend."

"Shirley no longer owes me any obligations."

Shirley felt desperate that something would happen to William because of her. To prevent William from being hurt and to give herself time to think, she decided to distance herself from him. Everything was happening too fast for her to absorb. She felt powerless. On the day she was discharged from the hospital, she mentioned to Chopstick and Crazy Mary that she wanted to take a vacation, and asked them if they would come along. It was time for them to take a break from the Red China and Jin Hu business and they both agreed. One week later, they flew from Kowloon to the Hawaiian island of Oahu.

Tension had been getting the best of her, ever since William had mentioned going to speak to Takamura. She had believed that the Japanese bastard wanted her to live the life of a mercenary. Yet Takamura was correct in his judgment about her not remaining with the Sons of the Sea. When she was still in the hospital, she overheard the conversation between Takamura and Lao Tung about her leaving the gang. She really did not belong with them anymore. Her revenge was done. Upon her return from the hospital, she consulted with Lao Tung on her departure first. Lao Tung supported her decision. Afterwards, she approached Ko Nan, who agreed with her and accepted her resignation from the Sons of the Sea with grace and respect.

They rented a house with a private beach on Oahu. Shirley constantly picked on Chopstick and Crazy Mary. Their display of affection for each other bothered her. She felt jealous of their ability to love. It was the afternoon of their third day on the island when Chopstick came from the beach and went into the kitchen to make a pitcher of iced refreshments. Crazy Mary and Shirley were wearing bikinis and followed him into the house.

Suddenly the quiet was broken by the sound of a car. Shirley went to the window. A red coupe turned into the driveway and parked. Wearing dark glasses, William, dressed in a bright aloha shirt, emerged from the vehicle. Shirley turned and cast her eyes at Chopstick who was stretched out on a chair sipping iced tea.

Momentarily, their eyes made contact. Chopstick spoke to her very directly. "You have been a pain in the ass ever since we got here. Let William in and take him to bed before you explode!"

Shirley went over to the door and opened it. When William saw her, he broke into a grin.

Coming into the house, William said, “Hi everyone. How is the sunshine? Shirley, you look simply enticing and beautiful.”

Shirley put on a pouting face. “William, why are you here?”

“I’m also on vacation. Chopstick said you needed me.” He crossed the living room to sit on the sofa and accepted a drink from Chopstick. “Tonight, we are going to dance.”

Crazy Mary spoke up excitedly. “Can we come along?”

“Sure, we’ll all have a ball!”

Crazy Mary rose off the sofa carrying her drink and walked towards her bedroom. Chopstick’s eyes follow her.

“Mary, wear that tight green bodysuit tonight. It’s so form-fitting that I wonder how you can get into it.”

She turned her head and gave him a sexy pose. “Try feeding me double scotches.” Chopstick, grinning from ear to ear, got up and followed Mary to her room.

Putting all the problems in her life aside temporary, Shirley was really pleased to see William. She started to relax as they spoke. The pair talked politely until they left for the club around 6 PM.

At four in the morning, the red coupe pulled back into the driveway of their rented house. Chopstick and Crazy Mary were in the rear seat very drunk. The pair leaned all over each other for support trying to extract themselves from the back seat. Once inside the house, Crazy Mary stated that she was going to bed. Chopstick, grinning like an ape, accompanied her into her bedroom and shut the door.

Shirley glared at William. “What are those animals doing?”

“Can’t you see that there is something more than sex between them?” Inflamed by his statement and feeling frustrated, she proceeded to throw a few punches at him. He blocked some of the punches and finally threw her over his shoulder. She landed with a thud on the floor.

“William, you animal! You hurt my shoulder!” He assisted her up. Eagerly they embraced each other and kissed for a long time. Shirley was afraid to let go of him.

He whispered in her ear, “Lao Tung said I should keep you barefoot and pregnant, but I know you’re too smart for that. It’s time for you to settle down. Takamura San erased your debt from him as our wedding present. Snow Flake Yuan, will you marry me?”

Shirley replied, “What will happen to the blood on my hands?”

“That was caused by settling an internal affair among the gangs in the districts of Hong Kong.”

Hearing her proper name, she tried to pull away from him but he restrained her. Their eyes searched each other's face.

"If you don't like that name, try a new one Mrs. Snow Flake Chu?" Tears filled her eyes. All that had happened in the past was over. From today onward, there would be a new beginning.

Looking straight into his eyes, she asked, "Will you love me forever and ever?"

"Yes, but tomorrow we will arise early."

"Why?"

"My dear, you are going to be a married woman and live a normal life."

Shirley Reclaims the Name Snow Flake

It was three days before the Chinese New Year, the Year of the Horse; Snow Flake and William had been married almost ten years. The Chu family was blessed with two children: Linda, age eight, and Robert, who was six. The family resided in a medium-size house in a middle-class section of Kowloon. They lived not far from William's sister, Jessica, and her husband, John, who was now a captain. Ever since their wedding, the new bride reclaimed her former name, Snow Flake, and became a stay-at-home mom. Her greatest passions were raising her children, cooking and gardening. William had been promoted to captain and stationed at a police precinct in Kowloon.

Though Takamura did not marry the two women he lived with, they accepted their relationship with him. Po Ling and Mai Gee each gave Takamura a son. The children were born days apart. Fatherhood altered Takamura's lifestyle. He became a family man, honoring each of his women. He relocated his whole family from the apartment in the rear of the Gates of the Hell Bar to a luxury house located on Victoria Peak. He devoted more time to his family and less to the bar and his other businesses. Mai Gee and Po Ling were great friends with Snow Flake, Ginger and Jessica. They often visited each other or conversed by phone. Takamura and William were bound together like brothers, and Lao Tung was like a father to them. They met very often.

Due to Ko Nan's erratic leadership, Lao Tung retired from the Sons of the Sea two years ago, living with his girlfriend, Blossom, in Kowloon. At his advice, some of his students and followers including his son, Fung Tung, and his nephew, Yu, also left the gang to seek a new life elsewhere. Fung Tung and his family lived near his father in Kowloon. From time to time Lao Tung's students and old friends would have a gathering, either for lunch or dinners or on holiday celebrations. But his attitude toward Ko Nan did not change. He continued to criticize the gang leader's drug dealings and senseless killings in public. Lao Tung gave Snow Flake his serpent knife, a family heirloom, as a present when she returned from Hawaii as a married woman. As a reminder that it was Lao Tung who gave her life a second chance, she treasured the knife and always kept it in her purse.

Ginger and Otto had been married five years but were still childless. They resided in Ko Nan's big house in Hong Kong. Kim, feeling uneasy ever since leaving the Sons of the Sea, moved to Canada where he met a Chinese woman whom he later married. He worked for his wife's brother in real estate.

Because the Tung family didn't approve of their marriage, Chopstick and Crazy Mary eloped and settled down in San Francisco. Following Chopstick's lead, his friend, Motai, also moved to the bustling California port city. With their combined share of the money from the Jin Hu affair, they opened a supermarket in San Francisco's Chinatown.

In the living room, Snow Flake used the coffee table as a desk where she inserted money into red envelopes in keeping with the Chinese New Year custom. Outside, the weather was cool and there was a hint of a late evening shower. At noon, Sway Tien, the Chu's live-in housekeeper, asked to be excused to visit a doctor. She appeared very tense, nervous and pale. Snow Flake offered to drive her to the doctor, but she refused the offer and left on her own.

Snow Flake continued her New Year preparations. In the middle of her work, a sudden uneasiness settled upon her but she paid it no mind. Staring at her wedding ring, she realized that her life was totally caught up in her marriage. Somewhere among her children, cooking and gardening, she lost the personality and fighting ability that was inherent in 'Shirley'. However, she had gained a new sense of what it was to be a total woman, a happy wife, and a mother.

The doorbell rang at 2 PM, disturbing the silence of the house. Snow Flake rose to answer it and opened the door. There stood Ginger and Po Ling. Pleased to see her friends, she welcomed them, ushering them into the living room. She was delighted to see Ginger especially, since the last time she saw her was two month ago, at her mother's funeral. The middle-aged woman had died suddenly of a heart attack during a meeting with Ko Nan in his study in his mansion in Hong Kong.

Snow Flake went to the kitchen to make tea. Po Ling followed her and spoke in a whisper. "Ginger needs your help. Her melancholy feelings over the loss of her mother and a disappointing marriage are eating away of her vitals. Her outlook on life is dangerously low. What she needs is a shoulder to cry on. Why don't you go out with her for an early supper?"

Snow Flake said, "I would like to go out with Ginger but my housekeeper is out sick and there is no one to take care of my children when they return from school."

"I'll look after your children for you, don't worry."

William mentioned in the morning that he would go to Lao Tung's birthday party in the evening and would be home late. She saw no reason for not spending some time with her friend.

"I'll go with Ginger. Thanks for volunteering to mind the children. I've made cookies for them. They are in the refrigerator. Don't let them eat all the cookies or they won't be able to eat supper." Snow Flake hugged Po Ling warmly.

A dejected Ginger peered off into space. She had drastically changed since they last met. It wasn't the expensive clothing, jewelry, French perfume, or hairstyle. It was her eyes. They reflected a loss of her soul, a sadness that was almost palpable. While Snow Flake served tea, she asked Ginger to accompany her for an early supper at the Crown Palace. She agreed and Snow Flake went upstairs to change her clothing. They left the house a short time later.

While on the road, Ginger squeezed her hand just as she did in the old days. She even managed a smile.

"Ever since mama's death, it's you that I love the most in this entire world. My dream of a blissful marriage has turned into a nightmare."

They squeezed each other's hand hard.

"You are my best friend. Talk all you want. I'll listen," Snow Flake assured her.

"Thanks for the sympathetic ear."

They entered the Crown Palace Restaurant and were seated in a booth. Ginger constantly talked about her late mother and recited what she did or said as well the foods she prepared for her. For the first time that day, Snow Flake noticed her friend's eyes sparkled as she recalled these fond memories, but without a warning, the smile faded. Her eyes went dead and bitterness crept in her voice while grievance after grievance against Otto surfaced.

To console her friend, Snow Flake related the agony of her own heartbreak when Gascon threw Charles Albert, her firstborn son, into the sea. That one instance had changed her life forever.

"After that tragedy, I was consumed with hatred. When the revenge was accomplished, I felt empty and lost. It was William who rescued me from hell. You and I went through the loss of loved ones but we have to continue to live. I'm sorry that you and Otto have disagreements. Give him a chance. I'm sure that he loves you."

Ginger's grim face stared back at her. Unseen by Snow Flake, Ginger's tightly compressed fists turned white under the table. Suddenly Ginger grabbed her drink and gulped it down.

"Otto refuses to communicate with me. I'm at a dead end. It's only a matter of time before we part. In one respect, he is still a child who can't make a decision unless his father gives him permission. On the other hand, he desperately wants to make a name for himself. Otto searches for fame while still under his father's protective wing. Too bad he'll never be able to wear his father's shoes."

The waiter arrived with their food. While they were eating, Ginger continued. "Otto is constantly away from home, sometimes for days. When he returns, the bastard doesn't bother to remove the lipstick from his ears and neck. Our marriage has been a disaster. I was so ashamed to tell anyone. Mother had warned me not to marry him."

Ginger drank her second glass of wine quickly. "Let's change the subject before I get really maudlin. My stomach churns thinking about him. I just want a way out of this nightmare."

"You certainly sound miserable. Otto must be giving you a really hard time. How about some marriage counseling? Maybe you two can resolve your differences enough to save the marriage."

She replied, vigorously shaking her head, "You're wrong. You just look at the bright side of life. I read the tarot cards for him after mother passed away. They revealed that evil is afoot. Darkness is descending on him and I don't want to be any part of it."

Eying her friend, the girl suddenly broke into tears. "I dearly miss my mother. She could see things clearly. I honestly believe that Ko Nan did away with mama. Did you know that mama could read minds? She wasn't a witch. She was an angel from heaven."

"You're suffering from rejection because Otto treats you badly. I really feel you should both see a marriage counselor and you should seek psychotherapy. Breaking up a marriage is a hard thing to do. Whatever you decide, I'll be there for you."

"You are right. I have fallen into a mean-spirited way of looking at my marriage and my life." She reached out again to give Snow Flake's hand another squeeze. "Just being with you has boosted my spirit." They paused while the waiter came and cleared away their dishes and filled their glasses with wine. After he was gone, Ginger touched her glass with a smile on her face. "Let's have a parting drink. I promise that after today, I'll partake no more, okay? I can't understand why people want to live a hundred years." Snow Flake was deeply touched and saddened by what Ginger had said, but there was nothing she could do to comfort her friend.

Snow Flake went to the ladies room. When she returned, she was greeted with a warm, friendly smile from Ginger. Her eyes glowed and when she spoke, her voice was once again soft and gentle. The girl's spirit was buoyant. She raised her glass to offer another toast.

"Here's to the hero who lies dormant within the Sea Devil. Let's drink to eternal friendship from beyond the grave." Snow Flake was alarmed by the strange wording of the toast. She felt a sudden chill as they touched glasses.

The Dark Side of Father and Son

Ginger was unaware of Otto's hidden aversion towards Snow Flake. Like all young lovers, he had once asked her a playful question while lying on their honeymoon bed in each other's arm. "Who do you love most in the world?"

Truthfully she replied, "Mama, Snow Flake, and...."

Otto didn't wait for Ginger to complete the sentence. The mere mention of Snow Flake caused an eruption inside his brain. Repugnance overwhelmed him as he vividly saw the woman strutting with Sasin's head in her left hand and the sword in her right hand. Fear once more gripped his heart, sending a tremor throughout his entire body. His mouth became dry and his hands trembled uncontrollably. Otto bemoaned his cruel fate. Snow Flake always showed him up. Even for the love of his wife. Whenever, the name of Snow Flake appeared, he would always be second best.

"Why must that Sea Devil always oppose and overshadow me?" He flew into a violent rage, breaking everything within reach. Ginger looked on in silence. Otto ran out of the bedroom and down to the bar. Grabbing the nearest bottle, he proceeded to drink himself into a stupor.

Ginger followed him and attempted to coax the bottle away. He brutally shoved her to the floor. Incoherence governed his babbling tongue.

"That woman from the deepest abyss of the darkest corner of hell always manages to ruin my dream of glory and now tries to take away my happiness! My friends couldn't talk about anything else besides Shirley's bloody fight with Sasin. They didn't see the grotesqueness of that scene. Blood soaked, carrying the head, and her triumphal screaming as she bent over drinking his blood after she killed him. How could I surpass her deeds after she killed Gavial and Gascon? Inside Snow Flake's body resides a Sea Devil. It was that Devil who outsmarted Jin Hu, the Old Fox. Father looks upon me as a failure. What chance does a mortal man have against a sea monster?"

Through a sleepy haze, Snow Flake's hand felt the empty space beside her in bed. Opening her eyes, she quickly rose to a sitting position but she had a sensation the room was spinning. When the vision cleared, she was shocked to find herself in strange surroundings. She was not in her house or any location she recognized.

"Is this a dream?" She stood on unstable legs and anger swelled at the thought of Ginger who was playing tricks on her again. She managed to reach the bathroom to splash cold water on her face.

Raising her head and looking into the mirror, she received a second shock. She had on a blue blouse and a string of pearls circled her neck. She recalled that the blouse and the pearls were Ginger's. Looking at her hands, she noticed her wedding ring was gone. Upset, she stormed back to the bedroom. A bright yellow envelope was taped to a dresser mirror. She tore open the envelope. There was a letter along with American money in it. She read the letter.

Dear Friend,

I do not have the luxury of time to argue. At times you're very head-strong. I wear your wedding ring and switched clothes with you to fool the killers. When you read this letter, I may already be dead and incinerated in your house. Lao Tung, Blossom, One Dollar, Fung Tung, Yu, and William also will be dead. Po Ling has gone to intercept Takamura to warn him of an ambush on him. I pray she reaches him in time. Ko Nan, my father-in-law, has resented Lao Tung whom he considers a relic of the past and an enemy of his ambition. His pride can no longer stand Lao Tung's criticism on his drug dealings and ruthless killings. He also fears the power of the combination of Lao Tung's followers and friends. He knows Takamura, William, and you would have avenged Lao Tung's death. That is enough of a reason for him to have you all killed. Then nobody will dare oppose his will and touch his ego.

Last night, while I was waiting for Otto to come home, I aimlessly examined the fireplace in the living room. Peering inside, I saw a knob covered with soot, and I pulled on it. When that didn't work, I turned it. A secret door opened into a dark passage. Taking a flashlight, I entered to explore the passage. It leads inside the walls and exits at the high hedges at the rear of the house. If you look carefully you can see another knob on the outside wall. It's on the right side of the garage and behind a bush. The place is very dusty and dark, filled with spider webs. On my return, the sound of a very loud voice caught my attention. I stopped to listen. I recognized the voice. It belonged to my father-in-law.

He was ranting and raving, "In order for us to take over all the Districts of Hong Kong, we must eliminate those who stand in our way. Tomorrow night, there will be Lao Tung's 75th birthday party in the Carnauba's restaurant. All his close relatives, friends, and students will be there. Send a team and mask you faces. San Lin will *lead you. Kill them all! Otto, you will kill Snow Flake and her children. Burn their house to the ground. Their maid will give you a key to Snow Flake's house. Don't fail me!" Ko Nan continued, "Five high-powered individuals have been hired from the outside to ambush Takamura during his daily walk tomorrow afternoon and they will burn his body. Rotten Melon will kill everyone in Takamura's household in the night. The time will be concurrent with the action at Lao Tung birthday party."*

After I emerged from the passage, I was shaking like a leaf in the wind. When I returned to the living room, Otto was there. Fortunately, he was stinking drunk and did not notice where I came from. I could not make a phone call from the house, and all I could think about was saving my friends.

There is something I have to tell you about the day of mother's sudden death during her meeting with Ko Nan. I was consumed by sorrow and suspicion; I confronted my father-in-law and said, "You murdered my mother! You must pay for her life!" Since then I had lost my freedom to contact my friends. That was why I couldn't reach you since my mother's funeral two months ago.

With my mother's heavenly guidance later this morning, I found an opportunity to leave the house without being caught. When I was outside and made sure that I was not followed, I called from a pay phone. Neither Lao Tung nor any of his relatives could be reached. I could not call the police because the entire force worked for Ko Nan. I dared not imagine the consequences, if I did. Racing against time, I finally reached Takamura's residence.

Po Ling and Mai Gee, Takamura's women, they are like you, dear Snow Flake. They don't panic. Mai Gee is flying with your children and theirs to a secret place in Japan. If Takamura survives, he will meet you tomorrow morning around 8 AM, at the Wong Da Shin Temple. You know the place. Don't try to contact William even if he is alive. Don't act recklessly to throw your life away. You must think only of your children and your husband. Be careful, my beloved friend. Ko Nan has grown very vicious. Protect your back and trust only your instincts.

Eternal love, Ginger."

Snow Flake was outraged at first, refusing to believe what was written in the letter. She was fuming. Ginger, as a preteen, loved to tell lies. The missing wedding ring embittered her. She looked around for her purse and found it on the floor near the bed. She picked it up and opened it. Her ID was gone but the serpent knife, a wedding gift from Lao Tung, was there. Her hand went to the phone and stopped. Instead, she counted the money in the envelope. It came to ten thousand U.S. dollars in big bills. Her eyes went to an open closet where a green jacket hung. She went there to search the pockets. She found a hand gun, a ring of keys and some change. Snow Flake satisfied herself by trying the key in the door lock. It worked, so she knew it could be used if she chose to return. She put the envelope in her purse and put the jacket on. Looking at her watch, she noticed it was 7 AM. She stepped outside and realized she was in a motel on the outskirts of the city limits.

At a newsstand nearby, she purchased a newspaper. The headline was enough to convince her that Ginger had told the truth. Police officer William Chu was shot in the leg in Carnauba's restaurant last night. Master Lao Tung, along with his son, nephew Yu, and some of his fellow students were all killed in the restaurant. A total of seventy bodies were found. Takamura's body was found burned beyond recognition in the park behind the Gates of Hell Bar. Coupled with a picture of William was the news article describing how his wife and children had been mysteriously burned along with their house. She felt helpless. She walked one block and hailed a cab.

Snow Flake was standing on the top stairs of the Wong Da Shin Temple with her right hand inside her jacket pocket holding the gun. It was early morning and the street was deserted, except for a squalid beggar lying near the bottom of the stone stairs. When the beggar lifted his head and saw the woman, he laboriously started to rise to his feet. Staggering with each step, he approached her. When he was a few feet away from Snow Flake, she noticed that his blotched face and watery eyes conveyed that life had crushed him.

With palms held like a cup, the beggar pleaded, "I haven't eaten for days. In the name of Buddha, give me some change." Uncontrollable shaking shook his entire body. Feeling pity, Snow Flake's left hand searched for some change. She tossed the coins on the steps at his feet. Dropping to his knees to collect the coins, he turned to display a face glowing from pleasure, thanking her many times in the name of Buddha.

Holding the coins in his hand, he said, "Bless you, Sea Devil, but could you spare enough change to buy some herb wine to go along with the food?" Flabbergasted, she froze standing like a statue. He rose and shook a finger at her.

"Po Ling is waiting on the street to the right in a green sedan. Are you armed?"

"Yes. I'm glad to see you."

Snow Flake got into the front seat, and turned around to look at the beggar who had entered the back seat. The sedan rocketed away from the curb. Takamura removed the soft rubber mask and placed it along with the overcoat in a soft plastic bag.

He commanded the driver, "Po Ling, keep a lead foot on the gas pedal."

Anxiety and concern made its way into her voice. "Are my children safe?" Snow Flake asked cautiously.

"Yes, at this very minute they are in Japan. We are leaving Kowloon this very night. William will be safe as long as Ko Nan believes that you're dead. Ko Nan's people have spread the word that the multiple killings were in conjunction with Gascon's death ten years ago; it was the act of revenge from the big boss of the Blood Brother Gang in India. In retrospect, what happened yesterday was the result of Ko Nan's ambition. He never felt safe with you, me, or Lao Tung alive. Po Ling, slow down or you'll miss the cutoff."

In a house on the north hill of Kowloon, the women changed into evening dresses. Takamura portrayed a rich businessman accompanying two beautiful women on a pleasure trip. In his inner pocket were visas, hotel reservations, and currency in big bills. Po Ling drove the car to the Kai Tak Airport where a private jet was waiting. As a precaution, Takamura and the women wore gloves so they would not leave fingerprints.

After That Deadly Night

When William was released from the hospital, his leg was sore but the wound wasn't serious. He could walk with the aid of a cane. Jessica brought him to her house. What had saved his life was a lone gunman who fired from the crowd, killing six masked assassins who had tried to rush over to shoot at Lao Tung, Fung Tung, Yu, and William, while William was reloading his weapon. The unidentified gunman melted into the crowd after the rest of the masked assassins fled. When he was in the hospital being treated, he heard the news from his brother-in-law, John. A fire had raged through his house and killed his entire family. Sadness and unanswered questions filled his head.

In the meantime, Ko Nan was busy providing his dead brothers with a big funeral. He honored Lao Tung as his reclaimed father. In public, he pledged to move heaven and earth to find their killers. He expressed sympathy for William as he shed tears for Snow Flake and her children at their grave site.

When he was mobile, William went back to the grounds of his residence to question his neighbors. Sway Tien, his housekeeper, had disappeared from the earth and was also assumed dead in the fire along with his family. An old woman sitting in a wheelchair, who lives across the street from his house, wheeled over to William as he was standing in the front of his burned down house. When he pressed her for information, she opened up. "Mr. Chu, I heard shots before the fire started and later I saw a car driving away."

He went to police headquarters to search the investigation reports on the death of his family. When he located the file and opened them, they were not completed. The x-rays of the skulls were missing.

William re-examined the case for any clues. It came back to him that on the deadly night, because of an added work assignment, he had arrived late for Lao Tung's birthday party. Just when he got there, from out of nowhere, bullets tore into his friends. His first reaction was to draw his gun and fire at the charging masked assassins. During the exchange of gunfire when he was reloaded his gun, he was hit in the leg and fell to the ground. He still managed to strike an assailant on the side of the neck.

Lao Tung, riddled with bullets, was dying. Summoning one last burst of strength, he managed to crawl over to shield the detective with his body. A little while later, he died in William's arms.

William tried to rationalize his thoughts about the tragedy in which he lost his entire family and his dear friends.

He asked himself where were Po Ling, Mai Gee, and their children? Did they simply vanish into thin air? It appeared to him that they just packed their suitcases and left. It was Little Moon's day off on that deadly date and she was away playing Mah Jong with friends. She had no idea where Takamura's family might have gone. Too many unanswered questions floated in William's mind. With a heavy heart and determination, he continued his pursuit into the affair of the underworld.

In a house off a mountain road along the northern coast of Japan, not far from the famous White Cloud Temple, Snow Flake had a joyous reunion with her children.

It had been one week since Snow Flake arrived in Japan and settled with her children in this house, which was prepared and arranged by Takamura and his women. Every day, her children asked about their father and when she couldn't answer them, she would break into tears. During the day, she sat and watched her children playing in their yard. They were warned to remain close to their house and never to speak to strangers.

As the days slowly passed, Snow Flake's love for her husband and the torment of losing her dear friends tore her apart. She had been having dreams that were vividly recalled upon awakening. Often, in her dreams, Ginger was dressed all in white with her arms out stretched, calling, "Shirley, where are you?"

One morning, Snow Flake drove five miles to Takamura's residence. Since returning to Japan, he had resumed his original name, Yagako Ohara. Po Ling and Mai Gee greeted her warmly, escorting her into the living room. In the middle of the room, in front of a low table, Takamura was painting with a brush on white rice paper. He raised his head and smiled at Snow Flake.

She bowed to him and said, "Thank you again for saving mine and my children's lives and all the arrangement you made for us to live here."

"Think nothing of it, Mrs. Chiang." That was the name Snow Flake presently used.

He carefully studied her face. "If there is something else on your mind besides appreciation, feel free to express yourself."

When Snow Flake cast her eyes down and remained silent, he continued. "I have been gathering information about Ko Nan and his company who believe you and I are dead. Also, I have learned that Ko Nan eliminated San Lin and the ones who joined in the killing of Lao Tung and his friends in Carnauba's restaurant on that deadly night. Under no circumstance will we let it be known that you are still alive. That tidbit would endanger William's life too." Snow Flake bit her lower lip. She didn't touch the teacup set before her.

Po Ling and Mai Gee were peering at Snow Flake. She said, "I want to avenge the deaths of Lao Tung, Ginger and my friends. I owe them my life."

Takamura seemed to be studying the picture in front of him. "Would your corpse floating in Kowloon Bay or Hong Kong harbor satisfy your obligation to Ginger and Lao Tung? When was the last time you fired a gun, threw a knife, or practiced your 'kung fu'?"

Snow Flake bowed to him asking, "Will you help me to get back in shape? If your answer is no, then I will do it alone."

There was not response while Snow Flake was waiting for his answer. Minutes later, he said, "Yes, I will, but only if you will listen to me. That's the easy part."

She asked, "Will you come with me?"

"Why should I exchange a safe haven for a watery grave? I'm over forty years old and my martial skills are in decline. Besides, I want to see my children grow and marry."

"I will be grateful for any assistance you can give me."

Again, it was deadly quiet for a full five minutes. Finally he said, "Come back tomorrow morning. You will begin running and exercising. I'll provide you with a martial arts instructor. There will be no duplication of your Gascon assault."

"Thank you, Ohara San."

After Snow Flake departed, Po Ling and Mei Gee came to look at what their husband had been drawing. He smiled at them and winked.

"Planning is the key factor. It must be based on detailed information about the climate in the Districts of Hong Kong under Ko Nan if Snow Flake is to have a chance to succeed."

Mei Gee asked, "Husband, are you allowing Snow Flake to go there alone?"

"What is the sound of one hand clapping?"

There were smiles on their faces. They both replied, "Cooperation. Why do you not tell her?"

"I, too, owe Ginger for saving our lives, and Snow Flake can't do this alone. Ko Nan took Lao Tung's life and, for that, he must pay the piper."

The Renewal

While they were eating lunch, Takamura spoke his mind. "It will take two years to get Snow Flake into her fighting form. We also need to wait for the massacres in Kowloon to fade away in the media."

Mai Gee looked upon her husband with pride. "I shall relieve you of the cares of this house and your children so that it doesn't interfere with your training. When you go to war, I shall send you off with a smile on my face and love in my heart. If you die, our children will be reared in a way that you would be proud of."

Po Ling said, "Before you leave for the Districts of Hong Kong, I want another child. Bring Snow Flake back alive."

"I, too, seek revenge," Takamura said. "Lao Tung was not only a good friend, he could see into my soul. I miss him. Ginger gave her life to save ours. It places me in her debt. The current problem is that Snow Flake isn't 'Shirley'. She is Mrs. Chu. Ten years of motherhood has changed everything. This afternoon, I'll go to the temple and speak with my brother."

Monk Hojo agreed to help Snow Flake get in shape. Takamura was pleased. "Thank you for your assistance in training Snow Flake. She is a good woman. But I have to ask you – as a monk, why are you helping us take another's life?"

"Did you mean, albeit in murder? Our belief is that no soul ever dies. We live in a dream world of our own creation. Our souls are immortal. Your task will be to send some misguided souls to their next reincarnation. There, I pray, these souls will learn to lead a more saintly life." Raising both hands and bringing them together, he continued, "Buddha, bless this household."

The following morning, the sky displayed signs of inclement weather when Snow Flake arrived with her children to Takamura's house. She was dressed in a yellow jogging suit with black running shoes and wore a cap. Po Ling invited them into the house. Snow Flake mentioned that she had made arrangements to send her children to a private school to resume their education.

"Bring your children here every day, and I shall take them to school and bring them back to our house." Mai Gee said.

Takamura emerged wearing a light blue jogging suit and a blue cap. He gave Snow Flake a look. "Are you going to dream this entire day away?"

Po Ling gave Snow Flake a shove as Takamura ran past her. "Go! Go, Snow Flake, and return as Shirley."

They ran all the way to the temple where Monk Hojo resided. Snow Flake followed him across the snow covered temple grounds into a darkened hall. She was out of breath. When her eyes grew accustomed to the dark, she noticed a seated old monk in a corner but he gave no indication of their presence. Monk Hojo entered the hall, greeted them, and asked Snow Flake from now on to speak only Japanese. He beckoned to the seated monk.

"Monk Fujimoto will teach this young woman the monkey style martial art." He looked at Snow Flake with a smile on his face. "May the Buddha have mercy on you."

Takamura laughed at the look on Snow Flake's face. Monk Hojo touched his arm. "Let's go. There is much work to do."

Two years passed quickly while Snow Flake became adept in the Japanese Monkey Style martial art and regained her top physical condition. She was also in better mental capacity. Later, she and Takamura practiced firing guns and hurling knives at moving targets.

In his mind, Takamura outlined a plan for re-entering the Districts of Hong Kong. One day, during their morning run, he paused to look at the scenery from the mountain road. "Our faces are too well known in the districts of Hong Kong. We need to change our appearance."

"Ohara San, I will do all that must be done to avenge Lao Tung, Ginger, and rescue my husband."

Takamura told her a story. "Over three hundred years ago, a Japanese man and woman named Masaru and Kufuyo together ruled the underworld. They lived by gambling and fighting and they gave the money they obtained from the rich to the poor. They were a hero and heroine for many Japanese people. Their legacy affected the thinking and behavior of the Japanese for many years to come. In modern Japan, there are many gangsters and even educated youngsters who would like to associate themselves with these two and use their names as their own."

Snow Flake did not reply so he continued. "Now, Ko Nan has a foothold in Macau, a gambling hall which is his base of financial operations and drug distribution. It's headed by Rotten Melon and managed by Jos Jung. We will add gambling and guile to our arsenal, and assume the names Masaru and Kufuyo, two professional gamblers, when we return to the Districts of Hong Kong. We will blend in with the crowd of tourists. Our strategy is devious but should provide what we need. We will incite hostility and chaos between the Sons of the Sea and the other gangs for a larger portion of the pot of gold. While under this cloud cover, we will be free to kill Otto, Rotten Melon, and

Ko Nan. Tomorrow, a master of this subject, Tota by name, will teach us how to gamble with skill."

Tota looked to be many years over sixty, with a short, slender frame. He wore thick glasses and his short hair was snow white. He accepted money from the two strangers who arrived wearing surgical masks, large dark sunglasses, and hats which covered their ears. They came to him to learn the art of gambling. Tota never asked questions of anyone who came to him for learning. He proceeded to teach his two new students the finer points of numerous games likely to be found in a gaming hall. Days passed quickly and Tota was pleased with the progress of his pupils.

They were fast learners with quick hands and sharp eyes. Every time he attempted to cheat, they caught him. With twinkling eyes, he voiced his approval. Tota had spent his entire life studying games of chance and reading body language. In his younger days, he had only gambled for high stakes. Tota enjoyed the thrill and adrenaline rush he got from such games.

Four years ago, he won a large amount of cash playing poker and one of the losers at the table took matters into his own hands. The larger man broke Tota's fingers. Since then, Tota began to teach gambling instead of playing it. So far, this man and woman were the best students he ever had. They learned all the rules of every game he taught them, knew how to beat the odds, and, just as importantly, understood the subtle clues to reading body language.

While shuffling the cards, Tota mentioned which gangs controlled the gambling houses in Japan. He related a story about his late friend who won too much money from such an establishment.

"It was about five years ago," he began. "Bisho the Bright had an extraordinary run of luck at the Red Moon Gambling Hall in Tokyo. The gods of gambling smiled down on him all that time but on the last day of his gambling life, the dour-faced gods of war were against him. After he departed the house with his big winnings, misfortune was close behind him. Bisho was attacked a few blocks away from the Red Moon Gambling Hall. A motorcycle gang beheaded him and took everything of value from his body. Since that time, nobody dared win too much money at The Red Moon."

Po Ling brought Snow Flake to a clinic for plastic surgery to change her appearance. Two days later, Snow Flake met Takamura and was not surprised to see that he also had his face bandaged.

After eight weeks, they were fully healed from the effects of the surgery which made both of them look ten years younger. Even their appearances were better than before. They looked like a leading couple in a love story movie. One was very beautiful and the other was extremely handsome.

In one afternoon, Snow Flake and Takamura drove a rented car to the Red Moon Gambling Hall. Once inside the establishment, they moved with the crowd and paused at the tables observing the play. Snow Flake watched the house man moving the tiles on the table. When the bidding was heavy, he would always revert to sleight of hand. Later that evening, Snow Flake entered the game but was cognizant of keeping her wagers low. On the way back to their hotel, Snow Flake told Takamura about a dealer who cheated. He merely smiled, praising her sharp eyes. “Tomorrow, if the same dealer is there, you will take action and I will back you up.”

All preparations were in readiness for their return to the gambling house the following night. Their recently purchased car was parked on a quiet street two blocks away. In the car there were a change of clothing and assorted weapons. Snow Flake was calm and ready for the inevitable fight. Her companion displayed his usual business-like demeanor. “From this moment on, you are Kufuyo and I’m Masaru if we need to call each other in public.”

Once they were inside the gambling hall, they separated. They located the cheating dealer who was working at a table and Snow Flake sat at an empty seat. She entered the game with small wagers. Soon the pile in front of her was multiplied by four. Later, some people left the table to try their luck at other games or went to the bar for a drink. Some losers complained to each other and left the table with long faces.

Watching the action at the table from the bar, Takamura saw Snow Flake’s signal. He carried his drink over to the table where she was playing. It did not take long before a space next to her was open. Placing money on the table, Takamura played for high stakes and won. The following round, Snow Flake increased her bet making it a high stakes pot. When the dealer saw the amount of money on the table, he smiled. Rapidly he moved the tiles while palming the winning pair. When he stopped, players eagerly reached for their tiles.

Snow Flake grabbed the dealer’s wrist and forcibly turned it over and with a blow to his wrist it opened the dealer’s fist. Two tiles were dropped on the table.

Seeing the tiles, the players grew angry, pointing at him, shouted, “Cheat! Cheat!”

Snow Flake released his hand then reached over to the dealer’s side of the table to rake in a great deal of the money, as Takamura did.

“This will cover your shamelessness,” she said calmly. “Where I come from, the ones cheating would have their hands cut off.”

Immediately, the security guards surrounded the table to prevent a riot. Observing the situation, the pit boss approached, beat the dealer to his knees. Graciously he allowed Takamura and Snow Flake to pocket the money.

The pit boss called out to the guards, shouting, “Carry him out and break his fingers. We want only honorable dealers in the Red Moon.”

Once the dealer was outside the back door, he was dispatched by his boss to alert the motorcycle gang and give them a description of Masaru and Kufuyo who just left the gambling hall.

Takamura drove their car at a slow speed while Snow Flake changed her jacket and shoes. He glanced at the rear view mirror often, observing the progress of the motorcycle gang who were still some distance behind them. Five blocks away from the gambling hall, the gang increased speed. Slowly, Takamura stopped the car in the middle of the street and looked in the rear view mirror. He saw a dozen leather-clad bikers hoping to make any easy kill. Two of them broke off from the rest and raced forward. Snow Flake screwed together the darkened, thick walled, aluminum tubes. Suddenly Takamura stepped on the gas and quickly turned down an empty street. This was where Takamura had previously chosen for the battlefield. The cyclists increased their speed in pursuit.

When two bikers pulled alongside the moving car, ready to shatter the side windows, Takamura and Snow Flake went into action. They shoved tubes through pre-drilled holes in the front door, jamming between the spokes of the bikes’ front wheels. The abrupt stop sent the bikers over the handlebars. The car stopped quickly. Takamura and Snow Flake emerged to cut the throat of the fallen bikers. Snow Flake spat on a dead body and gave it a kick. Takamura removed a sword from the hand of another corpse and viciously slashed at the body.

He turned towards the other bikers and shouted, “The odds are reduced now to ten to two. Is there any one of you brave enough to fight us?”

All the bikers revved their engines enthusiastically in response to the new challenge. Being eager for a quick kill, their leader drew a sword, and made slashing movements with it. On cue, four bikers entered the battle, racing their cycles forward to engage their prey. Snow Flake and Takamura got back into their car. Snow Flake twisted the handles of the pole protruding from the side of the car and removed two thin, blackened, foot-long blades. She handed one to Takamura.

When the bikers were within twenty feet, Takamura accelerated the car away from them. With an added burst of speed, the bikers raced forward.

Suddenly the fleeing car stopped suddenly and Takamura put it in reverse. He pushed the pedal to the floor and the car shot backwards, catching their attackers off guard. The bikers moved to either side the car, prepared to slash the tires. Two bikers screamed as sharp blades pierced their bodies through the open windows, knocking them off their bikes. Takamura slammed on the brakes again, bringing the car to a halt. The remaining two bikers circled back around for the kill. As Snow Flake impaled the third biker, her weapon broke as his body twisted to the left. The fourth attacker lowered himself between the bike handles. Quickly Snow Flake hurled a knife which pierced his neck. He fell off the bike as it went out of control. Takamura and Snow Flake now prepared for their next move.

Outside the car, they stood together with swords in their hands. Takamura parried a fifth biker who carried a chain and severed his arm. A scream filled the air as the assailant powered into a fire hydrant, breaking his neck. Takamura taunted the bikers.

"You dare send more shits to attack us? They are little boys who weren't even full grown men!"

Mata, the gang leader raised an arm holding a curved sword high in the air as a dramatic gesture to the rest of the gang. They revved their engines and spread out for the final charge.

Takamura whispered, "When they are within ten feet, shoot them." She nodded in response. Snow Flake and Takamura stood their ground and waited.

The bikers rapidly covered the ground, egged on by Takamura's taunts. Lowering their swords, Snow Flake and Takamura reached for their guns. Many shots rang out. Dead bikers fell onto the street as their cycles crashed into the side of buildings. The last biker alive was Mata, who managed to stand up and face his enemy bravely.

Displaying a gun and sword, Takamura called out, "Shall we fight as was fought in the days of glory? If not, would you rather I shoot you?" A high-pitched scream came from the biker's lips. Takamura, emulating his hero, 'Masaru', boldly walked forward.

Holding a sword in both hands, Mata rushed at him. The thrust missed the mark. Takamura's blade came under Mata's chin and went upward, sending his head flying ten feet away. Snow Flake walked over to remove the mask from the dead biker's head. When she pulled it off, she almost cried out in surprise. Mata was a young woman. They returned to their car, got the money, and departed on a useable motorcycle.

Back in the Districts of Hong Kong

It had been more than two years and four months since Lao Tung had been murdered along with his relatives and followers. Takamura had been reported killed and his body burned to ashes. William's wife, Snow Flake, and their children perished in a house fire. Yet no one had been arrested in this case, leaving all kinds of rumors flying on the street.

After William had been released from the hospital four days after that deadly night, he went to live with his sister, Jessica. Often he would look for an apartment only to be persuaded by Jessica to remain. She was lonely and her spirits sad ever since her young son's death. William drowned his sorrows at different bars in Kowloon, yet it couldn't relieve the pain. He needed his sister's comfort as much as she needed his.

William often lay in bed remembering the past. It had been Fat Gee Yeung, an officer with twenty-five years on the police force, who had introduced him to the pirate, Lao Tung. Their acquaintance changed his way of thinking about life and human nature. It took him a while under Lao Tung's influence to understand that there was no fine line between black and white. The scene faded from his mind and was soon replaced with a picture of Shirley that One Dollar gave him when Lao Tung asked him to look for her. The face was unsmiling but beautiful nonetheless. He remembered feeling his first serious attraction in his life after their initial meeting. He had put handcuffs on her at the time; however it was she who had stolen his heart forever.

William was chosen to head the investigation department in the police headquarters in Hong Kong. Two female detectives, Sergeant Lotus Koo and Sergeant Spring Su, were added to his staff. They were both women in their late twenties. Lotus was short, wiry, and pretty. She was also tough and street-wise. Spring, on the other hand, was tall and plain looking, but a good figure caused many heads to turn her way.

Although laden with work, he never stopped the investigation into the death of his family. He thought it was very strange that out of the vast numbers of informers, none admitted to have any knowledge of the arsonist who set his house on fire. Peering deep into those informers' eyes, he saw nothing but fear. William sensed that somewhere, there was a force exerting pressure on those men. In the past, those men used to speak freely to him but now they were silent and seemed to shy away from him. Who were they fearful of? He wasn't one hundred percent convinced that Ko Nan's hands were clean. Without proof, hunches and insinuations were simply conjecture.

After one year had passed without finding any trace of Ginger, Otto finally went to the police to file a missing person's report. During that year, Ko Nan had hundreds of his gang members searching for her without any success. He even hired private detectives to search as well. Otto was constantly overwrought and agitated. He couldn't keep the tears out of his eyes because, among all those women he encountered, Ginger had been his first love, the only true love of his life, and his wife. One thought festered inside him, however. He began to believe that his father was indirectly responsible for Ginger's disappearance. Bedeviled by a burning fervor, Otto continued using women and drinking in an attempt to quench his sense of loss. He even went as far as defying his father and moved out of the big house they shared.

The Sons of the Sea replaced the Blood Brother Gang, becoming the largest group in the Districts of Hong Kong. Ko Nan was the king who ruled the underworld of the entire region. His drug business and far-reaching power covered almost all the countries near Hong Kong, including Burma, Laos, Vietnam, Singapore, and Taiwan.

To establish his new image as a philanthropist and climb the high society ladder in British Hong Kong, Ko Nan donated large sums of money to local causes. Often his picture was shown in the newspaper during local charity events.

Masaru and Kufuyo

One day in May, a group of Japanese tourists arrived at Kai Tak Airport in Kowloon and passed through immigration and customs following a flag carried by a native guide to their bus. Snow Flake, who was identified on her new passport as Kufuyo Akemi, sat at a window next to Takamura. His new identify was Masaru Yagyo. Peering outside, Snow Flake watched as their luggage was placed in the compartment underneath the bus. She had mixed emotions about being in Kowloon again.

The guide spoke in fluent Japanese to describe the buildings they passed. To make some extra cash, the bus driver made a slight detour on the way to their hotel to stop at a shopping mall. Snow Flake fingered the charm Monk Fujimoto had given her. He had asked her to personally return it to him. His meaning was very clear. He wanted her to come back alive.

Their reservations in the five-star hotel contained separate but adjoining rooms. Takamura was thinking about his wives and children. On the night before he left, he talked to them about life without him. They listened without displaying what was on their minds. Quickly, he pushed that thought aside. Any indulgence in that kind of thinking could get them killed. He was too much of a realist to get caught in that web.

The first step of the plan was to make their presence under their new identities known to both the government and underworld of the Districts of Hong Kong. Then, to initiate the ill feeling, rumors would be spread that some rival gangs in the region were actively declaring that Ko Nan should be slain. After the gang wars heated up, they would sit back like a disinterested party, patiently waiting for an opportunity to strike.

In her hotel room, thoughts of her husband filled Snow Flake's mind. "How will I react when I meet William? Monk Fujimoto warned me not to recognize him, because that foolish act could bring death for both of us."

She wore black stretch pants, a tight red sweater, an expensive wristwatch, jade bracelets, colorful big earrings, and her steel tipped high heels. She looked at herself in the mirror. She saw a strange, pretty, young face dominated by hard features that definitely belonged to a Japanese woman. Her tight lips made her face look strong and showed that she was hard headed. Takamura wanted her to carry a small throwing knife in addition to the 'serpent knife' in her purse, and a derringer hidden in an inner pocket of her red summer jacket.

During their taxi ride to the Gates of Hell Bar, Snow Flake thought about the conversation she had had with Monk Fujimoto. The two of them had been standing on an arched bridge overlooking a pond when the old monk had tossed a pebble into the water.

Directing her attention to the ripples, he reflected, "Each present life consists of events from the past and your wishes for the future. They have their own cause-and-effect upon each other. Having free will, you can choose to ignore what must be corrected, but it will return later to haunt you. There is no such thing as linear time; everything happens at once. Every action causes a counter action somewhere off in a spectrum of your past, present, and future lives. You owe Lao Tung and Ginger a life. Now you have chosen to repay your debt."

"Reverend, sir, I accept my fate. In my heart, all I desire is to live in peace with my husband and my children. But I can't go to my husband nor have him come to me due to the evil surrounding us. I have tried to be kind and just to people, but that didn't prevent my first-born from being murdered. I have killed out of revenge and hatred. Now I'm thrust into something which I have no control over, in order to avenge my friends. How could I forget them? I'm the sole survivor so it's up to me to avenge them. If I must die, so be it."

"We are surrounded by karma. Doing nothing is one way of solving a problem. Actively doing good deeds can elevate the soul to a higher plane. There are thousands of solutions to a problem."

"Master, I was born to fight against injustice. I have no interest in money, power, or fame. I pray for my friends and am seeking guidance. I'm not sure the gods hear me. If I return alive, I shall never raise a hand in anger to any living thing. I shall allow the ripples of life to cleanse my soul."

"You express yourself very well. I do not bless your venture. Your way is not mine. Yet, I feel it's my duty to pray for your safe return."

When Takamura and Snow Flake entered the Gates of Hell Bar, they peered around. Takamura thought the place had changed little since he left more than two and half years ago. But according to his sources the only change had been at the ownership level. The bar now belonged to Ko Nan. That was enough reason to get even with that evil man, he thought. Takamura, now as Masaru, was dressed in a dark blue Chinese silk jacket, matching pants, and a wide open shirt displaying his well-defined, heavy, muscular chest.

The noise level of the bar was high with people shouting, drinking, and playing games. Almost all of the tables were taken. Takamura indicated to Snow Flake to follow his lead. He stopped at a table in the center of the bar and snapped his fingers. There were four French seamen at the table drinking. They looked up at him in a drunken haze.

Louis, a barrel-chested giant, moved his eyes from the man to the woman and spoke to her in French.

"Good evening, my lovely. Can I buy you a drink?"

With a sweep of the back of her hand, bottles and glasses were sent crashing to the floor.

She said in broken Chinese, "How dare you sit at this table!"

One of the Frenchmen understood a little Chinese and translated the remark to his friend. Feeling insulted, Louis rose, revealing a large belly overhanging his belt. Red-faced, he looked from Takamura to Snow Flake. An overabundance of alcohol made him suddenly brave.

"How dare this Japanese whore speak to me like that! I'll fuck her right on this table!"

Her fist slammed against the giant's Adams apple and he grabbed his throat, gasping for air. With a series of kicks to his stomach and chest, the Frenchman was dropped to the floor. His friends leapt to their feet to engage the new threat but the results were the same. They were all beaten to the ground.

She grabbed the arm of a passing waiter and spoke in fractured Chinese, "Remove this trash and clean the table!" A retort wasn't necessary. Soon Erh Hoo, the waiter, saw what she did to the Frenchmen. He obeyed. The waiter had worked here for eighteen months. During that time, he had seen many fights but this woman scared him.

This Japanese couple spells trouble with a capital T, he thought to himself. He had no choice but to appease them.

Scarred from many fights, the bouncer, Ah Wei, a large man in his thirties, was busy pulverizing a drunken Welsh sailor whose face was covered in blood. It was the Welshman's punishment for fighting with a Chinese man. Ah Wei stood six foot two with a firm figure and jet black hair. He took great pleasure in harshly subduing others in the performance of his job. The commotion caused by the two Japanese drew his attention away from the Welshman. Ah Wei released his victim and strode over toward the group of bodies lying on the floor in the middle of the bar. He stood over Takamura who was now seated at the table.

The bouncer roared in Chinese, "My fists are the law here!"

Takamura looking up at him replied in Chinese, "Get away from me. Your breath offends me. Go wash your mouth before speaking to me!"

The room went silent. Tension hung in the air like a dense fog. Working himself into frenzy, Ah Wei shouted, "I'll beat the skin off your soft body and cripple you for life!"

Quickly, Takamura was on his feet and shoved the slovenly man. His push propelled the bouncer backwards. Ah Wei grabbed at a table corner in order to prevent himself from falling.

Takamura shouted, "Is there something wrong with your hearing, goat? You offend me by speaking!"

Like an enraged bull, Ah Wei charged Takamura with out-stretched arms. His opponent launched a counter-punch which landed on Ah Wei's face, stopping the large brute in his tracks and sending him backwards. A stupid expression appeared on his face as he spit out broken teeth into his outstretched palm. Ignoring the pain, the bouncer shouted, "I'll kill you!"

He threw a series of punches at Takamura's body. Takamura avoided every blow, then he smashed Ah Wei's elbow with the side of his hand. Everyone in the room heard the sound of bones breaking. Coldly, Takamura pounded away at Ah Wei who stepped backward, then leaned forward and fell on the floor in a daze. He shook his head in an effort to clear his head, but it didn't alleviate the sharp pain shooting through his body.

From somewhere in the back of the room, a blood-curdling scream pierced the air. When Ah Wei managed to turn his head, he saw the Welsh seaman running towards him carrying a knife in his hand. The bouncer tried to sit against the wall and put his arm in front of him to ward off the attack. His eyes widened for the last time in his life as the Welshman's blade pierced deep into his heart.

The seaman, his face covered in Ah Wei's blood, grinned down at the body. A moment later he looked surprised when the blade resisted his efforts to extract it. He yanked harder. When he finally succeeded in recovering his knife, the exertion left him shivering and shaking so hard that he dropped the weapon. His teeth chattered as shock began to set in. His mates lifted him up and carried him out of the bar.

Invited for a Drink

At the right side of the Gates of Hell Bar sat five members of the Red Flesh Eater Gang. Woo Ma, the third-in-command, was in his early thirties with a short, thin build. He was young looking for his age, and dressed in a tailor-made suit without a tie. He was very impressed with the Japs' ability in the Yakuza style of fighting. He was a cold-blooded killer and loyal to his boss. He ordered his half brother, Chai, to invite the Japanese couple to his table for a drink. Chai was in his twenties with a strong build. He swaggered over to the table where Takamura and Snow Flake were drinking and snapped his fingers to get their attention.

While the woman's cold eyes scrutinized him, Chai addressed the pair in Chinese. "Come quickly. My boss, Woo Ma, wants to see you."

Takamura bent Chai over with a back hand to his stomach and grabbed his lips between his strong fingers and squeezed.

"Errand boy, where are your manners? Your words are an insult. Should I have Kufuyo remove your ears to atone for your sin?"

Chai's eyes widened in horror as the Japanese woman touched his cheek with the blade of a knife. Takamura released him and he ran back to his table, rubbing his sore lips. Woo Ma slapped him on the top of his head.

"Idiot, can't you do a simple thing such as inviting someone for a drink?" Chai cowered under the rebuke.

Woo Ma arose and walked over to the Japanese's table. He bowed. "My name is Woo Ma. I'm associated with the Red Flesh Eater Gang. Would you do me the honor of sharing a drink with me? I would like to make your acquaintances."

Takamura nodded, "We will be glad to join you. I'm Masaru and this is Kufuyo."

"Have we met before?"

"Not as far as I know, but there is a first time for everything."

Woo Ma bowed a second time, politely leading them to his table where the other men all rose to their feet.

Woo Ma introduced his men to Masaru and Kufuyo.

"Chai, the one with no manners, is my half-brother. Then we have Lover Boy Wang, Ken Yang, and Jan Chang." They all nodded at the Japs.

Lover Boy Wang was in his early thirties and nicely dressed. He was good looking and observed the woman with an appreciate eye. He moved over and sat next to Snow Flake, attracted by the woman's beauty. He couldn't take his eyes off her and thought he had never seen a Japanese woman who was built so well. Bold by nature, Lover Boy inched his fingers until they touched Snow Flake's thigh. Suddenly his head shot back and his hand moved away from her thigh. Snow Flake had placed the barrel of a derringer against his rib cage.

She spoke in broken Chinese, "You touch me once more and I kill you."

Woo Ma smiled to show he's everyone's friend. "Relax, Kufuyo. Lover Boy didn't mean to be impolite. He's under the impression that all women adore him. Today, you taught him a valuable lesson. Wang, apologize to Kufuyo."

Wang rose to his feet, displaying his charming smile and said, "Please forgive me. I was greatly attracted to your beauty."

She replied in fractured Chinese, "Mr. Wang, once is a mistake. Make sure it never happens again." The smile vanished from his face and then he sat, looking straight into his glass.

Ken Yang was a decade older than Wang, with a strong build and rough look about him. He was delighted with the sudden turn of events. He hated his younger rival because the boss favored him. All of Ken's achievements were in jeopardy as long as Lover Boy Wang was with the gang. Ken's eyes briefly went to Lover Boy, and thought it was said that a man's weakness for a woman might cause his downfall. He prayed that Kufuyo brought him nothing but grief.

Ken raised his glass in a toast. "To your health…"

Woo Ma asked, "Masaru, what brings you to the Districts of Hong Kong?"

"The climate in Japan was unpredictable and uncomfortable for us. We came here for the warm weather, to have some fun, and to change our luck."

Woo Ma was calculating their guests' ability. Although they both had shown to be capable fighters, Masaru was still the one to be watched. Minutes ago, he observed the Jap defeat Ah Wei without flinching.

Woo Ma said, "For some fun, come to our gambling hall while you are here. We have every game you can think of. Our place is called The Fragrant Gardens. It is located at Central Road in Hong Kong."

"It sounds interesting, doesn't it, Masaru?" Kufuyo had replied in Japanese.

Woo Ma asked, "What did Kufuyo say?"

"Gambling is what we do best." Takamura rose to his feet. "We must be on our way. The night is still young and Kufuyo wants to see more of the beautifully city." The group exchanged good nights and the Japanese couple left.

Woo Ma fixed his eyes on Lover Boy Wang whose head followed the Japanese woman as she left the bar. Knowing his nature, Woo Ma hoped that his boss's trigger man wouldn't try to force himself on this woman. Since he did not trust the Japs, he planned to have a private eye check on Masaru and Kufuyo. He knew people couldn't be too careful in this line of business. The couple could be Japanese undercover agents working in conjunction with the British Hong Kong Royal Police. If they are, we will kill them, he thought.

The following evening, Takamura and Snow Flake entered the Fragrant Gardens. From his office overlooking the action, Woo Ma recognized the Japanese couple who were circulating the hall. It appeared that they were checking the trend of the games. Snow Flake idly hung around the Pai Gow table and watched. She studied the way the dealer moved the tiles around the table. Woo Ma's eyes followed Masaru who now stood at the bar looking up at the two-way mirror. Understanding Woo Ma could be behind the mirror, the Jap raised his glass in a salute. Woo Ma ordered Ken Yang to go down on the floor to oversee the games.

The reports on Masaru and Kufuyo were given to Woo Ma by his informer who was a police sergeant. It stated that there were many Japanese gangsters known as 'Yakuza' going by those names. But there was a notation that this pair could have been involved in the slaying of a leading Japanese gambler in Osaka. Woo Ma felt that it would be interesting to know the real reason that brought Masaru and Kufuyo to this region.

Snow Flake settled herself at a Pai Gow table. She noticed the house man's hand movements were too quick for the average eye, exhibiting an over-confidence as he called the players to place their bets. At first, she won small amounts which were accumulated to six piles of chips. Ken Yang came to stand by the table where Snow Flake was playing. The action at the table was accompanied by lots of commotion as people got excited over winning and losing. Ken Yang edged closer to the house man and stepped on his foot.

He whispered, "Don't play cute. The Japanese woman is a pro." Snow Flake won again and, an hour later, she left the table with her winnings.

Carrying her chips, Snow Flake went to another table. Takamura followed her and stood nearby.

Ken Yang came to her. "Will you play cards with me, one to one?"

She replied in a mixture of Chinese words and Japanese. "We will play out in the open, if you don't mind?"

Seemingly amused, Ken Yang looked at Takamura, who appeared at her elbow. "Masaru San, did you hear what she said?"

"Never mind what she said. Just play twenty-one."

Ken Yang slowly dealt out the cards from the shoe. Half an hour later, Takamura touched her shoulder which caused her to immediately stand up and take a break from the game. The act did not go unnoticed by Ken Yang. The look in her eyes made him feel uncomfortable.

Takamura smiled at him. "We are leaving to go for dinner. Would you please cash in her winnings and tell your boss that we thank him for his hospitality?"

"You're welcome. Enjoy your dinner. Please come again. I'll bring the money right away." When Ken Yang went to cash in her chips, his hand was shaking. He was horrified by how much money the Japanese couple had won today.

The Empire Hotel lounge was sparsely populated. A young, pretty, Chinese woman wearing a low cut evening dress sang in English as she played the piano. A waiter stood chatting at the bar. Takamura spoke to Snow Flake in hush tones.

"An informer told me that there will be an all night card game this Friday night, at 10 PM, at the Old Tsa Fan Pier. It is a monthly social gathering of the Red Flesh Eater Gang. "Do you remember that place?"

"Of course."

"This is our opportunity to fuel the smoldering embers. The Sons of the Sea and the Red Flesh Eater Gang are undeclared enemies. This game will be held in a territory claimed by the Sons of the Sea. Once there, all the Red Flesh Eater Gang members at the game will be dead and we shall leave the evidence of the killings pointing at Ko Nan's men. These young Red Flesh Eater Gang members are feeling their oats and wish to stray into the territory established by the Sons of the Sea again."

He smiled while pushing the bowl of peanuts towards her. She shook her head.

He said, "Chow Liang is the boss of the Red Flesh Eater Gang. He keeps a respectable distance from Ko Nan ever since attempting to take over a disputed café one year ago. That encounter gave Chow Liang a permanent limp and now he needs a cane to walk. He seldom makes public appearances. Tomorrow is Wednesday. I shall trail Otto, and you go sightseeing with a group. I'll meet you back in the lounge. Say around eight in the evening? Now let's change and visit the Green Garden Gambling Hall in Macao, which is run by the Sons of the Sea."

Inside the Green Garden, they observed the action. Snow Flake hovered about a table where the dealer was unlucky. Snow Flake waited and took a vacant seat. She decided to play for small stakes. Takamura came over to the table where Snow Flake was playing and watched.

Rotten Melon was now in his forties with a big head and a large, tall body. He had a mechanical smile on his face and was dining among his henchmen. Jos Jung whispered in his ear that the two Japanese who fought in the Gates of Hell Bar were present. He directed Rotten Melon's attention to them. The house changed dealer at Snow Flake's table. This new dealer chased everyone away by winning every hand, except Snow Flake's. Takamura went to another table.

Filled with confidence, he stated, "Now you're the only one left. Please place your bet."

She answered in broken Chinese. "Please speak slowly or in Japanese. I don't understand Chinese very well."

The dealer replied, "I'm sorry miss, I don't speak Japanese very well but if you speak very slowly in Chinese, I'll understand you."

At the beginning, Snow Flake played small until the house's luck changed and then she played big. Between hands, Snow Flake peered about the hall. When she saw Rotten Melon, her blood went to her head. It was a struggle for her to keep her composure in spite of the lectures Takamura had given her about self control. She forced her mind away from Rotten Melon and back on the game. The level of the noise increased. Snow Flake collected her winnings and went over to the bar for a drink. Carrying her beverage, she approached Takamura.

While Takamura fingered his stacks of high denomination chips, he smelled the aroma of Snow Flake's perfume.

Without looking over his shoulder, he asked, "Shall we leave?"

They walked toward the bar and found a table. While the waiter serviced their drinks, Takamura asked a house man to cash in their winnings. The man counted half a million Hong Kong dollars and brought the chips to the cashier. While the Japanese pair glanced at the people in the gambling hall, a house man carrying large Hong Kong bills in his hand set the money before Takamura. He looked over at Snow Flake and pushed the bills to her.

Sensing Snow Flake's anger, he leaned over and whispered softly to her. "Mask your rage. Let's not show our hand. Look like the innocent apple, not the one with the poison concealed inside. He is coming our way."

Rotten Melon appeared before the Japanese couple. During the last few years, Rotten Melon had put on fifty pounds, mostly around the waist. He was clean shaven. When his head was tilted back, his face gave the look of a shiny ball. A tailored suit covered his body and several diamond rings adorned his fingers.

With a forced smile on his face, he addressed the couple. "Welcome to Macau, Masaru San and Kufuyo. I heard it was said that the climate in Japan was too unpredictable this time of year. I hope our nice breezes here will be more to your liking."

Takamura's eyebrows arched, "Who are you? How do you know our names?"

Rotten Melon felt slighted. "I'm Rotten Melon, second-in-command of the Sons of the Sea. My boss is Ko Nan. Your names have become well known, because you fought Ah Wei in the Gates of the Hell Bar "

"I have heard of you and your boss while I was in Japan. It's a nice place you have here. Please have a seat. I distrust people who stand over me while I sit."

A waiter hurried over with a Rusty Nail which was presented to the big boss. They toasted each other's health. Rotten Melon was silent while Takamura spoke to Snow Flake in Japanese. During that brief conversation she often peered at Rotten Melon with her lips curled. Rotten Melon was wondering if the two Japanese had been sent here by a foreign gambling boss or another gang who wanted to branch out to this part of the world. With their gambling skill, he thought it best if he could convince them to work for him rather than float around as freelancers.

Wetting his lips, Rotten Melon asked, "Would you be interested in mixing business with pleasure?"

Trying to establish an air of mystery, Takamura swirled the liquid in his drink without replying. Finally he stated, "It's common knowledge that you have very deep pockets. My motto is money up front."

Rotten Melon sent out a feeler. "What does Kufuyo have to say?"

"I speak for her."

Snow Flake replied in very rapid Japanese. Takamura chuckled, while Rotten Melon waited for a translation. Takamura merely shook his head back and forth.

"Do you really want to know what she said?"

The smile faded from Rotten Melon's face, followed by a sharp intake of air. "Is she that tough?"

"Yes, and she is very highly capable."

"Is she your woman?"

"She is her own woman. What else do you want to know, our life story?"

Rotten Melon, feeling insulted, abruptly rose. "Enjoy your stay in Macau," he said respectfully before walking away.

Touching her hand, Takamura whispered, "Rotten Melon hasn't changed in spite of his increased wealth and power. You should have seen his eye feasting on you. Woman, you missed a ready-made opportunity for an easy kill. Once alone in the bedroom with him, the rest would be a snap, but you didn't play your cards right."

A look from her was enough to let Takamura know what she thought of that idea. She understood that he enjoyed teasing as a means of lightening the atmosphere and to alert her of other possibilities, beside the knife and gun. Snow Flake ignored his wicked smile and suppressed the urge to kick him. Takamura became silent.

"What if Rotten Melon goes into hiding after Otto is killed?" she continued, "Shouldn't we act fast?"

He patted her hand. "Rest your mind on that account. Rotten Melon is an easy mark. Otto can be a problem. I found out recently that he is constantly surrounded by eight heavily armed men."

Triumphantly, she replied, "I know how to lure Otto to his death."

Jovially coming to his feet, Takamura said, "Let's get out of here and continue our talk on the ferry back to our hotel."

Plant the Seeds and Set Fuel to the Ember

Snow Flake explained, "When I lived in Lao Tung's house, Ginger and Otto often went to the beach, and sometimes Ginger would ask me to join them when I was free from practice and job assignments. Once on the beach, she would kick off her shoes, go dancing about on the sand, then run into the water. Her youthful, joyful, exuberant laughter would fill the air. Ginger favored wearing layers of thin white dresses, and she carried two long white veils. She liked it when the white veils billowed in the sea breeze. Dancing with the veils in her hands, she would sing and splash her feet in the water.

Otto enjoyed this very much, and he would follow her every movement on the sand and in the water. If we devised a method in which we could recreate this activity and it reached Otto's ears, he wouldn't hesitate to come to the beach to see if it was Ginger who was dancing or if it was her spirit."

"Woman, you've got something. Let me think about it. It's time for us to return to the hotel."

On Saturday morning Takamura waited in the Crown Palace Restaurant for Jack Eng to arrive for his ritual breakfast. Jack was a creature of habit. Every Saturday and Sunday at 8 AM sharp, he would sit at the same table and have the same waiter serve him the same choice of dim sum.

As usual that morning, Jack Eng automatically headed for his table. He was thrown off stride when he saw a Japanese man had appropriated it instead. Confused, he stared at the stranger. He stood in front of the table, shifting his weight from foot to foot.

Takamura paused from sipping his tea and said, "Will you join me for breakfast, Mr. Eng?"

"Sure, if you don't mind."

Jack Eng, a retired newspaper columnist, used to be one of Takamura's pay-on-request informants. The last time Takamura had seen him was four years earlier. He was still frumpish, but now his mouth was noticeably pulled to the left, which could have been caused by a stroke. Nevertheless, the stroke hadn't dulled his brilliant mind. Patiently he waited for the man in front of him to initiate the conversation. Jack Eng assumed that he was talking to a stranger, because he could not recognize the Jap. Takamura poured tea for his guest, who kept fidgeting nervously with his tie. He summoned the waiter and ordered Jack's favorite dim sum dishes and also ordered some expensive items from the daily specials.

With the food on the table, Takamura asked, "Is the story true that Ko Nan's daughter-in-law, Ginger, ran away with another man?"

The newspaper man didn't answer right away. He took one more bite of dim sum, savoring the warm, delicious taste. "It's the general consensus."

Jack began to relax slightly, aware of the stranger's intent. The man wanted information and Jack was willing to sell it...for a price. He abided by the rules of asking no questions. He watched the Jap set large bills on the table and he pocketed the cash.

Takamura asked politely, "Tell me more about Otto, such as his lifestyle, his interests."

"He is in constant search of new amusement. He is into hard drugs, reckless with women, and commits senseless killings. Because of his father's influence, Otto ranks high in the Sons of the Sea. He sought metaphysical assistance in search of his missing wife after all other searches failed. The current rumor is that his wife is somewhere in Europe."

Jack continued to eat, while eyeing his guest attentively. Takamura pressed him. "Does Otto have many enemies?"

"There's a long list of enemies. Recently Otto ordered his bodyguards to beat the cook of The Monkey King Bar and Grill. Kwong Yip got a broken nose because he didn't prepare his fish right. I could go on for hours. Are you looking for anything in particular?"

Takamura abruptly rose, set large bills on the table for a second time and wished him a good day. Jack looked at the Jap's retreating figure and regretted that he had asked questions.

Looking at the food on the table, he decided it would be a crime to let it go to waste. Jack leisurely ate and smoked at the same time.

Takamura spent the entire morning searching for more information about Kwong Yip. He wanted to find a way to approach him without scaring him away. Money loosened tongues. Takamura learned that, in addition to his cooking job in the late afternoons and evenings, the man worked most of the mornings at a food stand called 'Little Lai Lai' in partnership with a cousin. Following directions provided to him, Takamura located the place.

At a nearby newspaper stand, Takamura noticed Kwong Yip standing by a hot stove and wearing a strip of tape across his nose. Carrying a Chinese newspaper under his arm and a bottle of wine in his hand, Takamura sat at a small table. Kwong Yip came over to take his order. While Takamura was eating, he loudly complimented the cooking.

Flattered, Kwong Yip joined his customer when he was free from cooking. Takamura invited him to have a drink. Kwong Yip toasted to the stranger's health. Being a friendly sort of a person, he started a conversation and freely mentioned his second job cooking at a restaurant. Takamura interjected, explaining that he was seeking a master chef who would expand the menu of a new restaurant in Hong Kong. He stressed partnership; the chef would control the kitchen. Kwong Yip saw this well-dressed stranger as a supplier of capital and who might bring him good fortune.

In order to accomplish his lofty dreams, Kwong Yip invited Takamura to his apartment for further talks after he got off from his work at the Monkey King Bar and Grill that night. They agreed to meet at midnight in his apartment and he gave Takamura his address.

During their late night rendezvous, Takamura identified himself as Kashin Soto from Japan and clinched the deal by producing cash to open a luxury restaurant in Hong Kong. He stressed to Kwong Yip that he would have his lawyer work out the details and draw up a contract for their joint venture. They drank until the bottle Takamura brought was empty. In a jubilant frame of mind, Yip brought out a bottle of his own.

Takamura inquired how he got his nose broken. Kwong Yip's resentment surfaced, his face turned red, and the veins in his neck bulged. He said that Otto ordered his bodyguards to rough him up. Slurring his words, he explained, "The beast shows nobody respect. That day he was in a very bad mood and complained that the fish he ordered was not cooked right." His hand went to his sore nose. Takamura knew this was the proper moment to plant the seed.

"Would you like Otto to lose face as retaliation for your broken nose?"

Blood-shot eyes sparkled from the suggestion as Kwong Yip pounded the table top. "That would be a pleasure, but how?"

"The plan would require a fabricated tale. Everyone in the Districts of Hong Kong knows that his wife ran away from him with another man." Takamura went on to explain,

"Otto must hear rumors of people seeing a woman on the North Point Beach during a full moon wearing a white dress and holding long white veils dancing into the surf. This will lead Otto to go to the beach to look for his wife on a full moon night. If this story is shown on the news with his picture chasing a ghost, Otto will be the biggest fool and joke of the region of British Hong Kong for years to come. Otto will certainly lose face."

The cook liked the idea. Banging the palm of his hand on the table again, he agreed to do his part. Glancing over at the clock, Takamura noticed it was 3 AM. He stood up, and as they said goodbye, Kwong Yip promised he would not forget to do his part in this drama.

Friday morning, Takamura and Snow Flake drove to a rented house overlooking the North Point Beach. In a locked closet, they stored their soft body armor, weapons with silencers, knives and a white dress with two long white veil sleeves. On their way to the car, Takamura was silent but kept staring at Snow Flake. This made her very uncomfortable.

Later, he explained, "On that day, arrange your hair in the style that Ginger wore before she married Otto. I have devised a way to conceal the guns and throwing knives."

While they drove back to their hotel, Takamura brought her up-to-date with the Jin Hu affair.

"After Jin Hu's son died, Red Lantern could foresee her father-in-law's intention. She secretly placed Yee Hu with her parents who lived under an assumed name in Taiwan. Under the guidance of a communist party official in Red China, and with support from Li Wang, they planned the conspiracy very carefully on a grand scale. The grandson Jin Hu got was an orphan whose legal documents were authenticated by a large bribe. The communist officials arranged his paperwork to show him as 'Yee Hu'. Red Lantern, her handsome prince, and the communist party officials shared the money she obtained from Jin Hu with their beloved mother country, the People of China. After you brought Yee Hu to Jin Hu's house, he lost his ten millions US dollars and the lives of his men. Using Jin Hu's money, I found someone who came from Hu village years ago. Later, he lived in Kowloon and I sent him back to his village. That was how I uncovered the scam."

He smiled as he continued his tale. "I was determined from the onset of the operation that the trouble would occur at his house and not in Red China. It's impossible for Jin Hu to change a lifetime habit. He wasn't honest with anyone. The biggest mistake of his life was to team up with Ko Nan. Resentment festered for years and Jin Hu sought underhanded ways to get back at you and me. Later, Jin Hu became Ko Nan's banker and financial consultant. However, Jin Hu met up with an unfortunate accident last year."

Scornfully, she replied, looking at his eyes "What kind of accident?"

"One that left Yee Hu's substitute a very rich heir."

"I see how you operate. How do your women put up with your obsession to play tricks?"

"They are too smart to be caught in my games. Those women are far ahead of me in any game I chose to play. They laugh at my efforts and enjoy the drama."

In her hotel room, she stated, "I'm glad that you are here, because the closer I get to William, the more my mind begins to cloud." She peered into his eyes and was very touched by what she saw. It was clear to her that he was willing to die to save William and to avenge Lao Tung.

"Good night," he said. Rising from his chair, he left her room.

On Friday night around 11 PM, a fog drifted lazily along the Old Tsa Fan Pier. In a dilapidated warehouse, a card game was in progress. There were ten men sitting around a table talking loudly with piles of money in front of them. Bottles and old playing decks were on the table. The building was owned by a distant relative of Ken Yang. The ten men were members of the Red Flesh Eater Gang. Takamura had been at the place scouting the area since the early evening. The only lights in the otherwise dim warehouse grounds came from the shed and guard post.

Takamura parked the dark van one block away where, with his night vision goggles, he had a clear view of the front gate and the shed. He handed Snow Flake the night vision goggles to study the area. The gate watchman appeared to have fallen asleep in his chair.

"After tonight, the Red Flesh Eater Gang will be at Ko Nan's throat," he said.

Wearing padded ski masks, they approached the warehouse gate. Takamura broke the neck of the sleeping watchman and moved his body under a bush. Quietly they secured the area before making their way to the shed. From there they could hear loud shouting and insulting language. Takamura glanced through the dirt encrusted window and noticed that all the men wore shoulder holsters with their jackets hanging from the back of their chairs. A player rose, hurled the cards on the table in disgust, and headed for the door. "Use a new deck! I didn't win a fucking hand all night. I'm going outside to piss away my bad luck."

Takamura signaled Snow Flake that someone was coming out. The door was thrown opened and slammed shut behind him. A man walked into the bush area. Looking about with an annoyed expression on his face, he unzipped his fly. Takamura killed him with a blow to the back of his head with his gun, carried the body behind a bush, and set it on the ground.

A voice called out, "Hsun, it's your turn to deal. What is keeping you so long?"

Moving forward, Takamura knelt behind a bush ten feet from the door and alerted Snow Flake with a hand gesture. Quickly, she burst into the room, firing. Within seconds, the gang members were all down. He entered and made certain they were dead. Then he went outside and dragged in the other two bodies.

Back outside, he removed a match box which advertised the Green Gardens from his pocket and dropped it on the ground fifty feet away from the building. After insuring that nothing was left behind, he turned out the lights. Given the signal, Snow Flake took out an inflatable foot pad from a side pocket and activated the charge. They both ran out of the warehouse and, when they noticed the street was empty, silently they made their way back to the van.

North Point Beach

Seated at his usual table, Otto was in the Monkey King Bar and Grill accompanied by two women and his bodyguards. All were engaged in heavy drinking, sprinkled with loud talking and laughter. Rock and roll music blared from the stereo system as the DJ working himself into a sweat. On the stage were dancers gyrating to the music and pumping their arms in the air. Otto pushed himself to his feet, indicating to his bodyguards that he wanted to go alone to the toilet.

By looking frequently through the kitchen window, Kwong Yip had Otto under surveillance. When he saw Otto weaving his way heading for the men's room, he left the kitchen and also made his way there. Once inside, he saw pants protruding from the furthest stall. The rest of the toilets were empty. Washing his hands, he pretended to be speaking to another person.

"Dah Nain, did you see that a young woman on the North Point beach during the last full moon wearing a white lace dress?"

He deepened his voice. "I see and hear so little these days since my dog died. What did you say the woman was doing there?"

He returned his voice to normal. "She, carrying two white veils, was dancing barefoot on the sand into the surf."

Deeping his voice again, he said, "Who was the first one to see her?"

Softly he said, "Tim Yen."

"Have you seen her yourself?"

"Yes, I saw her last full moon. According to Tim Yen, she was always there at each full moon. She could be crazy." Leaving the water running, Kwong Yip returned to the kitchen.

Otto's mind was dulled from drinking too much liqueur, and he couldn't believe his ears. With his pants around his ankles, he attempted to rise but almost fell. He wanted to question the men, but by the time he got out of the stall, they were gone. Otto was bathed in perspiration. The conversation fascinated him. He splashed cold water on his face and looked at himself in the mirror. It wasn't the face of a young man. This face sagged too much.

He remembered how Ginger used to dance on the beach while they were in their teens. How she loved the wind which blew her hair against her face and the sound of the surf flowing onto the beach.

Tears spilled from his eyes and his mouth turned down at the corners. He wiped his tears away using a paper towel.

"Is it possible that Ginger has returned? Am I looking into the shadows? Why should I let every drunkard's babble excite me?" Great lamentation burst forth as his hands violently trembled.

"Ginger, I miss you dearly. Even in death, that Sea Devil still eats away at my soul."

Vividly he recalled that night years ago, when silently entering Snow Flake's house, he found all the lights out except the one on the desk where she sat. He had aimed his gun at the back of her head.

He looked bitterly at the image of the man in the mirror. That fucking Sea Devil cast a protective spell which paralyzed me, he thought. With bitterness in his heart, he recalled how he froze with fear, unable to pull the trigger. One of his men shot the devilish woman instead. They doused the body of the Sea Devil with gasoline and set it on fire. Shamefully, he was dragged out of the house and into the car, still unable to turn his head to look at his enemy.

His lips curled into a sneer. He remembered how he later killed the men who were with him on orders from his father. He felt he would have killed them anyway for they might have inadvertently said something to his father about his cowardice.

Whenever Otto thought about 'Shirley' or Snow Flake, an image appeared in his mind. She was holding the sword in one hand and Sasin's head in the other. Recently, in his dreams, the scene changed. She was holding his severed head in her hand. Jolted by the shock, he vomited all over the bed.

"Why did Ginger leave me without a word?" Resentment swelled inside him and his eyes dilated into pinpoints.

"Someone is pulling my leg." Otto smashed the toilet mirror with his fist. He ignored his bleeding knuckles and the small piece of glass in his flesh. Crying from despair, he dropped to his knees and held himself.

"Ginger, I desperately need you to cleanse me of the Sea Devil's curse. Only the secret witchcraft your mother taught you can help me. I have tried everything from drugs to therapy, but without success. Since you are gone, when I try to sleep in the quiet of the night, I hear within my brain that Sea Devil's laughter and her blood-curdling scream! It drives me mad! I can't continue to live like this any longer. Please return to me if you ever loved me. I don't want to die like Sasin with my head cut off."

Back at his table, Otto grabbed his bodyguard and whispered to him, "Find out when the next full moon is due."

"Yes sir." The man left and sought the information for his boss's son, thinking about the strange request. Shortly he returned, said, "This coming Sunday night will have a full moon. Today is Friday."

Otto gulped down his drink, rose from his chair, and pulled one of the women at his table to the dance floor. She cried out, "Please, Otto, you're hurting my wrist." He didn't care about anything or anyone right now. His thoughts were fully consumed by what he might see in a few days time.

At noon on Sunday, Otto was certain that somebody was fooling with him. With no intention of leaving the house, he started to drink again in the afternoon. By evening he was drunk. He sat in his house, continuously fingering his wedding ring. The loss of Ginger made him feel powerless and insecure. Suddenly he was filled with a desperate compulsion to find out if this rumored woman was indeed his beloved Ginger. He drew himself out of his chair and shouted for his car.

It was close to midnight as Takamura and Snow Flake waited in a sedan with darkened windows at the side of the road by North Point Beach. From their vantage point they could see headlights of a car coming along the road but the car didn't stop. Ten minutes later another car's headlights came from the same direction. Through his spy glass, Takamura read the license plate. It belonged to Otto. While they were waiting, Snow Flake had grown restless. William and her children crept into her mind along with images of Lao Tung and Ginger. It was Takamura's detached coolness that gave her consolation. From time to time, he would pat her hand. This time he gave her hand a sharp rap.

Out of the car, Snow Flake ran in a crouched position to the beach. She stopped behind some rocks and removed her dark shawl which covered the white dress. The gun with silencer and the throwing knives were secured flat against her body within easy access by slits in the outfit. For reassurance, Snow Flake's hands touched the cool steel of her weapons.

The car stopped and some men got out. They stood in front of the car and looked around. On the sand, Snow Flake rose to a standing position. The ocean breeze caught the white veils in her hands, bellowing them out. Separating her arms, she danced towards the water's edge and splashed her feet in the surf. Then she ran across the sand giggling just like Ginger used to do. The sight of the white veiled woman held Otto spellbound. He wet his lips while his eyes riveted onto the dancer's movements. The woman's high piercing giggling sent shivers down his spine. Otto took several steps forward and eight guards followed him.

Otto stood transfixed staring at the woman who was dancing across the sand. He began humming a song Ginger often sang. Snow Flake duplicated Ginger's exuberance. Otto watched the performance and became weak in the knees, breathing heavily.

One of his bodyguards asked, "Do you want me to catch that crazy woman for you?"

Otto's eyes glared at the man and snapped, "Touch her and I'll strangle you! You all stay put here!"

Otto came down from the road with sand filling his shoes, but he never felt it. What had set him off was the trick that Ginger used to do by wrapping the veils around her face. Then she would spin round and round. To Otto, that was no coincidence. The woman on the beach was doing too many things similar to Ginger's movements. He walked downward towards the woman and stopped to rub his eyes. The wind carried the woman's perfume to him. Snow Flake slowly turned to face Otto. The transparent veils blurred her features.

With the blood pounding in his ears and his face flushed, Otto trembled. "Ginger, is that you?"

The response came in the form of the woman's hands making circles from the wrists. A sigh of relief bursting forth from his lips as his entire body relaxed.

"No, it's Snow Flake, dear Otto."

His face instantly turned crimson. The saliva in his mouth dried up and the hair on the nape of his neck bristled.

Otto compressed both hands into tight fists and screamed, "Snow Flake is dead! Do you hear me?"

The breeze changed direction and wrapped the veils around her body.

"I'll bet death came from behind. You haven't the backbone or the guts to look into Snow Flake's eyes because you can't face the fact that she is superior to you."

Anguish contorted his face into a snarl as he stamped his foot on the sand. He tried to clear his blurred vision.

"Why taunt me? Snow Flake wasn't human. Didn't I tell you that my father beat me that morning after the battle for not challenging Sasin? How could I tell him that I was afraid of that Sea Devil who is capable of casting powerful spells? Didn't Sasin try to flee from her and look what happened to him! "

Perspiration burned his eyes and covered his body soaked his clothing as he trembled.

Pacing back and forth, he said, “Snow Flake made my life a living hell!” Hate flashed from his eyes and reshaped his face. Tears streamed down his cheeks.

“Ginger, how could you say to me that you loved Snow Flake more than you loved me? I tried to tell you it wasn’t love. It was bewitchment. Your witch mother’s magic wasn’t powerful enough to counter Snow Flake’s spells. She robbed me of your love and your mother paid the price for it with her life!”

Snow Flake advanced within twenty feet of him. “Ginger is dead and you killed her.”

He hesitated, as tremors surged through his body. “You’re not Ginger.”

“No, I’m not. The night you came to take my life, I had already escaped with my children. It was Ginger who was in my house at my desk.”

The words released all restraint. He opened his mouth and bared his teeth. It was a warning of an impending attack. Incoherent sounds came from deep within his throat. Deep inside his unraveling mind, Snow Flake’s bloodthirsty yell once again reverberated, calling for his head.

One of the men shouted, “Otto, are you alright?” When there was no reply, they started down on the run. Bullets from a sniper rifle dropped them in their tracks.

Otto’s brain obliterated the sound of gun fire. Wariness and heated passion engulfed him.

“All the elders praised you long after you left the Sons of the Sea. I noticed that they cast sly glances at me. They were thinking it was too bad Shirley was only a female. I understood what they would have preferred – a Sea Devil from the deepest and darkest portion of the ocean. I shall kill you and then eat your heart, even if it takes me a hundred lifetimes.” Malice unfettered him from fear as he dashed forward lowering his head.

He howled like an animal with arms extended and hands opening and closing.

Snow Flake withdrew her gun and fired at his head. His body dropped like a puppet whose strings had been broken

Feeling some sadness, she said, “Ginger, I’m sorry I had to kill your husband.”

A sharp retort stung her ears. “Your grief is overdone. Get on with it. The incoming surf will remove all traces of your presence.” Snow Flake reacted to Takamura’s orders.

The headlines and pictures in the following day’s paper showed the bodies of Otto and his bodyguards lying where they died. It was hinted in the newspapers, though not in so many words, that this killing was in retaliation for the death of the Red Flesh Eater Gang members in the warehouse at the Old Tsa Fan Pier. After he read the newspaper at his food stand, Kwong Yip's hands started shaking. His teeth were chattering and all color drained from his face.

"What if Ko Nan uncovers my part in this plot? It was that son of a bitch, Kashin Soto, who set me up. In reality, he never wanted to go into the restaurant business and have me as a partner. I'm a dead man."

Frightened, Kwong Yip sought refuge in a bottle. In the afternoon, his cousin dragged him into the restaurant where he sobered up enough that he could work in the kitchen.

In the evening, a messenger arrived at the restaurant carrying a small package for Kwong Yip. He tore open the package and saw what was inside. Quickly he stashed it carefully until he was ready to leave. When he got home late that night, he opened it once again, dumfounded. In the package were bundles of cash in big bills totaling fifty thousand Hong Kong dollars. This bonanza represented a chance at a new life.

He called his longtime girlfriend, Lucia Guo. "Let's pack." The next evening, they left Kowloon for Taiwan.

Ko Nan in a Frenzy

Upon hearing the news that his son was dead, Ko Nan broke everything in sight and attacked anyone within his reach. In his eyes, the blame for Otto's death fell squarely on the shoulders of the Red Flesh Eater Gang and their boss. He ranted that nothing but all their deaths would satisfy him. Fearing that he would also be held responsible, Rotten Melon sent out many men to kill every Red Flesh Eater Gang member they could find. Corpses soon littered the bars, restaurants, and streets. The police were out gathering suspects to question.

Before the week was up, Rotten Melon suggested to Ko Nan they should get outside help. When he was given the go-ahead, he called the hotel where Masaru was staying. He became vexed upon learning from the hotel desk clerk that the Japanese couple was out on sight-seeing tour.

In the evening, when Takamura returned to the hotel, he ignored the urgency of Rotten Melon's request. Instead, he accompanied Snow Flake to a hot spot in Hong Kong to dance the night away. They didn't return until the early morning hours. Snow Flake was thankful that Takamura had kept her busy, not giving her time to think about her problem. When she lay down in bed, thoughts of Ginger filled her mind but she soon fell asleep from sheer exhaustion.

After lunch, Takamura returned Rotten Melon's call and agreed to meet him at the Wong Village café at 6 PM.

In the car, Takamura was silent as they made their way across town. Just before Snow Flake emerged from the vehicle, he asked, "Do you think you will have any difficulty in handling the business with Rotten Melon? We are only into the first phase of this operation. Will you be able to handle the stress? Be honest if you can't. Go back to Japan and I'll do what must be done."

A look of determination burst forth from her eyes.

"Although I'm fighting conflicting emotions, I'll never let you down. The life of my husband is at stake and the revenge for our friend's death must be accomplished. It was I who begged you to come, not the other way around."

"My dear Snow Flake, when I look into your eyes I want to see Shirley staring back at me. She is here with us now. Let us not lose her until this sordid affair is over."

Rotten Mellon arranged the meeting in a private room. He explained to the Japanese couple why he wanted to put them on Ko Nan's payroll and that they would work for the Sons of the Sea. He suggested they should remain neutral by appearance. When Takamura readily agreed, Rotten Melon set money on the table. Without counting, Takamura passed the big bills over to Snow Flake who put them in her purse. Rotten Melon strutted out of the restaurant as the food arrived. Takamura touched Snow Flake and they both arose. Takamura threw some money on the table to cover the meal and tip.

After they left the restaurant, he placed his arm around her shoulders and whispered softly in her ear. "When we return to our hotel, you shall place the money in their safe and get a receipt. Then you will go alone sightseeing. Be highly visible in the crowd and don't relax your guard. We are being watched."

Snow Flake arranged for the tour with the hotel desk, before retiring to her room. An hour later, she emerged with a group of twenty guests and boarded a large bus. Sergeants Lotus Koo and Spring Su of the British Hong Kong Royal police followed behind in an unmarked car. This surveillance was ordered by Captain Chu. The Japanese couple had come to his attention when the report of the bouncer's death at the Gates of Hell Bar landed on his desk. William was seeking answers as to what brought this couple to the Districts of Hong Kong. He also sent a request to the Japanese police asking for Masaru and Kufuyo's rap sheets.

In his office, William was studying the pictures of Masaru and Kufuyo that were pinned on a bulletin board. He asked himself what their motives were in picking a fight at the Gates of Hell Bar. Why has the bloodshed been increasing in this region since their arrival? He didn't believe it was a coincidence. Every one of his people he sent to tail them had either lost them in quick fashion or reported no evidence of their wrongdoing. A mere tourist wouldn't have that talent, he thought. The reports he got back from Japan were of no help either. They were very vague.

He decided that he wanted to have a face-to-face talk with Masaru and Kufuyo. He wanted to draw his own conclusions.

Snow Flake grew bored with the tour and left the group at the Botanical Garden to see the zodiac statues. Lover Boy Wang had a man tailing her from the beginning of the tour. Once in the park, Lotus recognized the man as a member of the Red Flesh Eater Gang. She phoned Captain Chu to inform him where to find Kufuyo, but omitted telling him about the gang member's interest in her target. She calculated that her boss would arrive within fifteen minutes. Down the path, Lotus saw the man speaking on a phone so she and Spring Su hung back and dogged him.

Snow Flake stood by the rail, looking at the zodiac statues. Her eyes caught sight of a flunky who stood five feet away from her. He turned away as she glanced towards him. She also spotted two women by the refreshment counter. They had the appearance of police imprinted all over them. She had noticed they were following her ever since she got off the touring bus. Now she could see their faces clearly for the first time, and she recognized them from Takamura's descriptions. The women were Lotus Koo and Spring Su. They were collecting paychecks from both the police department and Ko Nan.

Snow Flake's stroll brought her to an outdoor restaurant. She sat at a table and ordered tea to take her mind off the anger she felt towards the two turncoats.

Standing apart from his underlings, Captain Chu observed Kufuyo who was leisurely sipping tea.

He soon became aware that Kufuyo was looking directly at him. Abruptly, she stood and left.

The appearance of her husband made her nervous. She pondered whether he would recognize her. Snow Flake hadn't covered forty feet before William came abreast of her. He called out in Japanese, "Kufuyo, could I have a minute of your time?"

She tried to force herself not to panic. Instead of stopping, she increased her pace. This time William came in front of her, blocking her way. He displayed his police identification to her.

"I am Captain Chu of the British Hong Kong Royal Police. Can we speak or must I arrest you? Either way we shall have our talk."

Speaking in fractured Chinese, she replied defiantly to mask her normal voice. "Captain William Chu, if you take me in, my lawyer will have me out before you can complete your paperwork. Since it is a lovely day, I'll talk provided that you speak in Japanese." William's respect for this woman escalated. She not only knew his first name but she also knew that he spoke Japanese.

Walking leisurely side by side, she avoided eye contact with him.

"What is a Yakuza of your caliber doing in the Districts of Hong Kong?" he asked.

"Believe it or not, I'm on vacation."

"What was the need for a demonstration of your skill at the Gates of Hell Bar?"

"I live an adventurous life. Sometimes I need to practice my skill." She paused before she spoke, sensing William's eyes flowing over her body.

"Have we met before?"

"Isn't that the oldest pickup line in the books?" She held on tightly to the railing. "I'm sure a man of your intelligence can do better than that."

She smiled, directly looking at him. The sight of him made her want to cry. He had a terrible appearance, there were bags from lack of sleep under his eyes, his face was haggard, and his shoulders were tense. As a diversion, she went over to a machine to purchase bird food. Opening the bag, she tossed handfuls of seeds on the ground and watched the birds eat.

"Your rap sheet states you are a convincing liar, card shark, and a skilled fighter. I believe that you have used many aliases. What is your real name?" Snow Flake crumpled the empty seed bag and tossed it into a trash can.

"End of your free time, Captain Chu. I'm doing nothing illegal but enjoying the Botanical Park."

Realizing he was at a standoff, he bowed. "You may go wherever you like. It is certain that we shall meet again. By the way, is it Miss or Mistress?"

Flames burst from her eyes and tongue, "It's Kufuyo!" Quickly she walked away.

"Ouch," said William with a smile on his face.

Watching this Japanese woman walk away, William judged her on what he saw. She was highly intelligent, nervy, street-wise, tough, and definitely not a common tourist. Walking back to his car, he thought about her some more. The street talk was that Masaru and Kufuyo won a lot of money from the gambling halls belonging to the Sons of the Sea and the Red Flesh Eater Gang. Could there be a connection? Did they win the money or were they being paid for services rendered? "Sooner or later, the cleverest criminals make a mistake," he said under his breath. "When that happens, I'll be there."

Another question popped into his head. With a clenched fist, he asked himself if Masaru and Kufuyo were the rumored outsiders that Ko Nan had mentioned. Entering his car without starting the engine, William made a mental note to have a talk with Masaru. In order for him to meet the Japanese man, he had to remain close to Kufuyo. Desperate for a cigarette, he reached for his pack with trembling hands.

Shaken, Snow Flake went blindly along a path. Her sixth sense alerted her that there was danger ahead. Seated on a bench was Lover Boy Wang dressed in a dark blue silk suit and a red shirt opened at the neck. Three henchmen stood behind him. He gave her a grand greeting. "Well, if it isn't Kufuyo. Come sit by me and we'll have a nice chat."

"I'd rather be alone, if you don't mind."

"I see you prefer the company of the police to me. Are you a Japanese undercover agent?"

Scornfully she saw his gaze pass over her, so she continued to walk. Lover Boy Wang shouted to his bodyguards, "Shu, Tai, drag the bitch back!"

Snow Flake stopped and turned to face the men. They had expected her to attempt flight and were taken aback by the nerve of the woman. From a pocket in her jacket, she removed leather gloves and put them on. Her small purse went inside a zippered pocket. The men came towards her from opposite directions. When they were within kicking distance, Snow Flake lashed out with a foot striking each man on the chest. Without breaking stride, she punched their faces. Powerful kicks knocked them to the ground. Lover Boy Wang did not anticipate this woman to be so tough and skillful.

He was annoyed and with a wave of his hand he sent his strongman, Zang, after the woman. Zang, confident in his ability, walked toward Snow Flake. When he was close to her, he separated his arms for her to kick his chest. Instead, her foot struck his kneecap hard, tearing cartilage. He sank to the ground holding his shattered knee. As she tried to chop his throat, Zang grabbed her wrist. Without hesitation, she shattered his nose with her other hand. He released his grip as he brought his hands to his face.

From the corner of her eye, she saw two policewomen idly standing around.

"Why don't they stop the fight?" Contemptuously, Snow Flake spat on the strongman and coldly eyed Lover Boy Wang. With the last of his bodyguards out of the picture, she came at Lover Boy. Her face displayed disgust.

He removed his butterfly knives from his pocket and used quick wrist movements to flash the sharp blades in the air around him. He wanted to demonstrate that he was not to be trifled with. Lover Boy shouted, "I'll carve my initials on you, Japanese whore!"

He made several feints in an effort to frighten her. He swung the knives high then low before making a quick thrust at her. She caught his wrist and violently twisted it. She kept the pressure on forcing his hand open. He made a half-hearted try to strike at her with his other hand. With his face contorted in pain, he screamed as she broke his wrist. People stopped to watch, but the two policewomen still did nothing. In one quick motion, she kicked the side of his jaw and broke it. He fell to the ground withering in agony. Contemptuously she stomped on his knee caps. Loud screams pierced the air as he rolled on the ground.

It was in their Chinese blood. Lotus Koo and Spring Su hated Japanese and were disappointed with the outcome of the fight. They had hoped to see Kufuyo beaten or carved up by Lover Boy Wang. They watched Kufuyo breaking the gangster's bones and punching his body but did not intervene.

Snow Flake kicked Lover Boy Wang while he was on the ground but she stopped short of killing him. After brushing herself off and straightening her jacket, she rapidly walked through the parting crowd. She went to the nearest phone box and dialed a number. At the sound of Takamura's voice, Snow Flake recited a message and listened. Looking at her wristwatch, she left the park and hailed a cab.

Takamura absorbed what Snow Flake concisely related about what just had happened in the park. He congratulated himself on the success of his perceived plan for her. It was logical that she would be tailed by the police. Now the police tail will become her alibi. The meeting with William was inevitable and she had handled herself very well. On the phone, he told her to forget about Lover Boy Wang, go see a movie and retain the stub. After the movie, she was to go to dine at the Royal café in the Hilton Hotel. He reminded her to be a generous tipper at the restaurant so she will be remembered. After he hung up, he used his contacts to learn some of the names of Lover Boy Wang's enemies. Quickly he formulated a plan to kill Lover Boy. Since he was going to be hospitalized, immediate action had to be taken that very night.

Shan Pak lived with facial scars, a product of Lover Boy Wang's handiwork. As he looked into the mirror each morning, the sight fueled his dream of revenge. Takamura learned of the gangster's attack on Shan Pak and decided to use the victim's revenge for his own purposes. Takamura called every hospital until he located the one where Lover Boy Wang was taken. Then he went to the bar where Shan Pak was known to hang out.

The following morning, newspapers headlined the story that Lover Boy Wang and his three bodyguards were slain inside a hospital. Pictures of the dead assassins also were on the first page side by side. Shan Pak and his brother were killed by police after they murdered Lover Boy Wang and his men. A gun battle ensued and three policemen were killed as well. The newspaper articles hinted that Ko Nan employed Shan Pak and his brother to kill the Red Flesh Eater Gang members in retaliation for his son's death.

There was not one word in any newspaper, however, mentioning the fight in the park which sent Lover Boy Wang and his henchmen to the hospital. It would have injured the pride of the Chinese to admit they were defeated by a lone Japanese woman. William was disappointed that Shan Pak was dead. He would have liked to talk to him. William was certain that the two Japanese were implicated in those murders in some way.

When William scanned Lotus's report on Kufuyo's fight, he was annoyed. He asked himself why they didn't they stop it. Later, a phone call from another informer told him that, after she left the park yesterday, Kufuyo was alone in the movie and afterwards she had dined in the Royal Cafe. The policewomen who tailed Kufuyo also mentioned she took a cab back to her hotel alone later in the evening and went directly to her room. There were no phone calls in or out.

"Ingenious." William concluded that Kufuyo had established an airtight alibi. She knew what was going to happen.

"You have to give credit to this woman. Who could give her a better alibi than policewomen?" He tugged at his nose in an unconscious gesture.

"What made Lover Boy Wang think that he could abduct Kufuyo in broad daylight?" Shoving the reports across his desk, he called in the two female sergeants for a tongue lashing. While the women stood rigid, he strongly reprimanded them for not preventing what happened in the park.

The Gangs Must Unite

Chow Liang was in his fifties, a tall, lean figure hobbled with a walking cane. He was the boss of the Red Flesh Eater Gang and has spent the last several days reeling from the constant attacks by Ko Nan and his men. The recent assassination of Lover Boy Wang was the last straw. The situation forced him out of his hideout to seek an alliance with Ting Don, the leader of the Shandong Tiger Gang.

Ting Don was a tall, slender man, ten years younger than Chow, and eager to unite his forces against the Sons of the Sea. This arrangement would double their manpower, he realized, and serve to put him in a better position for eventual takeover as the new boss of the underworld.

To beef up their force against the aggression of the Sons of the Sea, Ting Don sent a representative to speak to Masaru. Ting Don wanted someone with experience and skill in fighting and who wouldn't be a threat to him. Aware of the arrangement between the Jap and Rotten Melon, he decided to offer more money as an inducement to change Masaru's mind. He reasoned that Masaru was a gambler by nature, and only money talked. No, it shouted.

The following morning, Takamura and Snow Flake went on an excursion and didn't return to their hotel until the evening. Takamura dropped Snow Flake off in front of the hotel. "Meet you in the lounge later," he said, before crossing the street to talk to one of his informers.

After entering the lobby and getting her key from the desk clerk, Snow Flake turned and saw William reading a newspaper on a lounge chair. If he was here, there must be others around as well, she reasoned. She let her gaze wander across the lobby and saw the two policewomen near the shop's dress window.

When William caught sight of Kufuyo, his heartbeat quickened. It bothered him because she attracted him like no other woman since Snow Flake. Leaving the paper on the chair, he rose to follow her. Kufuyo walked towards the lounge. William noticed that she sat at a table in the center of the room. He came and sat across from her. The policewomen came and sat on either side her. Snow Flake signaled the waiter and when he came, she ordered a Japanese beer.

With a challenging look, she asked her guests, "Have your people stolen anything from our rooms while we were away?"

"Good evening," William replied calmly. "How was your sightseeing trek? I don't know why you bothered to order anything. We are taking you in."

"What is the charge?"

"A complaint of assault was filed against you. That beating you gave Lover Boy Wang and his bodyguards landed them in the hospital resulting in the murder of four men and the deaths of three policemen."

She sat up straight. "Really, Captain William Chu, we're both street-wise. Lover Boy would never sign anything like that, especially after being beaten by a Japanese woman. It would make him lose face among his friends. He wouldn't give police the right time of day. The way he treated women, that animal had a long list of enemies who would be anxious to put him away and do a favor for all the women in the Districts of Hong Kong. Your policemen died in the line of duty, not by my hand. Imagine what would happen if the newspapers printed a story about an attack on a Japanese tourist in a public park in broad daylight as two policewomen sat on their hands watching. Your boot lickers neglected to properly perform their duty. How would that look on your police blotter?"

William pieced together the gist of what she said using Japanese with added Chinese words. It amused him. Lotus Koo and Spring Su were giving Kufuyo sharp looks. The waiter came and poured beer into her glass, then left.

"Your case is filled with holes. It won't fly."

William replied in Japanese, "No need to brag. It isn't over."

She drank some of her beer. Looking at his weary face, haggard from lack of sleep and the daily pressures he endured, her heart was broken. Her eyes caught sight of a moving figure standing at the bar. Takamura walked over to the female pianist and placed some money on the piano. She smiled at him and began to play. Catching Snow Flake's eye, Takamura raised a finger and left the lounge. It was a sign for her to leave as soon as possible.

William said, "True, the people of the entire region will not shed a tear at the loss of Lover Boy Wang."

He mentally tried to index the Japanese woman's face with the others he had in his memory bank. He couldn't come up with a match, and it riled him. He did not know this woman, yet he had this strange feeling that he had seen her before. She affected him in the strangest way and did indeed remind him of someone.

Meanwhile, Snow Flake was looking at the ceiling. She was silently counting. When she reached fifty, she abruptly rose and exited the lounge. That act caught William and his people off guard. Within seconds, she was out of the lounge.

William gave an order. "Bring her back!"

Takamura was near the lounge and heard what William said. He realized he had to do something to distract William's attention away from her. He accosted the two policewomen just by the exit and escorted them back into the lounge. William saw that his policewomen were trying their best to free themselves of a man's grip and were failing. Takamura released the policewomen, went toward the table where William was seated. He reached for Snow Flake's glass and sipped it.

"I am Masaru. You must be Captain William Chu of The British Hong Kong Royal police. What the hell did you order for Kufuyo?"

"It's Japanese beer. She ordered it, not me." Takamura signaled the waiter and ordered a bottle of Italian red wine. In the meantime, he picked up Snow Flake's glass and deliberately spilled it on the floor and smashed the glass.

Takamura said to the waiter, "I'll pay for the drink and the glass. Clean them up. Here is something extra for you." The man's eyes widened at the sight of the overly generous tip. He dropped to his knees to remove the broken glass and clean up the spill.

The policewomen rubbed their wrists and were glaring at Takamura who asked, "Captain Chu, will you join me for a drink?"

"No thanks," William answered warily.

Takamura poured wine into two glasses and shoved one across the table towards the police captain. The pianist was playing another tune. William was measuring this man.

This is the coldest, self assured person I have ever encountered, William thought to himself. He radiates a deadly kind of power.

Takamura held up his glass to the light. "Tell me Captain Chu, do you like sad songs or happy ones? Cheer up, my dour-faced captain. In life, everything can be changed. The quickness of the hand can fool the most experienced eyes. Would you send away your people so we can talk?"

William realized that this was his chance to learn more about the Japanese couple. "Sergeants Koo and Su, leave us alone." After the women left, he reached for the wine glass.

"I'm off duty now." They raised their glasses in a silent toast and emptied them. William set his glass on the table.

"Is the woman yours?"

"No, she belongs to someone else."

"Why are you traveling with her?"

"For the sake of friendship. Her husband and I are good friends and twin brothers but without the same blood."

"Are you here on business, pleasure, or something else?"

"I'll pass on that one."

"Were you both in here three years ago?"

"Yes." A deep silence ensued as William studied Masaru's face. Those icy eyes gave away nothing.

"Why don't you ask me the question which is foremost on your mind?" William stiffened. "Did Kufuyo or I have anything to do with the death of your friends or family? The answer is no."

William rose from his chair standing over the Japanese man. Takamura peered up at him.

"I can read the newspaper in three languages. It was a sensational story. My paid informers tell me you are also fluent in Japanese and English. Am I to assume your people found nothing out of the ordinary in our rooms, or have you planted something?" William sat down and poured himself another drink.

"You're a very clever man. Let's see if I can match your brilliance. Are you playing both ends against the middle? Do you always travel with a friend's wife and allow her to share the blame with you?" Takamura didn't take the bait.

"Are you trying to dampen a friendly conversation?"

Takamura thought William appeared as tight as a drum, showing little emotion about the world.

The Japanese man said, "I heard that trading with the enemy is as old as war." Takamura raised his hand signaling the waiter to bring the check. He dropped some bills on the table and stood up.

"Good night, Captain Chu. I'm certain we shall meet again." Takamura walked toward the elevator.

William muttered, "You got that right."

After the Jap left, William remained at the table. He tried to fathom what was behind this man's words. It was clear that Masaru had more to say, but the main reason for the Japs being here still eluded him. Then he noticed a matchbook with pin holes on it, near the wine bottle on his table. Like all cops, he picked it up and put it in his pocket. Casually he finished the wine in his glass and headed for home.

In his bedroom at home, William took out the matchbook and examined it. He was curious about the series of pin holes on the matchbook's cover. William looked around and located a dictionary with Braille character translations. He drew the pin marks on a paper pad and then compared them with those in the Braille alphabet. It spelled out in English, "You are living in a fish bowl."

"Damn, this message is for me. Masaru knows what has been going on in the police department. Just what kind of a game is he playing? Why is he warning me?" He tugged at his ear.

Six months later, on a Wednesday night, the tremendous power of Ko Nan was shaken to its core. The allied gangs bombed the Sons of the Sea's gambling hall, the Fragrant Gardens in Macau. Rotten Melon was away when the attack occurred. In that raid, forty Sons of the Sea gang members were killed. Half the gambling hall was destroyed. A gauntlet had been thrown in Ko Nan's face. Rumor on the street was that the allied gangs had a secret pact with Masaru, who would receive twenty percent of what Ko Nan took in a year.

During the following days, the gangs demolished several warehouses belonging to the Sons of the Sea. Soon afterwards, two of Ko Nan's subordinates, rising stars in the Sons of the Sea, Tien Mu Bao and Lia Yan Lee, were gunned down on Sunday morning as they emerged from their homes. Headlines in all the newspapers detailed the gang war. Pictures of the battle scenes appeared on the first and second pages of the newspapers.

Reading the news, Takamura was pleased. His action had succeeded in producing a smoke screen which veiled the true purpose of the killings. He left the hotel early Monday morning with Snow Flake. When Captain Chu sent his men to the hotel to bring Masaru and Kufuyo in, they returned empty-handed.

Rotten Melon was willing to pay more money to the Japs in order to change their minds again and become active members of the Sons of the Sea but Ko Nan distrusted them. He didn't want Masaru within a mile of his back. He thought the crafty foreigner was probably sent as an agent for the leading gambling syndicate in Japan to test the waters here. Ko Nan announced to his direct subordinates that Masaru and Kufuyo under no conditions were to be used by the Sons of the Sea in their fight. However, Ko Nan decided to seek outside help from other sources. Within days, two high ranking martial artists arrived at Ko Nan's office. The Japanese female fighter went by the name Otowa and the Korean man was named Soong.

Rotten Melon Is Next

Using the power of money, Takamura roamed the entire region in search of information about Rotten Melon's daily routine. Takamura recalled that years ago at the Gates of Hell Bar, the gangster liked to boast of his many female conquests. Since his nature didn't change and good fortune seemed to be smiling at him all the time, it was logical to assume that Rotten Melon had mistresses.

From several informers, he also learned that Ko Nan had imported outside talent for his personal protection and enhance his power. One of the names was familiar to him. He recalled that, five years ago, he killed a Korean by the name Soong in his bar. He wondered if this Soong could be related to the Soong he killed. Why did he not come seeking revenge then? This youngster must have been practicing Korean Martial Arts for the last five years.

His detective work was paying off handsomely. Takamura was able to locate Sway Tien, the Chu's housekeeper. She had been missing since the day the Chu family house was demolished by fire. Now she worked for Sony Cosmetic at Tong Choi Street in Hong Kong. He passed himself off as a friend of her ex-boyfriend, On Hou. An appointment was arranged for that night at the Royal Grill Restaurant.

There was plenty of food on their table and a handsome display of cash in his wallet. With greedy eyes, she immediately surrendered herself to him. During the course of their eating and drinking, she mentioned that years ago she was cheated by a friend who asked her for a favor. Sway Tien bitterly denounced her ex-boyfriend and her unlucky dealing with Rotten Melon, who promised her big money which she never received. As the night of drinking went on, Sway Tien mentioned Rotten Melon's threat.

Vehemently, slurring her words, she said, "That two-faced bastard sent men to kill me, but I was too smart for them. I'm really no dummy, though I might look like one."

Sway Tein then described how on that deadly day, she faked being sick and left the Chu house at noon. Later, she met Otto on the street and gave him the key to the Chu's residence on the condition that Rotten Melon would give her $10,000 U.S dollars.

Bitterness filled her voice. "Not only didn't I receive any money, but giving him the key made me an accomplice."

After the meal was finished, Sway Tien suggested they continue their talk in her apartment. While she went to the ladies room, Takamura dropped some powder in her drink. In her apartment she passed out and Takamura made a quick exit.

Two days later, in the late afternoon, an informer gave Takamura a juicy item concerning Rotten Melon's present love interest which he kept hidden from his wife. This new woman, May Meng, lived in the New Territory near the Kowloon border. She was a television actress, whose brother, Henry Meng, acted as her agent. These days, Henry could be usually found at the Lily Pond Mah Jong Parlor in Kowloon.

Upon hearing this news, Takamura began to visit the parlor. One day when a new round game was about to start, he was able to procure a seat next to Henry Meng. The young man was in his late twenties, thin, and expensively dressed. He wore a gold Rolex watch and a jade ring. His clothing spelled money. Takamura sat down and introduced himself as a businessman from Malaysia. Takamura had heard that Henry was a happy winner but a sore loser. Takamura ordered a round of drinks for the table. While playing, he calculated what tiles Henry was holding and fed him the tiles he needed to win. Henry was slightly drunk, and feeling very upbeat from winning, mentioned where his famous sister lived and boasted about her boyfriend, Rotten Melon, the second-in-command of the Sons of the Sea Gang. Two hours later, Takamura embarked upon a mission to kill Rotten Melon.

In Snow Flake's hotel room, they discussed the next target on their list. She suggested having the alliance gangs attack Rotten Melon's house. Seeing him inattentive, her temper began to flare. Unruffled at her display of nerve, he stood up and slowly inched closer to her. He gave her a pat on her back that did not calm the stormy waters.

"Why are you acting so silly?" He softly chided her. "Do you know that women are man's downfall?"

She threw her hands in the air and retaliated, "You always have to blame defenseless women for your shortcomings." Exasperated, she went to look out the window.

"Rotten Melon will come to us."

Her blank stare changed to disbelief.

With his eyes twinkling amusement, he explained, "I have the address of Rotten Melon's mistress in the New Territory. Without fail, Rotten Melon arrives every Wednesday at noon to visit his lady love."

"Every week..?"

"Every Wednesday morning, he is driven in a van sporting 'The Bank of Kowloon' logo to his bank office right inside the border of Kowloon for a routine business stop before he visits his mistress. Our plan will start with taking over the van after he enters the building. When he comes out the building and enters the van, we will have him. Then we'll drive to a quiet location where you will send him to join Otto. As a precaution, we will wear soft body armor under our clothing and change our looks. Let the rival gangs fight for an unworthy prize." She seemed impressed with the plan.

It was at a Christmas party more than two years ago that Rotten Melon, then a movie producer, was introduced to May Meng, a young beautiful actress who enticed him. He showered her with expensive gifts. The man soon produced a movie in which she was the star. Rotten Melon appeared to May Meng as an old-age policy consisting of yearly dividends. The courtship had being spanning eight months now. It took a king's ransom in presents to finally convince May Meng to accept him. A high-rise apartment building was purchased in her name and furnished in top fashion. An allowance was agreed upon. Every Wednesday at noon, Rotten Melon could have three hours with her. He was pleased with the arrangement that allowed him to have this beauty without his wife's awareness.

It was the first weekend of the month when Snow Flake and Takamura went to the New Territory. They stayed in a hotel in the downtown area for five days. They located the building called the Capricorn where Rotten Melon's mistress lived and then proceeded to study the nearby streets and traffic in detail. During that time, Takamura rented a secluded house three blocks away from the Capricorn. Their new hideaway was surrounded by a tall stone wall and had a spacious yard with a two car garage and a belly stove. When Takamura came here to rent the house, he disguised himself as a sixty year old rich man from Japan here on business.

With a detailed plan, they laid out all the preparations needed for the job. They decided the date of the action would be on the fourth Wednesday of the month. Returning to their hotel, the pair reviewed the plan, step by step, many times.

On the given day, Takamura and Snow Flake left their alternate residence in Kowloon before sunrise and rode motorbikes into the New Territory. They arrived at the rented house where Takamura had stashed electrical equipment, uniforms, and all the items needed for this day's operation. In the house, they put on soft body armor and prosthetic makeup to thicken their faces. Snow Flake's hair was tucked under a wig. Finally, they put on their electrician uniforms. They rode to the Capricorn building grounds and began their operation early in the morning. The apartment complex staff could be seen outside cleaning the street as well as the yard of the building.

Takamura and Snow Flake parked their motorcycles around the street corner. The pair placed caution signs at each end of the street. Snow Flake chose a location near a utility pool 100 feet from the apartment building. She laid a tool box of instruments on the ground, selected a few and stored them on her utility belt. She snapped a two way transmitter on her belt as well, so she could communicate with her partner. Snow Flake then scaled a pole, opened an electrical panel and pretended she was working on it. Takamura walked between electrical poles looking at a yellow box he was carrying. At 11 AM, Snow Flake descended from the pole and the pair walked down the street and ate their lunch at the curb. Thirty minutes later, Snow Flake scaled the utility pole again, carrying the yellow box. Takamura stood nearby, observing the street as they waited for their target to arrive.

Not long afterwards, a van with a Bank of Kowloon logo on it stopped at the entrance to the Capricorn building. A portly man dressed in clean coveralls emerged from the passenger side of the van carrying a briefcase. Without breaking stride, he glanced at the workers on the pole then continued to walk to the side door of the building. Using a key, Rotten Melon opened the steel door and went inside. The van was parked half a block up where the driver, Iron Hand, had an unobstructed view of the building's door and the street. He turned off the ignition, briefly looked up and down at the two repairmen on the block, one who was working on the pole and other one on the ground. He reached for a newspaper and turned to the racing section.

Snow Flake, from her perch atop the pole, signaled to Takamura then tossed down a small electrical part. He caught the part easily and pretended to check it with an instrument. He shook his head to indicate it wasn't working. They were acting like regular repairmen for anyone who took notice. Takamura keyed the transmitter and spoke a single word to Snow Flake – a pre-arranged signal asking for information on the target. She looked over at the van and its occupant, then gave her reply in Japanese. "He's reading a newspaper."

Going into action, Takamura walked towards the van, then stopped, raised an eyebrow, and pointed towards the vehicle. She nodded. Boldly, Takamura approached the driver's side window. The driver saw the repairman in his mirror and became alert.

Takamura asked apologetically, "Friend, could you lend me a hacksaw blade? Mine's broken."

Iron Hand shook his head and turned back to his newspaper. Immediately Takamura pounded on the side of the van door.

He shouted, "It won't kill you to lend me your fucking hacksaw blade. It doesn't come out of your pocket."

The driver shook his head again. Takamura displayed both middle fingers. The gesture triggered anger and Iron Hand threw the newspaper on the next seat and got out of the van, ready to fight. Takamura backed away.

Iron Hand shouted, "Get the fuck out of here before I cripple you."

Using a heavy north Chinese accent, Takamura replied, "Nobody talks to me like that without feeling the strength of my fists!"

Assuming a fighting stance Takamura spit on his palms, them made fists. Iron Hand came at him and received a swift kick to the midsection. He bent over and Takamura hit him from behind the neck with a wrench he had in his pocket. Iron Hand dropped to the ground, unconscious. Meanwhile, Snow Flake descended from the pole, entered the van, and opened the rear door. Takamura picked up Iron Hand and carried him into the rear of the van and set him down inside with his head near the door. Takamura shut the door from the inside with such a force that it crushed Iron Hand's skull.

Later, Takamura went outside and brought the motorcycles inside the van. He sat in the driver's seat and Snow Flake sat in the rear just behind him. They were waiting for Rotten Mellon to return.

Turning her head, Snow Flake glanced at Iron Hand whose body was stretched on the floor motionless.

"Shouldn't we tie and gag him?"

"Iron Hand won't ever awake in this world. Don't feel bad. His hands weren't clean in his own uncle's death and the Lao Tung affair. Now we shall wait patiently for the Big Fish. Before we do that we will bring in all the signs."

Five minutes after 3 o'clock, Rotten Melon exited from the building. With his head held high, he gave the appearance of the one who owns the entire place. Waiting at the door, he gestured for the van to come to him. Irked that Iron Hand hadn't started the engine, he walked towards the van and came to the passenger side. Annoyed at the lack of response from his driver, he opened the door, dropped the briefcase on the floor, and got into the van without bothering to look at the man next to him.

From the rear seat, Snow Flake slapped him with a blackjack and Takamura relieved him of his weapon, bound him to the seat, and taped his mouth, keeping his head away from the window. Takamura made it appear to any curious motorist or individuals on the street, that the man was asleep. Takamura drove the van to their rented house and Snow Flake emerged to open the garage door. After the van was driven inside, she shut the large door behind her.

Rotten Melon awoke to find himself bound, and in pain. His neck ached and he couldn't move. He struggled to free himself, but all his efforts failed. Rotten Melon looked at his attackers but didn't recognize his heavily made-up captors.

In staccato tones, the smaller of his captors said, "Everything in life comes back in circles. Now it is your turn to face the gun. Lao Tung was your teacher. You were one of his students the others were your fighting brothers. However you chose to turn your hand against them. You betrayed them to make yourself rich. I'm fed up with your immoral behavior. This is where we part."

Takamura touched her arm and said, "Snow Flake, do it now!"

Upon hearing the name, Rotten Melon began to shake and wet his coveralls. He was in a panic when he felt the pressure of a gun against his temple.

"You gave Lao Tung and the others no chance. Therefore you get none. Send my regards to Otto when you see him." Takamura turned up the radio's volume while Snow Flake squeezed the trigger. The automatic weapon kept firing and Rotten Melon's head was blown apart. There was silence, before Takamura spoke. "He is dead and good riddance to him."

They carried the body to the van and threw it in back, where it laid beside Iron Hand. After changing their clothing, they burned the overalls they wore on the job along with other size clothing in a pot belly stove in the house, and returned to Kowloon.

She Is My Good Friend's Wife

Takamura sent Snow Flake out to see the town with orders not to lose her police tails. She boarded a bus downtown on the pretense of a shopping trip. While the bus was moving, she noticed that she was familiar with this part of Kowloon and soon exited the vehicle. Feeling hungry, she walked a short distance to a Chinese restaurant where she, William and their children used to come for dinner. Entering the Molly restaurant, she felt uneasy. If it weren't for Takamura's presence, she would have fallen apart after the killing of Rotten Melon. He warned her many times not to get too close to William. The words rang in her ears. William was an experienced policeman. You won't be able to fool him for long, she told herself. She became upset knowing that, but she knew in her heart Takamura was probably right.

After being seated, Snow Flake ordered food. While her gaze circled the restaurant, she spotted William who was few tables away. Upon seeing her, he rose and approached her table, just as her food was being served.

"Where have you and Masaru been for the last few days?"

"Is it a crime to lose one's police shadow in your districts?"

"I thought you hardly spoke any Chinese, yet you speak like a native."

"It has its advantages to have others think you don't understand what is being said. Either sit down or get away from me. I don't care to be looking up at you as we speak."

He sat across from her. "Kufuyo, cut out all this shit. Why are you and Masaru here? It was not a coincidence that the gangs in the Districts of Hong Kong had been uprising since your arrival."

She asked the waiter to bring another set of dishes. She poured him a cup of tea and placed food on a plate and shoved it over towards him. William's eyes never left her face.

"I have this strangest feeling that we have met before," William pressed.

"Isn't memory a policeman's best tool? Stop thinking so hard, relax, and I'm sure it will come back to you later. Either eat something or leave me alone."

He grunted, "We don't like your kind here. Leave within the week."

"I thought you were going to say 'anything you say can be used in a court of law against you.' Yet, I haven't admitted directly or indirectly to any involvement in any crime. Are you going to blame us for all the crimes committed in the districts? Let's get one thing straight. My lawyer will have your ass on the carpet for threatening me."

William rose and reached for some money. Angrily she said, "No! I'll pay my own way! You don't scare me, Mister Policeman, and I didn't have a hand in killing your family!" Hearing those words, he felt like a sharp knife had just cut into his heart.

William leaned forward light-headed. He almost touched her face with his nose.

"Masaru's message on the match cover said I was being watched. Who is watching me and for whom?"

Looking down at her plate, she forced herself to eat slowly. She replied, "Everyone around you is on Ko Nan's payroll."

The news didn't take him by surprise. She touched his hand.

"Captain Chu, don't repeat what I just told you. You will place my life in danger so please back away. Lover Boy Wang wasn't the only person interested in me."

He grinned and replied, "Kufuyo, don't lose any of my men again or I'll send out warnings to the police bulletin to become aware of you."

He racked his brains about where he possibly encountered this strange woman. William, for a brief second, considered that Kufuyo was toying with him. Then he completely rejected the idea. On his way home, he entered a bar. While his mind sorted through the facts related to the Japanese couple, someone came to his table and set a bottle on it. He raised his head and recognized Masaru.

"Captain Chu, what is bothering you?" He filled two glasses with wine.

"I had a talk with Kufuyo today."

Takamura reached for the nut bowl on the table. "You and Lao Tung were attacked not too far from this place," he remarked casually. "Too bad the old pirate didn't make it."

"Did you know Lao Tung?"

"In a way. We lose many things in our lifetime. There's that look again. No, I didn't kill him."

William shrugged. "What does it matter?"

Takamura changed the subject. "Kufuyo is very tough, isn't she?"

"Are you sure she isn't your woman?"

Takamura laughed while shaking his head. William drained the glass of wine.

"She's my good friend's wife. I'm looking after her for my friend." He refilled William's glass. "Look the other way for a week and we will be gone."

"You're a very clever but dangerous man. You are implying that I shouldn't look a gift horse in the mouth." He hunched his shoulders.

"Something like that."

"What is going to happen?" Takamura shook his head.

"Are you related to Takamura San?"

"Have you given consideration to the theory that it was the Sons of the Sea inner circle who killed your wife, Lao Tung, his relatives, his students, plus Takamura? I have heard a rumor that Ko Nan lost some men around that time. A key to this mystery is where is San Lin? I fear neither he nor any of the gang members who joined to do the killings will ever be found. A good night's rest should clear your mind. Think hard about Ko Nan's nature and character. That will bring everything out in the open." Takamura got up and walked away from the table.

Ting Don and Chow Liang procured heavy weaponry and recruited help from the ranks of ex-servicemen from Vietnam in Hong Kong and Kowloon. Weapons were purchased from an agent working in the Philippines and stored in deserted warehouses. The two gang leaders gloated over the scope of Masaru's thinking. The Jap envisioned cannonades blasting down the front gate and iron fences, while Ko Nan's men would be firing and running as they covered the ground. They had visions of Ko Nan shaking behind a crumbling protective layer of bricks.

In their meetings, Masaru, Chow Liang, and Ting Don went over the plan of attack on Ko Nan's building for the tenth time. Masaru suggested the day of the battle to be set on the fourth Sunday of the next month at midnight. Unbeknownst to the others, the reason Masaru chose that day was that it had been four years exactly, after his beloved friend Lao Tung and the others were gunned down. They agreed that Masaru and Kufuyo were to remain on the sideline for the time being. Before Masaru departed, he elaborated to the men about the riches they would acquire. Their eyes were filled with greed. They left with images of gold and riches dancing in their heads.

An anonymous call alerted the police that there were two bodies in a van parked in a locked garage of a private house and gave the address. The bodies were identified as Rotten Melon and Iron Hand. Ko Nan was called to the police station. He said that they were his men but he had no knowledge of their murder. Since Captain William Chu was assigned to this case, Ko Nan approached him as he and his lawyer were leaving police headquarters. The gang leader asked William to help solve the murder of his men.

From the autopsy reports, William learned that Iron Hand showed signs of trauma to the head and back of the neck. It was the blow to the head that killed him. Immediately he thought of Masaru but said nothing. With the head blown apart, Rotten Melon was identified by his fingerprints. William wondered if Ko Nan could be next. It was in the back of his mind that the Japanese 'Yakuza' wanted to branch out into a lucrative field. He would not bet his last dollar that neither Masaru nor Kufuyo were undercover police or paid killers. Another thing that bothered him recently was why the couple was so well-versed in what happened to his family and friends about three years ago. Could they have ties with Takamura?

Two weeks later, another anonymous call alerted the police that there was a burned body found in a garbage dump near Kowloon bay. It was identified as Chow Liang, the boss of the Red Flesh Eater Gang.

Learning of Chow Liang's death, Ting Don was frightened. Faintheartedness overrode his current ambition. At a meeting of the two gangs, he told Masaru to call off the Sunday raid on Ko Nan's base. Masaru's sarcastic laughter and his sneering face made Ting Don react with false bravado.

"Are you licking wounds which you never received?" Takamura asked mockingly. "Just a small setback and you're ready to flee."

Looking around at the men's faces, he continued, "Why throw away a sure victory before a single shot is fired? If you don't hit Ko Nan now, tomorrow he'll brutalize you, your relatives, wives, and children. Where will you hide that money can't find you? Who will you be able to trust? I thought you were a high-stakes gambler. You have the combined strength of both the gangs behind you. Use them or concede the entire region to Ko Nan. Remember, he's not a forgiving man. You'll be hunted down no matter where on earth you go."

Encouraged, one of the gang members joined in eagerly. "Boss, we can win. We should be running forwards rather than always looking over our shoulders."

Takamura directed their eyes to his plan on the table for all to see. "Adhere to the original battle plan. I have recruited ten high-powered fighters from Thailand who are now living here, and they will join us for the battle. Friend, Ting Don, emulated the fox, but sprang like a tiger. Men, are you in the game?"

The Lull before the Storm

William was in the hotel where Masaru and Kufuyo resided in Kowloon. The desk clerk informed him that the pair had not returned for several days. He sent out an all-points bulletin to have them brought into the police headquarters for questioning. Rumors had said that Masaru and Kufuyo won a third fortune at the gambling tables. The word from the street was intentionally circulated as a red herring by well-placed bribes by Takamura. An informer from the airlines reported that two people matching the Japanese couple's descriptions were seen boarding a flight to Taiwan three days ago. William contacted Taiwan's immigration office for records of their entry, it was confirmed that they had arrived at Taiwan three days ago.

In Taipei, the local police were alerted and went to the hotel where the Japanese couple was listed in adjoining rooms. However, the police only found their suitcases. There were no signs of either Masaru or Kufuyo. A sergeant in the Taipei police department stated that a Japanese woman fitting the description of Kufuyo was seen spending a lot of money on expensive items in numerous stores.

William entered Kufuyo's hotel room in Taipei, and he stood inhaling the faint aroma of a lingering perfume that had been used by Snow Flake. The sadness that had held him in its grip for almost three years suddenly vanished. He examined the entire room and came to the conclusion that Kufuyo never spent any time in this room. Searching the closets, which were full of clothing and shoes, revealed nothing.

"Do lies come in colors?" he thought to himself. "Logic indicates we have never met, yet my senses overrule my brain. I have a strong attraction to this woman."

Going through the adjoining door, he went into the next room. He examined every item of Masaru's. He had to smile when he noticed all the labels had been removed. William asked himself, for whose benefit is this sleight of hand being played? Is the deck stacked against Ko Nan? Masaru had said both of them would be gone in one week, but I think they never left the Districts of Hong Kong, or else they returned to be part of the game.

Returning to Kufuyo's room, William examined each garment in the closet a second time. Every item a woman would need was lying around, but everything was brand new. He recalled reading a story about a British secret agent who never existed. William said aloud, "Kufuyo, is your sole purpose for being here to draw attention away from something that happened in the districts?"

Absent-mindedly, he examined Kufuyo's toilet items and his mind suddenly conjured up Snow Flake's memorial tablet. White-knuckled with both hands, he held tight to the basin of the sink. He dared not look into the mirror for fear of seeing the past.

"Could the dead be trying to tell me something, or am I hallucinating?"

Covered with sweat and shaking badly, William hurriedly left Kufuyo's room in dire need of a drink. At the bar, William rolled the nearly emptied glass between his palms and looked at ceiling.

"Besides the fight at the Gates of Hell Bar, there was no concrete evidence of any wrong doing by either Masaru or Kufuyo. There is no law against having multiple residences, but the motive for having them is unclear. Masaru clearly gave me hints that he knew Ko Nan's background and the cause of Lao Tung and his followers' death as well. Why is this closed-mouth person talking to me so much lately?"

Since Masaru warned him that he was in a fish bowl, William took precautions of never placing his random thoughts on paper. He had also heard about interdepartmental rumbling over missing evidence. William rationalized that no police official was immune to corruption or abuse of power. Looking at his watch, he decided to go and spend the night in Masaru's room to have some rest.

In recent months, William's people had logged lots of time on the investigation of Masaru and Kufuyo's involvement on recent gang war and killings in the region. However they didn't come up with any results. He reported to the commissioner that Masaru and Kufuyo didn't have anything to do with the recent gang killings because they were away from the area at that time. Suddenly it came to him as he rose to leave his office. This could be the lull before the storm.

On the Day of the Raid

When all was ready for the raid at 10 AM, Ting Don met the men at his base in Hong Kong. With Takamura stroking the man's ego by stating that they had a two-to-one advantage over the Sons of the Sea, Ting Don was satisfied. Emulating a general, he allowed Masaru to instruct all the men in the group to attack Ko Nan's stronghold and to reiterate the plan.

Takamura reminded them, "I, Ting Don, and ten men will dress as police officers and attack the rear of Ko Nan's estate to draw their fire. Xu's team will crash through the front gate in heavy trucks. Wo Kok Ai's team will follow, enter the estate from the front door, and fire heavy weapons at the house and the windows. A third wave, led by Yew Wa, will alight from the trucks, spread out, and fire their automatic weapons as they advance towards the house. When we are certain that Ko Nan is dead, you will form a new gang with Ting Don in control. Hear this, all of you! The one who kills Ko Nan will receive the biggest bonus and become a rich man. Each group knows their position. The attack time is 12:00 midnight."

Smiles appeared on many faces as Ting Don said, "Kill as many of the Sons of the Sea as you can find." He handed out pictures of Ko Nan.

That evening around 9 PM, in a quiet street corner not too far from Ko Nan's estate, Takamura sat with Snow Flake in a sedan with tinted windows. He cradled his high-powered rifle across his lap, confident in his preparation. He glanced over at Snow Flake, who was honing Lao Tung's serpent knife.

Jokingly, he said, "I believe that William's on the verge of discovering your identity. Now it's time for you to disappear into the tunnel in Ko Nan's house." Pointing to a satchel in the back of the car, he continued, "I have prepared a backpack with everything you need. A radio locator is in there too, in case you get in trouble. If you aren't killed, I'll find you."

Snow Flake replied, "I've come a long way for revenge. I shall do everything within my power to reach my goal." She knew in her heart that he wanted her out of harm's way even for this last battle.

In the dark of night, Ko Nan's men were out on the streets looking for their rivals, leaving eighty men at his base along with his bodyguards.

Blending in with her surroundings and carrying the backpack, Snow Flake silently climbed over the iron fence and raced across the rear lawn of the huge estate. With the sniper rifle in readiness, Takamura covered her from a distance in the shadow. Snow Flake stealthily inched along until she reached the entrance to the tunnel and began searching for the brass ring. According to

Ginger, it was behind a bush at the right side of the garage. A guard by the pool walked away to circle the area. Within minutes, she located the ring and gave it a tug.

Once inside the tunnel, she pulled another brass ring from inside to close the entrance. Her pen light revealed mice scurrying for safety. Broken spider webs were everywhere indicating that someone had been here. Carefully, she checked the area. The tunnel was high enough for her to walk upright. Her heart fluttered at the sight of foot prints in the thick dust. She forced the thought of Ginger from her mind. Slowly, she made her way along the tunnel, stopping every few feet to listen. All was quiet. She arrived at a place where Ko Nan's name was written in Chinese on the dirt encrusted wall. She froze and listened.

"Boss, since we gave the fucking Red Flesh Eater bastards a hit in their head, the rest of the small fry have been in hiding. Ting Don must be somewhere with his head between his legs."

Another voice loudly said, "Jack Soong, do you know why I keep you near me?"

"Am I a handy kind of person?"

"No, it's because there are no dogs here and I need you to bark. I don't want Ting Don's head between his legs. I want it separated from his shoulders."

Another voice asked, "Boss, why do you not ask Masaru and Kufuyo for help?"

"I don't trust them. Look what they did to Lover Boy Wang."

A third voice said, "I would like to take on Masaru. It grieves me that I didn't come sooner to kill that Jap Takamura for what he did to my brother. Otowa, don't you want to fight Kufuyo?"

"I'm not a common street brawler or a trophy collector. I fight solely for money. It had been said that your brother lost to Takamura because he couldn't handle defeat so he killed himself. Are all the Soongs that weak?"

Ko Nan yelled, "I pay you only to fight my enemies. I'm going to sleep."

Now, Snow Flake had found the location of Ko Nan's office and set her backpack against the wall. She tied a handkerchief over her face to prevent herself from sneezing. From time to time, she glanced at the illuminated dial on her wristwatch. During her waiting hours, she mediated to pass the time.

The night had turned very dark but the rear gate was illuminated. Twelve men dressed as police alit from two sedans and headed directly for the rear gate to Ko Nan's estate. Takamura noticed that Ting Don started to tremble.

Ironically he thought, "This fucker is all mouth. How can he ever think of filling bigger shoes?"

After the trucks crashed through the front gate, thirty Sons of the Sea members laid down a steady pattern of gun fire. As bullets flew back and forth, men on both sides were dying. Bazookas blew holes in the house's wall and soon a big area was wide opened.

When a bullet grazed Ting Don's cheek, he put a hand to his face and his fingers came away red with blood. Panicky, he shouted, "Let's run! We are outnumbered."

Takamura shot Ting Don in the head. Growling, he turned to the men.

"The death of Ting Don is an example to anyone who dares to run away. We didn't come this far to flee. Take out the fucking lights."

Four men fired at the lights. He pointed at a heavy-set young man. "What is your name?"

"Nam Foo, sir."

"They said you used to be a soldier, am I right?"

"A fighting fool, sir." Takamura reached inside his overcoat pocket and tossed him three grenades.

"Ting Don was a coward. Who among you will take his place?" Nam Foo threw three grenades at the rear gate. The gate blew apart and Ko Nan's men fell back. They rushed inside the grounds. Takamura spurred the men into action. More Sons of the Sea went down, and soon the last of the resistance came to an end. They moved on until they reached the pool. Six men grinned at each other, looking at Takamura for direction. Takamura fired at the men's heads because they were useless.

At the first sound of gunfire, Snow Flake went to the entrance of the tunnel and opened it and waited. To her surprise, she found that Takamura was on his hands and knees when he was entering the tunnel. She had never been so glad to see him in her life. They walked to the section of the tunnel where she left her backpack.

She whispered, "Behind this wall is Ko Nan's office."

Voices could be heard amidst the gunfire. "Boss, we have been double crossed! Masaru and Kufuyo must have thrown in their lot with Ting Don who promised the Japs the world!"

"Let them come! We'll hold out until the police arrive."

Someone said, "I have already called the police, they are on their way. Those rats outside will be caught in a crossfire."

Takamura removed a device from his left pocket, setting it against the wall. Since he had already removed the police uniform before he entered the tunnel, he now wore a skin tight, black knit suit. He signaled to Snow Flake to back away to the opposite side. He placed a tiny flashlight on his hand, ready to activate the charge.

He whispered, "After the wall caves in, kill everyone except Ko Nan and his two bodyguards, the Jap and the Korean." He pressed the button and the wall exploded inward.

A dull thud was followed by a section of the wall collapsing into a dust cloud. Takamura ran into Ko Nan who was on his feet and rubbing his eyes. A blow on his face from Takamura took the fight out of him, dropping him into a chair and blood coming from his nose. All the bodyguards were shot except for the Jap and the Korean, who were still standing.

Takamura said to the two, "Earn your wages or flee right now. The choice is yours."

Soong removed his shirt displaying his muscular body. "I'll fight to the death!"

As Snow Flake approached, Ko Nan glared at her. The young woman pointed a gun at the gang leader's head. "Blink and you're dead!"

Takamura asserted, "Three minutes is all you have." Snow Flake wondered why he was deviating from the original plan.

The Korean attempted to head butt his opponent, but failed. Takamura, the veteran of numerous hand-to-hand contests, avoided Soong's kicks and punches. Soong landed a solid punch to Takamura's midsection, only to receive a kick to the face that rocked his head back. Snow Flake watched while keeping her gun on Ko Nan's head and eye on Otowa. The match seemed to take a long time. Takamura took the offense and kicked Soong over the sofa. Soong came jumping back over it and dove at Takamura. Quickly Takamura's finger speared Soong's throat in midair. As he landed on the floor he fought a losing battle to breath.

Snow Flake said, "Time is up." She fired three bullets in Soong's head. She asked, "Otowa, what have you decided?"

"I'm paid to fight, so I'll fight."

Otowa and Snow Flake squared off as Takamura watched them while covering Ko Nan. They advanced towards each other. Thinking he was unnoticed, Ko Nan reached for a gun on the floor. Takamura stepped on his hand.

"I wouldn't touch the gun if I were you. Where is your payroll ledger you used to pay off the police?"

"It's in the bottom drawer." Ko Nan pointed at it as he spoke.

"If it isn't there you'll live as a basket case."

There was heavy pounding on the office door. Otowa rolled away from Snow Flake, removed a knife from her pocket, and she threw it at her opponent. Snow Flake caught the knife and hurled it back at her, striking her thigh. A shot rang out and Otowa lay dead.

Takamura said, "Play time is over. Let's get down to business." He located the ledger, opened it and scanned the contents. Satisfied, he placed it in a zipper pocket.

Ko Nan said, "Let's make a deal. Let me live and billions are yours. Nobody but I can run this region. I'm Ko Nan, the leader of the Sons of the Sea, the king of the District of Hong Kong. My word is law here!"

Takamura looked down at him with contempt on his face and said mockingly, "Snow Flake, did you hear this line of shit?'

The gleam in Ko Nan's eyes bore into them. Words covered with venom spat from his mouth, "Snow Flake is dead! My son killed her three years ago. He wouldn't dare cheat me!"

Ko Nan's voice rang of assurance. Snow Flake leveled her gun at Ko Nan's heart. The blood was pounding in her head.

"You misjudged your son. Otto thought I was dead before I sent him to hell. You're guilty of driving your own son to slay his wife."

Ko Nan, thwarted, roared, "Whatever that dog, Ting Don, paid you, I'll multiply it a thousand fold!"

Scorn ruled her face. "You shouldn't have killed Lao Tung and your sworn brothers!" The pounding on the door increased. It showed signs of giving way.

Takamura said, "Kill him." He went into action removing incendiary devices from a pocket and set them around the room. Snow Flake displayed the serpent knife to Ko Nan.

"You can never fool me," Ko Nan mocked. "Snow Flake is dead. Where did you find that knife?"

"Shall I sever your head as I did to Sasin to convince you that I'm Snow Flake?" She punched him in the face. The blood ran down the side of his mouth.

Astonished, he said, "Snow Flake…then Takamura lives."

Takamura set the timers. "Today you pay for what you did to Takamura. I'm his cousin."

Ko Nan pleaded. "Be realistic! What will you gain by killing me? I represent the future. Lao Tung represented the past and he was holding me back from taking Gascon's place as the kingpin in the districts of Hong Kong. Lao Tung was always criticizing me about my drug dealing and ruthless killing. But drugs are a cash cow and ruthlessness represents power." Fear shook his body as he saw the sneer appear on Takamura's face.

The gang lord continued to plead for his life. "There were spoils ripe for the taking. It's a cardinal rule that the strong rules the world. Look around you! It attests to the truth. Everyone is fighting for power in their own way."

A spark of cunningness shown in his eyes as he continued, "Snow Flake, you can remain here without any questions being asked. People will respect you, for you shall have wealth beyond your wildest dreams. You can have a leadership position, as the Queen of the entire region. Why do you throw all this all away?"

Coldly, she replied, "The complete cardinal rule states, there is only room for one at the top. You had your day. Your blind ambition brought the Sons of the Sea to ruin. As a brother and leader you pledged a blood oath that you violated!"

She hurled the knife at Ko Nan's heart from three feet away. His hand moved in an attempt to catch it, but he had no chance. The blade embedded in his flesh. He grabbed the hilt to remove the weapon but his efforts were in vain. Snow Flake's foot came to rest on the hilt, and she pressed down hard. His mouth twisted in pain and his face was a mask of agony. Yet, he was determined not to die.

When he was unable to overcome her pressure on the knife, he cried out, "I shall be waiting for you at the entrance to the Gates of Hell."

Hatred inflamed her blood as she rammed the knife blade into his heart.

"Be sure to tie a red ribbon around your neck to distinguish you from the rest of the demons."

Takamura fired three times into Ko Nan's head. "That was for Lao Tung and for you taking over my bar."

He turned to Snow Flake. "You know what I admired about Ko Nan was that he wasn't interested in a celestial home. None of his ilk would be there to welcome him. Don't leave Lao Tung's serpent knife behind, it's a clue to your identity. Let's flee." Into the tunnel they ran with Takamura taking the lead.

Once outside, they ran past the dead bodies that littered the area around the rear gate into the street. In the dark, Takamura pushed Snow Flake in front of him. After they ran about two blocks to the east, they made a turn into a side street. There they stopped by the sedan which Takamura had parked at the corner earlier after Snow Flake had entered the compound. They got into the car and Takamura started to drive further away from the burning building, heading east. After five miles, they heard police sirens.

Ko Nan's Ledger

Takamura drove on for another five miles before they reached a stone wall surrounding a large, darkened house. At the driveway, they got out of the car and walked towards the residence. Snow Flake wondered who owned this huge building. Its garden path was being repaved with tiles, but part of it was not completed. Takamura knocked four times on the door. It was opened by a woman who pointed a pistol at them. Surprise registered on Snow Flake's face.

Po Ling said, "Come inside."

Takamura took the stairs two at a time. On the top of the stairs he stated, "Snow Flake dress in an evening gown. Po Ling will take care of your hair. We haven't much time." While they were cleaning themselves, Po Ling collected the discarded clothing in a plastic bag, dropped it outside in a hole beneath the unfinished paved path, and covered it with crushed stones.

A highly polished, red roadster drove along the road. Seated inside were three people dressed in evening wear. As they passed the police cars at the instruction of Takamura, the women waved colorful streamers. Snow Flake thought this was complete madness. Why does Takamura want to call police attention to us? She thought about it for a while then saw the wisdom. The best place to hide is out in the open where you can be seen.

Po Ling spoke to Snow Flake. "I'll drop you off at the Hyatt Regency Hotel and will come back for you later. William will be there waiting and you will give him Ko Nan's ledger."

Takamura handed her a gift-wrapped package and instructed her, "Warn him not to keep the ledger and burn it immediately after reading it."

"Why should I give this deadly ledger to my husband?"

"Once William reads the ledger, he will see that it's impossible for him to stay in the police force. With that road closed, the only avenue open for him will lead him to you."

"Takamura, beneath that icy exterior you present to the world beats a romantic heart."

He grinned at her. "Don't let your guard down. Po Ling will return for you in one hour. This adventure isn't over until we are out of the airport and the jet is in the air."

Snow Flake skeptically turned the package over and over in her hands.

"Isn't William your best friend?"

"I rely on his good judgment and sagacity to come to the solution to his own problem."

Half a block from the Hyatt Regency, Snow Flake was let out of the sedan and she walked towards the hotel. She spotted Lotus Koo and Spring Su in a car parked nearby. When they saw her, they got out. It was three hours after midnight, A few strollers were on the street and a man was walking a small grey dog. He paused as the dog went to smell the fire hydrant.

The two policewomen had held a grudge against the Japanese woman for her complaint to Captain Chu over the fight in the park with Lover Boy Wang. When Lotus came closer to Snow Flake, she swung her heavy purse at Snow Flake's head. Avoiding the attack, Snow Flake countered with a resounding slap across Lotus face. When Snow Flake feigned a kick to the midsection, Lotus made the mistake of bringing her head forward in anticipation of the attack. Grabbing a handful of Lotus's hair, Snow Flake gave it a strong pull. Then she followed up with a flurry of punches which broke Lotus' nose and knocked out teeth. Lotus dropped to her knees protectively covering her face with both hands.

Spring Su yelled, "Bitch, I'll kill you for what you did!"

The man with the dog was struggling to control the excited animal which was wildly jumping and barking. People on the street stopped to watch the battle. An old lady let out a piercing scream for help. Spring Su swung a blackjack at Snow Flake's head. She caught the weapon giving it a downward tug. Spring Su's wrist was twisted by the strap and she couldn't let it go. Snow Flake spun her around and tossed the policewoman's head long against a wall. Spring Su hit the wall hard and fell down.

Again, both Lotus Koo and Spring Su rose to their feet and charged Snow Flake who took some blows but gave many more in return. After the exchange of fists and kicks, the policewomen dropped down to the sidewalk with blood covered faces. Snow Flake had won another fight.

Hearing the screaming, a hotel doorman alerted the desk clerk. "There's a fight outside! Call the police."

William was in the lobby waiting for Snow Flake to arrive. He ran outside and surveyed the scene. Spring Su and Lotus Koo were on the ground with Snow Flake standing over them. What William saw displeased him. His two policewomen had clearly disobeyed his orders. While Lotus was reaching for her gun, William blew his police whistle, and pointed his weapon at her.

"Sergeant Koo and Su, if your hands come out with a gun, I'll shoot you! Just look at what you have done to yourselves! Get yourselves to a hospital! I want to see you in my office first thing in the morning!"

They arose and saluted William then went to their car, started it, and roared away.

William turned to the crowd. "The fun is over. Go on your way!"

Snow Flake picked up her package. William escorted her into the hotel.

He said, "I'm sorry about this unfortunate episode. You handled yourself well. Masaru was right. You are an experienced fighter."

Snow Flake bit her tongue to prevent her from saying something she might regret. She examined herself in the lobby mirror. Her hair was loose, and her gown was torn.

Angrily she said to him, "Those women are your responsibility. They started the fight. Did they act under your orders? Was the fight staged as an excuse to arrest me?"

"Why indulge in childish games with me? Those women are highly trained police officers"

"Oh, shut up! I want you to buy me another gown."

When William extended his hand, tried to lead her to the lounge, she kept pulling away from him. Finally he managed to get her into the lounge and seated at a table. Curious people were staring at them.

William said to her. "You have won plenty of money at the tables. Why cry over this gown? You have dozens more hanging in your closet."

Noticing the bartender staring, he shouted at the startled man. "Two stingers!" Turning to Snow Flake, he asked, "Why didn't you hit them in places they wouldn't bleed?" He saw that her eyes were still full of fight. She kept looking at herself in the mirror on the wall.

"Making money is no shame," she said evenly. "This world is filled with people who want to try their luck at wherever it might be." She shoved the package at him.

"That's Masaru's parting gift. Read it and burn the damn thing."

Without touching the package, he asked, "Just what is inside?"

She averted his eyes. "Death, money, power, greed..."

He leisurely sipped his drink trying to establish eye contact with her while she averted his eyes.

"Are you both Japanese undercover agents?"

"Forget about us. Soon we'll leave as you ordered."

He shoveled a handful of peanuts into his mouth. She saw his gaze rise from her breasts to her face.

She continued. "Would you like to hear a story?"

"I am tired of your lies. Who hired Masaru to bring Ko Nan into conflict with the other gangs?"

She raised her eyes to the ceiling. "Did it ever occur to you that I want to be alone?"

"Did Masaru call me just to have you deliver this?"

"Yes and no." A dual answer.

"Are the inside pages lined with poison?"

Annoyed, she replied, "You have read too many crime novels. Wear rubber gloves and a mask if you think that it has been poisoned." She rose, opened her small purse, and dropped some bills on the table.

"I must be off."

Frustration caused him to grab her wrist. With a twist, she freed herself. Ashamed, he exclaimed, "I'm sorry. I haven't gotten over my wife and children's deaths. I'm certain there are things in your head that I must know in order to retain my sanity."

The package bulged in his jacket pocket. He followed her out of the hotel and stood some feet away from her. Along came a blue sedan with tinted glass which stopped by the curb where Snow Flake stood. The hotel doorman came and opened the rear door for her and received a tip. She entered the car and he closed the door behind her.

Po Ling asked, "Have you given William a clue to your identity?"

"No."

"Blow the cobwebs from his brain." Down came the rear window of the sedan. William was looking directly at Snow Flake's face.

She stated in Chinese, "William, you animal, you hurt my shoulder again!"

The words stunned him like thunder and he became light-headed as he realized he was looking at his wife. She smiled at him and then Po Ling drove away. He ran twenty feet after the sedan and then stopped. His heart was pounding and the words in his head whirled around." My wife is alive. My wife is alive and my children are alive."

William assured himself that his bedroom door was locked before opening the package. He immediately noticed that it was some kind of payroll ledger. It listed columns for year, month, name, job classification, and amount of monthly payments. While reading page after page, he grew depressed discovering the entire British Hong Kong Royal police staff was in Ko Nan's pocket, including his brother-in-law, Captain John Hung, and the commissioner. Only two names were missing from the list. They were Lieutenant Wei Cha and Captain William Chu. "Masaru was right saying I am a fish in a bowl." William shut the ledger in disgust.

Putting the ledger back in his jacket pocket, he went silently to the kitchen. Pausing to listen, he made certain that the house was quiet. Jessica and John were asleep. He found a bottle of rye and opened it for a drink.

Down went the sharp liquid into his stomach. It did nothing for him. Frustration, anger, and a sense of hopelessness settled upon him. The reason he chose to be a policeman was to protect the innocent and make the world a better place to live. All was futile. Human nature couldn't be changed. His entire police career amounted to no more than an ill-timed joke. He took the bottle and went back to his room.

Fully clothed and lying on the bed, William thought about the recent events. Snow Flake returned to the Districts of Hong Kong as Kufuyo to avenge Lao Tung and her friends. Ko Nan ordered Otto and the others to initiate the killing spree, to eliminate his rivals. Ko Nan believed that he was king of the region covering the eighteen Districts of Hong Kong, because the entire police force was in his pocket. His ego could not accept "No" but Lao Tung often criticized him in public over his drug dealing and senseless killing.

Furthermore, he killed Lao Tung in order to prevent revenge and he had to kill anyone who was close to Lao Tung. That was why he ordered the massacre at Lao Tung's birthday party where I was shot in my leg by a masked man. It was the reason he ordered the killing of Snow Flake and Takamura. Everything Ko Nan said were lies. Since Snow Flake is alive, who was the corpse in my house? It came to him in a flash—it had to be Ginger. Poor Otto. He never could locate Ginger because she lay in Snow Flakes grave.

Aloud he said, "Why didn't Snow Flake contact me? Yes, my every movement was under constant scrutiny. Any sudden change in my usual behavior would set off rocket signals. Masaru must be Takamura San, the only one who could have thought up this brilliant scheme. I must pay my respects to Ginger. I owe her a debt of gratitude. Why did she do it? I'll never know."

In his bedroom, William turned the radio on low. He soon heard that there had been an armed assault on a grand scale at Ko Nan's base. Bodies littered the grounds and the building was one big inferno.

William digested the information. He concluded the living combatants would implicate Masaru as the organizer. Knowing how Takamura operates, Snow Flake would be designated to a safe place. It would only be a matter of time before the commissioner sends for me.

Protecting his wife was paramount. Without any way to link past events with the present incidents, the police department will fail to make the connection of Kufuyo's part in the crime, he thought. Let the commissioner believe the gang wars were simply an internal power struggle. My days as a policeman are over. I'll find Snow Flake or she will find me. Before retiring for the night, he pulled the phone plug out of the wall. At last, he had a restful sleep.

William Resigns

It was 11 AM the next morning when William woke to the sound of a knock at his bedroom door.

"William, a squad car is here." It was Jessica's voice.

Through the closed door he replied, "Tell them to go away. I'm not going in today. Say I'm sick or tell them to get lost." He rose from the bed, emptied the last of the rye on his hand, and then rubbed it over his face and neck.

A half hour later, another knock rapped upon the door. It was Sergeant Fon.

"Captain Chu, are you alright?" William opened the door. The aroma of alcohol was strong on him. The sergeant observed that the captain hadn't shaved. It appeared that he had slept in his clothes and his hair was uncombed. He saw that William's hands were shaking.

Through bleary eyes, William screamed at him. "Sergeant Fon, do you need your ears cleaned? I'm not going to work today!" He slammed the door in the startled man's face. Jessica was standing behind him and burst into tears.

It was mid-afternoon before William emerged from his bedroom. Jessica was in the living room dusting when she heard the door open. She stopped what she was doing, startled. Looking very worried, she went over to him.

"William, it's all over the newspapers that Ko Nan was murdered last night. They claim dead bodies are everyone on the estate. A group of men, some of them in police uniforms, attacked with heavy weapons. Ting Don was found dead too. It was the biggest gang related war ever to take place in the Districts of Hong Kong."

William merely glanced at the newspaper on the table but didn't pick it up. Jessica looked at her brother. "William, can I make you something to eat?"

"No, I'm going for a walk." He gave her a big hug and left the house.

He walked through the streets, checking that he wasn't being followed. Coming upon a small, sidewalk food cart vender, he sat on a high stool. The cook was feeding charcoal nuggets into the uncovered stove. William ordered a bowl of noodles. The cook covered the stove with a lid and prepared his customer's order. Slowly he ate. He looked at the stove lid and tapped it with his chopsticks.

"Open it," he said to the cook. Looking at William with suspicion, the man removed the stove lid.

William took the ledger from his pocket where he proceeded to tear out pages, crumple each one into a ball, and toss them into the fire. He continued the same process until the entire ledger had been completely burned. The cook thought this man was crazy, mad.

William handed the cook a hundred dollar bill. "Stir the ashes until they break apart then close the lid." Williams watched until all paper balls were reduced to a powdery ash then asked the man to stir them again. With a smile on his face, William went about his business. The cook shook his head as his customer left. He removed the bill from his pocket and checked that if it was real money.

It was 2 PM the next day when he finally made an appearance at his job. William was greeted by his staff and his associates as he entered police headquarters and walked to his office. He returned their greeting half-heartedly. Outside his office, William snapped his fingers at Lotus and Spring. Displaying the signs of the terrible fight on their faces, Lotus Koo and Spring Su jumped to their feet. They followed him into his office, where they stood at attention. He shut the door and sat, looking down at his folded hands. The silence electrified the air. Gradually he raised his head until his eyes beheld them. Hardness set in.

What should he do with these women? Letting out a sigh, he said, "For blatantly disregarding my orders, I should dismiss both of you. Your conduct makes you unfit as police officers. You brought disgrace to the department and tarnished the public image of the British Hong Kong Royal Police. I shall place this incident on your records. You're professionals, not street brawlers! As of today, you're reduced in rank and transferred to another department. Consider yourselves lucky. I have saved you by talking Kufuyo out of pressing charges." Shaking his head, he said, "Report to the Personnel Department for your new duty when you are fit."

The women stood at rigid attention. William locked his cold eyes on them. "You would never have made the kill. Kufuyo palmed throwing knifes. If I hadn't intervened, you would be dead. Lotus, can your aged mother live without you?" Turning to Spring, he looked at her face. "How could your younger sister enter college with you dead? For smart women, you made some stupid choices. Dismissed!" The chagrined women left the office.

Carrying a cup of tea, Sergeant Ying entered and set the cup on William's desk. "Sir, it's the commissioner's office. His secretary has been calling every ten minutes since 8:00 AM. It's about Ko Nan's case. Masaru and Kufuyo are still at large."

"You can inform the commissioner's lady-in-waiting that I'll be there later. You may go."

William, flanked by Lieutenant Wei Cha, approached the secretary's desk.

The woman behind the large desk said in a stern voice, "Captain Chu, the commissioner was looking for you for two days. Where have you been?"

"I'm here now. That's what counts." William entered the commissioner's office. The Englishman glanced up from the papers on his desk.

"Captain Chu, you are late! Why have you kept me waiting?"

William wasn't standing at attention. He was slouching. "Sir, I request time off for personal reasons."

"Out of the question!"

William removed a sealed letter from his breast pocket and dropped it on the desk.

"Here is my resignation."

As William walked towards the door, the commissioner shouted, "William what is the matter with you? Are you still mourning your wife and the children? Pull yourself together, man!"

William left the office without answering the astonished commissioner, who was shouting at him. "William, you can't quit! I need you!" The commissioner was on his feet and kicked the wastepaper basket over, sending its contents flying. With the back of his hand he knocked his favorite tea cup off his desk and it crashed against the wall.

"The finest police mind I've ever met in twenty years. Damn this bloody job!"

His secretary came in and looked around the room.

"Sir, what happened here?"

He took his anger out on her. "Can't you see that I'm upset?"

Jessica and John were exchanging words in the kitchen as she prepared supper. Since the death of their son, the couple had been growing apart. They heard the outside door open and shut. Jessica left the kitchen and went to the living room with John following her. William gave her a bright smile and a hug, but didn't say a word to John. It bothered John that he was snubbed by William.

Jessica asked, "Is it true that you have resigned?" He took her hand, leading her to the sofa.

"I need a rest and a change of scenery. The police department became my entire life after Snow Flake and the children were no longer with me. There must be a better life than the one I've been leading." Jessica began to cry. He gently brushed away her tears. It didn't stem the sobs. William encircled her with his arms.

"You're all the family I have now, but I need to straighten out my life." There, in the hallway, stood John. He turned to him and nodded. "You, as well as I, need to start living again."

She replied, "I can plainly see Snow Flake and your children are on your mind. Are you going off to some place to kill yourself?"

William tenderly massaged his sister's hands, "Jessica, I'm off to finally bury Snow Flake and the children. I reached a fork in the road." A smile replaced the sadness he saw on her face. It bothered William to lie to her, but Snow Flake and the children must be protected. Jessica wiped her eyes with her apron and returned to the kitchen.

William followed her and watched Jessica stir fry the vegetables in the wok.

"Kufuyo was more like Snow Flake when she was Shirley in so many ways." He was amazed that Jessica, from only listening to him talk about Kufuyo, was able to make the connection. He took a bottle of beer out of the refrigerator and changed the subject.

"I remember when I was a child you use to scold me for fighting." John entered the kitchen and also took a beer. William wondered about John. Since he accepted Ko Nan's money, was John aware of the pending attack on Lao Tung?

Jessica put the cooked food on a platter. "Would you please set the table?" she asked her brother. "The food is ready."

"I could eat a horse. How about you, John?"

The weeks passed slowly. Without a job to go to anymore, William loafed around the house and played cards with his sister. She was very excited over the pending adoption of a little girl. John had accompanied her to the orphanages where they found a three year old whom they liked. They agreed upon a name, Wild Wind. Jessica showed William pictures and described to him how shy, pretty, and bright the girl was. He was elated for her and understood that this was the change his sister needed. Now she and John could share something again. When John had confessed to her about the son he had fathered by another woman, there were bad moments between them, but in the end she finally forgave him. She accepted his promise never to break his marital vows again.

Two and half months had passed since William left his police post. One evening, Wei Cha came over to Jessica's house. Wei Cha had been promoted to captain to take over William's responsibility as the head of the investigation department. He wanted to talk to William about Ko Nan's case, and was immediately pulled into their card game. It pleased him to see William drinking moderately and laughing at his jokes. Wei Cha saw that being away from the department without all its emergencies and stresses had proved to be a good tonic for William. Wei Cha thought that William looked years younger than the last time he had seen him. Eventually, Wei Cha steered the conversation to the Ko Nan case.

"It has reached an impasse. Masaru was mentioned as being the planner of the attack which brought down the Sons of the Sea. We don't believe Masaru is dead because no body was found, yet where is he? As of today, no one has stepped forward to take Ko Nan's place." The captain looked to William for his opinion.

William drank his tea slowly. "I'll say that all your leads to Masaru and Kufuyo came up against a blank wall. The only evidence against them was the fight at the Gates of Hell Bar. All my conversations with Masaru revealed nothing. The department should rejoice that such a man has died or left the Districts of Hong Kong."

Jessica brought in a bowl of fruit from the kitchen. She mentioned Wild Wind, the girl she was going to adopt.

Looking at William, Wei said, "You mentioned that Kufuyo returned to Japan. Why did she leave behind all those expensive gowns and clothing?"

"Jessica, can you answer that question from a woman's point of view?"

"You already said that Kufuyo was going back to her husband," she continued, "Therefore, bringing back any expensive items would give her husband the wrong impression. Now what if you unpacked your wife's suitcases after she returned from a long trip without you and found goodies that weren't usual to your financial condition and standard of living?"

"I see your point."

One day in March, a travelogue was delivered to the house addressed to William. The envelope was hand-written. Jessica brought it to William in the living room while he looked at a series of pictures of Wild Wind. She handed him the travelogue and he examined the sender's name. He didn't recognize it. Inside the envelope were pictures of the hotel on Waikiki Beach and a hotel in Tokyo.

On the back of the picture of the hotel in Tokyo, written in Chinese, was the simple phrase "See you in April". It was signed "Mai Gee".

He showed the pictures to Jessica. "I'm going on vacation next week, first to Hawaii then to Japan. " Jessica smiled at William. The next morning, he ate a large breakfast like he did years ago which made his sister very happy. He soon headed out the door to visit a travel agent.

Following a Trail

On the first day of his arrival in Hawaii, William spent the entire afternoon sightseeing and browsing in Oahu's gigantic shopping mall. When he returned to his hotel, he found a package on his bed with an address from the Royal Imperial Hotel in Tokyo. He recognized Takamura's fine handwriting on the face of the package. It contained boots, shirts, pants, and a winter jacket, all in his size. William ordered a six pack of beer from room service. He took a shower and thought about the upcoming days ahead.

Someone had been following him ever since he arrived on the island. He gauged his activities so as not to cause alarm. Most days he went on group tours. On the days he wasn't traveling, he would jog five miles in the morning and lay on the beach in the afternoon. One day, he received a letter from Jessica stating that she changed her new daughter's name to Lisa Ann. She wrote how happy she had been with the little girl in the house.

William wrote back to her. "I wish you and John all the happiness in the world with your new addition. I'm certain that the girl will have a good life with you. I'm leaving Oahu in a week and shall send Lisa Ann gifts from Japan. Give my regards to John."

It was about time that he mended fences with his brother-in-law even though he didn't respect him.

After William registered at the desk of the Royal Imperial Hotel in Tokyo, a bellboy collected his luggage and escorted him to his room. Later, he called room service for a meal. The attendant brought up his food and drink and also brought him Chinese and Japanese newspapers. In the Chinese paper, there were brief mentions of stories about the gang war in the Districts of Hong Kong. As of today, no arrests had been made and no one had claimed responsibility. The next morning, a hotel serviceman came to his room to deliver a letter. It was from the commissioner of the British Hong Kong Royal Police. The man requested William to send him the evaluated data on the Ko Nan case. William threw the letter in a wastepaper basket.

The following evening while watching television, an envelope was slid under his door. Inside the envelope was a picture of a Japanese Buddhist Temple. He turned the picture over and found a written note in Chinese. Walk on the trails of the famous Silver Bells Monastery and take your time to enjoy the spring weather and beautiful scenery. William peered at the Chinese characters. There was no mistaking that it was Snow Flake's handwriting. He called the hotel desk and asked for directions to the Silver Bells Monastery.

William became impatient with the long bus ride along the mountain road. Sore from sitting, he promised himself never to travel by bus again. The weather was mild and the bright sunlight reflected off the snow-covered hillside. William got off the bus to walk about half a mile to the monastery. He stopped in front of the entrance to purchase a drink from a vendor. Casually, he strolled up the stairs towards the temple and saw a group of tourists standing on line to get in. William spoke to a monk in Japanese about the cost of a tour to the monastery. The monk said there would be no charge and invited him to join the group.

When they stopped in front of a rock garden, he saw a high stone wall to one side. Behind him, a young monk touched his arm and said in Chinese, "Please come with me."

Eagerly, William followed the monk to a door in the stone wall. The monk opened it and signaled William to go through. He went out only to find himself on a street. Looking around, he noticed two women sitting on a bench across the road. As he walked over, the women rose before he got close to them and walked towards a red sedan. William recognized them by their body movements and followed them. He got into the car and put his luggage on seat next to him.

"Po Ling, please, no jet take-off today." Mai Gee laughed. "Po Ling was grounded for a month after she broke the sound barrier." The car moved slowly away from the curb and then sped up on the open road.

"William, it's nice to see you again."

"Yes, Ko Nan had me bottled up." After ten miles of driving along the mountain road, the car finally came to a stop.

Po Ling asked, "William was that slow enough?"

"Yes. I didn't leave my stomach anywhere. Thank you kindly."

Mai Gee pointed to the other side the road. "It's the house facing you."

After he got out, the car immediately rocketed away. He took a deep breath.

"This modern technology is much too fast for me", he mused. "I must be growing old."

William had left his luggage in the car but he didn't care. Increasing his pace, he walked over a small wooden bridge spanning a fishpond. The sound of children's laughter reached his ears; it sounded like beautiful music. In the yard, William stood still watching the children at play. Linda was playing with a small dog, which turned to stare and bark at him.

She broke into a smile, shouted, and came running. "Dad is here!" In no time William had his daughter in his arms.

Hearing the shout, Robert, who was playing soccer with two boys in the yard, stopped and stared at the newcomer. Being shy, he peered at his father with big eyes.

Linda said, "Mama mentioned that you would be coming soon." Then his son ran to his father and held onto his waist. This was the happiest moment for him in more than three years.

He saw a woman on her knees digging in the garden.

William said to his children, "Play with your friends. I want to speak to your mother."

He walked over as she stood up to face him.

"Why are you here?" she asked.

"For you, for the children…." He removed her wide-brim hat from her head and dropped it to the ground. Husband and wife embraced, feeling the warmth of each other. Passionately he kissed her. William extracted a small box from his breast pocket. He popped open the lid to show her a wedding ring and he placed it on her finger. "Forever and ever, my dearest Snow Flake."

She cried. William kissed her warm tears as she said, "You must be hungry." He followed her into the kitchen. Even the sight of plastic surgery on her face didn't dampen his enhanced spirit.

"I like to watch you cook."

She turned red, touching her hair. "I must look awful."

"You're a wonderful sight to behold."

She went to the refrigerator for a beer, poured it into a glass, and handed it to him. While she prepared the meal, Snow Flake slowly related the long tale about how she and the children escaped from death.

That night in bed, William thought back to the times he spoke to Masaru. He had asked the question. 'Why are you traveling with this woman?' The answer echoed from the past in his mind. "For friendship…"

She rubbed his chest and William kissed her.

Snow Flake asked, "What are you thinking?"

"You and Takamura could have lost your lives."

"There were debts to be repaid. William, I love you. Only death can keep us apart. Yagako—that's Takamura's real name—loves you in his own way. You should feel proud that you have such a friend. In reality, you both are very much alike."

"That may be, but we are also many worlds apart."

The next morning, William couldn't find a change of clothing because his luggage wasn't returned. He questioned Snow Flake, who shrugged her shoulders. William sensed Takamura's fine hand had not finished with the gambit. She replied, "There are some new clothes in the closet. Go get changed. Today is Sunday and we are having visitors over for lunch."

He gave her an interrogator's look, which she ignored. "Woman, what is going on? I smell another of Takamura's sleight of hand." She kissed him and pushed him away. That was a signal to him that Snow Flake wanted him out of the way.

"Go for a walk but be back before noon." He went for a stroll with the children and the little dog whose name was Shau Dee.

When the clock struck the noon hour, the outside gate was opened and William went out of the house. He saw a tall Japanese man whose face resembled that of Takamura and Masaru. Behind him came Po Ling and Mai Gee and two children. Each woman was carrying a baby in her arms. The two older children resembled their father. To bind the friendship between the two families, Takamura had made William the boys' godfather and Snow Flake their godmother. Snow Flake greeted them and introduced them to William.

"This is Yagako Ohara San, a Muslim and his wives. The baby girl is Daio and the baby boy is Koji. The other two big boys are your godsons who were born in Hong Kong. You met them but they are taller and bigger now." William shook the strong hand. He complimented to the women that all the children were very beautiful.

William ushered them into the living room. Snow Flake brought in a bottle of herb wine and a tray with glasses. Yagako used his fingers to break the seal and extract the cork. He filled all the glasses with wine and handed the women their drinks. Yagako Ohara San said, "This one is for you, Hosokawa San."

William took the glass and replied, "Hosokawa. My last name is Chu, Captain William Chu of the British Hong Kong Royal Police."

Shaking his head, he replied, "That's impossible."

Yagako picked up a newspaper clipping from a nearby desk and handed it to William. His eyes went to the section highlighted in red. Captain William Chu of the British Hong Kong Royal Police was accidentally killed while hiking on the Fu Zee mountainside in Japan. The date on the newspaper was April 10th which was the third day after he arrived in Tokyo.

The paper stated that a section of the snow-covered mountain broke loose, entombing an entire group of hikers under tons of snow and rocks. When the bodies were recovered, Captain William Chu was identified by his police academy ring. William raised his eyes to peer at this man's grinning face. He remembered it was years ago that he exchanged that ring for the Takamura's jade pendant to bind their friendship.

"In case you have forgotten, Hosokawa San, your profession is a writer." They all drank to each other's health.

William jokingly asked, "What is the title of the next book I'm supposed to write?"

Takamura replied, "The Nine Dragons Saga."

William reached over to grasp Yagako's hand. "I'll begin writing the story tomorrow." He paused and looked into the man's eyes. "I owe you my life and that of my family. How can I ever repay you?"

"Friendship for friendship will do."

The Family Reunites

Twenty five years had lapsed since William returned to his wife. Upstairs, Jessica was dressing to take her granddaughter to the park. Lisa Ann was downstairs removing the breakfast dishes from the table. Two young girls, ages five and three, were running up and down the stairs. They were calling their mother. "Mama, is grandma ready?"

"Be patient. She will be down soon." The girls ran outside to play.

Lisa Ann came to the door and shouted, "Don't get dirty." From the living room window she saw a taxi stop in front of her house. A couple got out of the cab and came to ring her doorbell. She came to the door and opened it.

The man asked her, "Does Mrs. Jessica Hung live here?"

"Yes, she is my mother. Who are you?"

"We are Mr. and Mrs. Ziu from the old neighborhood."

In the living room, Jessica greeted them and asked Lisa Ann to takes the girls to the park since she has visitors. After Lisa Ann left with the girls, Jessica turned and smiled at her guests.

"William, you and Snow Flake look wonderful." William embraced his sister and she held tight to her brother, tears flooding her eyes.

She looked over his shoulder. "Snow Flake, you will never know how much I have missed you, your children, and William over the years." Snow Flake came over to embrace her.

"My greatest concern," William said, "was what the shock of discovering I was alive would do to you." Jessica released Snow Flake and brought them into the kitchen to make a pot of tea.

While she filled the kettle with water and put it on the stove to boil, Jessica replied, "I knew you both were alive. When John came home with the news of your death in Japan, I was heartbroken. When he mentioned how the Japanese government official identified your body, he unwittingly revealed the hoax. I recalled that you had told me years ago about exchanging the tokens of friendship with Takamura. Do you remember? Hence, the obvious reason for the mock death was to protect Snow Flake, your children, and yourself. I realized that they were alive and you were with them. Knowing that you distrusted John, I said nothing."

William commented, "Jessica, you should have been a detective."

Snow Flake said, "I'm sorry that John is no longer with us."

"I miss him. Ever since you left, he was a changed man. We made peace with each other, and he made peace with himself. John was a model father to Lisa Ann. He died of a heart attack on the job at his desk. Years ago, John revealed to me of the time he learned of the pending attack upon Lao Tung, his relatives and his students. He tried to prevent it, but he arrived too late to the restaurant to stop the killing. It was John who fired at the attackers from the crowd and saved your life. His blazing guns killed six of the masked men and drove the rest of the assassins away."

"Jessica, why didn't John tell me?"

"I guess he had his own reasons. After you were gone, he tried to live up to your image. I like to think that he made it. It was no secret at that time Ko Nan had almost the entire police force on his payroll. Some of the police officials were just as bad as those animals whom they arrested. John took it upon himself to weed the bad ones out of the service. William, my John was a strong and honorable man. I am very proud of him."

The tea kettle whistled. There were tears in her eyes as sadness gripped her heart. Snow Flake put her arms around Jessica as a comforting gesture.

In the living room, while they were drinking tea, Jessica inquired, "How long will you be staying here?"

"A few days," William replied, looking intently at Snow Flake.

"A few days! But it will be the beginning of forever for me. This time there will be no interference of any kind."

"We can stay here as long as you want us to stay!" Snow Flake said.

Glossary

WORD	DEFINITION	ORIGIN
Yakuza	Gangster	Japanese
Lao	Elder	Chinese
Sifu	Teacher	Chinese
Amah	Babysitter	Chinese
Kung Fu	The art of fighting	Chinese
Kuomintang	Political party established by Dr. Sun Yet Sun	Chinese
Kata	Sequence of movement in some martial arts	Japanese
Kown Yen	Buddha of Mercy who can see suffering of humans, can hear their crying, and has compassion	Chinese

CPSIA information can be obtained at www.ICGtesting.com
Printed in the USA
BVOW06s0146291215

431258BV00007B/51/P